"What

Jenna's cheeks grew ~~ro~~ ~~sh~~
recognized as female chagrin. "There's time for that,"
she said, not meeting his eyes.

She rose then and braved a smile.

He saw deep, unbridled compassion in her eyes. "I want
to know now. Tell me."

"I was hoping you'd recall all on your own," she
admitted softly, clearly uncomfortable with his question.
"I was hoping it would come back to you."

He waited and lowered his arm, releasing her wrist, glad
to have made the move but needing the relief resting his
arm would ensure. Her eyes darted away, the tawny gold
picking up sunlight as she looked through the window,
biting her lip and seemingly gathering up a dose of
courage.

"You came to Twin Oaks…to marry me."

* * *

Winning Jenna's Heart
Harlequin Historical #662—June 2003

Praise for Charlene Sands's previous works

Chase Wheeler's Woman
"A humorous and well-written tale,
this book belongs on your reading list!"
—*Romance Reviews Today (romrevtoday.com)*

Lily Gets Her Man
"Charlene Sands has written a terrific debut novel—
this is an author on the road to success!"
—*Romance Reviews Today (romrevtoday.com)*

"A charming historical debut…"
—*Affaire de Coeur*

**DON'T MISS THESE OTHER
TITLES AVAILABLE NOW:**

#659 THE NOTORIOUS MARRIAGE
Nicola Cornick

#660 SAVING SARAH
Gail Ranstrom

#661 BLISSFUL, TEXAS
Liz Ireland

CHARLENE SANDS

WINNING JENNA'S HEART

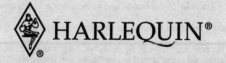

HARLEQUIN®

TORONTO • NEW YORK • LONDON
AMSTERDAM • PARIS • SYDNEY • HAMBURG
STOCKHOLM • ATHENS • TOKYO • MILAN • MADRID
PRAGUE • WARSAW • BUDAPEST • AUCKLAND

ISBN 0-373-29262-7

WINNING JENNA'S HEART

Available from Harlequin Historicals and
CHARLENE SANDS

Lily Gets Her Man #554
Chase Wheeler's Woman #610
The Law and Kate Malone #646
Winning Jenna's Heart #662

Other works include:

Silhouette Desire

The Heart of a Cowboy #1488
Expecting the Cowboy's Baby #1522

Please address questions and book requests to:
Harlequin Reader Service
U.S.: 3010 Walden Ave., P.O. Box 1325, Buffalo, NY 14269
Canadian: P.O. Box 609, Fort Erie, Ont. L2A 5X3

To Robin Rose,
my dear childhood and forever friend.
We'll always remember #18,
high school football games and "Turtles Rule."

And to Mary "Poquette" Hernandez,
my other forever friend.
Here's to wonderful school memories, all of those great
family vacations and our Laughlin gambling runs.

Friendships like ours are both rare and enduring.
May our memories never fade.

Special thanks to my editors,
Patience Smith and Tracy Farrell.
It's always great working with you.

Chapter One

Twin Oaks Farm
Oklahoma Territory, 1869

"You're playing with fire, sugar," the injured man mumbled in a soft, low drawl.

Jenna Duncan snatched her hand away from his chest. Slowly, he eased his eyes open. Relief swamped her immediately, thanking heaven above he was still alive. She'd looked after the wounded man for days, praying for his recovery and hoping she knew enough about doctoring to keep him breathing. She'd found him way up on the road, past Turner's Pond, slumped over, unconscious and bleeding. Nearly dead.

Dragging him to her homestead hadn't been easy, one woman on her own, but she knew she couldn't have left him there to die. He was strong; she'd give him that, surviving her tugging and pulling, hauling him over the terrain, bumps and all.

He'd groaned and grunted but hadn't regained con-sciousness…until now.

She dared a glance at his bruised face. His eyes were on her, as intense and blue as a deep river at midnight. Lord above, his eyes were rich with color, even in his weakened condition. They were just as she'd remembered. If there'd been any doubt as to whom he was exactly, seeing those eyes just now, brilliant in hue, indigo with traces of turquoise, as exquisite as they were unusual, left her certain that she was tending Blue Montgomery.

She turned and rinsed the cloth she'd used to bathe his wounds in a bowl beside the bed. When she returned to wipe his face, he'd drifted off again. It was only then that she'd thought about his voice, the deep resonating sound of it, pained yet threatening. Jenna shook her head. The man was not himself, she thought plainly as she pro-ceeded with his care.

With a tentative touch, Jenna continued rubbing his skin clean, washing away the remnants of blood. He'd been shot, the bullet going clear through his shoulder. She'd bandaged the wound, managed to keep the seeping down, but it would take weeks for his body to heal properly. So many patches of skin were discolored. It hurt to look at him, to see the pain and injury that he had suffered.

He was a stranger by all rights, yet not a stranger at all. Blue Montgomery had been due to arrive in town any day. They'd been writing each other since the age of twelve, when they'd met during happier times in their lives, before the war and all the devastation. All throughout, Blue had written; sometimes she'd only received a letter once a year, but more recently he'd been writing regularly. And something amazing happened between the prose, between the words of solace and talk of such inane things—if the weather would hold or the river would flood again. Between all the small talk that made the pages of a letter nearly a living thing, to hold and cherish in her hands when things looked so dreary that Jenna could barely hold on. Yes, something wonderfully amazing had happened. They fell in love.

With words.

Between two hearts.

Two lonely people sharing their most intimate yearnings.

Jenna had prayed and prayed for Blue's recovery. Goodwill, Oklahoma had no doctor to call its own. It was a town that had no real preacher or schoolteacher, either. There was no goodwill left in Goodwill. The town was dying except for a few hangers-on, like Jenna at Twin Oaks and others who had crops to raise but not much else.

Blue Montgomery had come to her. It graced her heart to know that. He'd been a man of wealth once, but that didn't matter now. He was here and together they'd planned on making Twin Oaks what it once was.

"Sleep now, Blue. Sleep," she said softly enough to soothe, daring to stroke a dark wisp of hair from his forehead. "There'll be time for us."

Jenna sat in the hollow foyer on the third step of the wooden staircase, the only stair that wasn't in desperate need of repair, and hugged Blue's long coat to her chest. She'd managed to wash out most of the blood and grit that had soaked through the dark wool material.

Dread had taken her voice when she'd spotted him that day, out there in the cool morning air and she'd half-prayed it wasn't Blue that she'd found. But hours later she'd managed him into her bed, with the help of Ben, her family's onetime hired help and now Jenna's most trusted friend. He and his wife Rosalinda tended the fields with a few others, helping Jenna keep Twin Oaks from failure.

Jenna had fumbled with the long coat, feeling something solid in the inside pocket. Stealing her hand inside, she'd pulled out a frayed leather-bound Bible. Blue Montgomery's name was written on the front page.

It was then she suspected she'd rescued the man she'd met only one time before, when he was just a boy.

He'd been shot and badly beaten. He'd been penniless when she found him, robbed clean of all his possessions and left for dead.

Jenna's heart had taken a tumble, but she'd had

no time for tears. She had to help him and she would continue to do so, until he was up and around. That he'd awakened once, if only for a short time, had to be a good sign, she mused.

Clinging to his coat, she sent up another prayer to the Lord. "Let him live. Please, let Blue live."

"You say somethin', Miss Jenna?" Ben appeared in the doorway, his gray irises marking his wide-eyed expression.

"I was praying," she replied.

"That man gonna live?"

"That's what I was praying for," she said with a small smile. Blue had to live. Jenna couldn't abide anything else. She couldn't let him die and all of their dreams along with him. They'd shared so much in the span of years, written about their dire wants and needs. They were kindred souls, she believed, and should be together on this earth first before meeting up in the hereafter.

"Rosalinda and me's been sending up that same prayer, for your sake, Miss Jenna. We was praying that man would come and put a big smile on your face again. Just like you used to."

Jenna smiled wide for Ben. "I'm smiling now, aren't I? I have faith in the Lord."

"That's good, Miss Jenna. Faith's always a good thing."

Jenna heard a groan, a low-pitched sound of pain and stood up instantly. "I'd better go check on him now, Ben. He needs me."

* * *

He opened his eyes again, this time braced and ready for the pain that one act would cause. One eye opened easily enough, but the other felt as though it was weighed down with an iron bar. Still, he managed and for the first time took in the room he was lying in. Nothing looked familiar. Not the threadbare, soiled curtains that must have once been cheerful white or the rickety pine chest by the wall and certainly not the bit of ivory lace lying across that chest. He didn't recognize the bed he was in, but instinct told him he'd woken up in plenty of unfamiliar beds in his time. Yet he held no such exact memory.

Squinting to block sunlight, he looked out the window, taking in the full measure of the place. He couldn't see much, just flat land and out farther a pair of towering oaks, their low-lying branches arching toward one another, the leaves fluttering gently in the breeze and touching like a lover's caress.

Nothing familiar.

He closed his eyes and immediately felt better.

A pleasing scent surrounded him. It had been the only pleasant sensation he'd had in days. The soft soothing aroma of something fresh and alive. Magnolia, perhaps? It wafted throughout the room airily, filling the area with its sweet fragrance.

Oh, if only he could lose himself in that scent.

And then a woman appeared. She sat right down beside him and the scent intensified.

"Blue," she breathed out.

He knew instantly that her soft hands were the ones that had nursed his injuries. She'd had a gentle touch, just like her voice, tender and soothing.

"You're finally awake. I hope you don't mind me calling you Blue. We'd decided months ago to use our given names...in our letters."

"Who's Blue?" he rasped out, through teeth that fairly ached. He hadn't as yet spoken and now the sound of his voice seemed strange, unfamiliar. "What...letters?"

"Why, you are, of course. Blue Montgomery. And I kept all your letters, Blue. Every one you ever sent me. Twenty-seven letters in all."

He didn't recall any letters. And she'd called him Blue. Blue Montgomery, she'd said. Mentally, he shook his head, the name not sparking even the smallest kindling of recollection.

He stared at the woman, hoping for some shred of memory to return. Her clothes weren't comely, looking worse for wear, but that wasn't near enough to mar her appearance—the undeniable quality to her delicate features. She smiled and two dimples appeared, lighting up her face almost as much as the striking hue of her amber eyes. The ovals were such an extraordinary tawny color, gleaming bright and shiny. Long hair in a dozen shades of gold, streaked by the sun no doubt and pushed back off her face made the picture complete. Whoever she was, she was memorable. Yet he didn't know her.

"I'm Blue Montgomery?" he asked, dubiously. She nodded.

"And who are you?"

She placed a cool cloth to his head and kept it there. Amazingly, he felt better, just from her touch.

"Why, I'm Jenna Duncan. Don't you remember me?"

Lord, if he'd known her, he doubted he'd ever forget her. She held a stately poise, although he'd already surmised she wasn't a woman born of refinement. And her gentle as a summer breeze touch and tentative smiles left a man to wonder and to hope. He'd only seen her for a brief moment, yet he'd supposed all these things about her, and he didn't believe for a second he'd been wrong.

"I'm afraid not."

"Oh," she said, drawing in her lower lip.

"But I'm not remembering much right now. Everything's all muddied up. Where am I?"

Jenna brought the cool cloth down along his jaw and rested it against his neck. She sat so close now and her flowery scent grew increasingly stronger. "Twin Oaks in Oklahoma, not overly far from the Texas border—the right side of the border," she said with a smile.

He tried to concentrate on what she'd said,

where he was, who he was, yet nothing she'd said meant anything to him. Not one thing.

"You've had a terrible…accident," she whispered, as though saying it aloud would cause him great pain. "Do you recall anything?"

"No. Was I shot? Feels like I was." A pain pierced through his shoulder just then and his gut told him all he needed to know.

"Yes, you were shot. Robbed and beaten," she said quietly, as though it pained her. "Oh, if I hadn't gone out that morning, there's no telling what might have become of you."

"Someone wanted me dead?" He knew the answer already. No man who felt what he was feeling could label his injuries as an accident. It was deliberate. Someone had tried to kill him. That much he surmised. But who and why were the real questions. Who would want him dead? And more importantly, why? What kind of man was he, to have been beaten and shot? Right now, he had all questions and not one answer. Hell, even his name didn't seem to fit.

"I don't know. I found you out past Turner's Pond and dragged you back here. That was six days ago."

Six days ago? He'd been here at the place Jenna called Twin Oaks for six solid days? She'd been tending him for all that time, keeping him alive. He wondered who else lived on this farm. Or was she alone? Had this woman been his sole nurse-maid?

"I don't remember. I don't recall anything. I don't…know you," he said reluctantly, realizing this was not what the woman would want to hear. She certainly thought she knew him, but still, as much as he tried, he couldn't bring any memories to light.

He watched her inhale, the breath filling up her lungs. "I don't know for sure since I'm not a doctor, but I suppose the injuries to your head caused your lapse."

The reference to his head reminded him of the pain there, the constant throb that knifed through as though a randy stallion had kicked him to hell and back. And the lapse she referred to was more a complete and total memory loss. He only knew what she'd told him, which wasn't much. "What am I doing here?"

Her cheeks grew rosy, a slow burn of color that he recognized as female chagrin. "There's time for that," she said, not meeting his eyes.

She rose then and braved a smile.

He lifted his arm and caught her wrist before she could turn away. Agony shot through him from a move any well man would give no mind. He winced and saw deep, unbridled compassion in her eyes. It was all the more reason for him to halt her departure. "I want to know now. Tell me."

"I was hoping you'd recall all on your own,"

she admitted softly, clearly uncomfortable with his question. "I was hoping it would come back to you."

He waited and lowered his arm, releasing her wrist, glad to have made the move, but needing the relief resting his arm would ensure. Her eyes darted, the tawny gold picking up sunlight as she looked through the window, biting her lip and seemingly gathering up a dose of courage. "Oh, Blue."

Still he waited and met her eyes with patience. "You came to Twin Oaks…to marry me."

Chapter Two

He sat in the kitchen, the effort taking a good deal of strength, yet he was determined not to go back to that bed. Leastways, not too soon. He'd been here for two weeks, letting Jenna wait on him, worry over him, cater to him. He hated it, the being useless part. He wasn't accustomed to having anyone tend him so, but how he knew that he wasn't certain. He only knew it for fact.

But Jenna. He didn't mind having her around. No, sir. He'd spent his time watching her flutter about the room, feeding him, tending to his wounds, her hands on him every day. He sure liked Jenna putting her hands on him. Fact is, he liked just about everything about Jenna Duncan. That was one reason he wasn't about to take advantage of her good intentions another day. It was about time he did something around here to help out.

He lifted a coffee mug to his lips and sipped it easily enough. Simple things, coming slowly, but they were coming. For four days now, he'd been out of bed, walking the room when Jenna wasn't in sight. The stretch of his legs felt good and he'd been getting stronger every day. She'd be bent if she found out, pampering him too much. Like he deserved it or something. Yet he was recovering. Thanks to Jenna.

The woman saved his life.

He owed her.

He still couldn't get around the marrying part, though. She said he'd come here to marry her. A man should have memory of those feelings, shouldn't he? Gut instinct told him he wasn't a marrying man. But that's all he had to go on these days. He had no real memory of anything. Not one solid thing.

She gasped when she saw him at the table, her rosy cheeks flustered, her eyes blinking wide. "B-Blue, you're up."

"Yes, ma'am." He sipped his coffee, then narrowed her a look. She was staring at him. Hell, he'd struggled into his pants, but she wasn't looking there. Her gaze was fixed on his bare chest. Shocking her hadn't been his intent, yet he didn't have any choice but to come into her kitchen this way. He had little to call his own, a shirt being foremost on the list.

Slowly, she lowered an overflowing basket of eggs to the table. He'd seen her coming away from the henhouse minutes ago.

"I couldn't find any clothes," he said.

Heat rose up her face, her cheeks reminding him of an overripe peach. Her flushed look stirred something in him. And when she drew in her lip, his gaze followed the movement. He thought of all the times she'd sat down on the bed to tend him. If he'd been more than barely conscious, he would've enjoyed having her there. He pictured her there now and the stirring became a near physical thing. Made him real uncomfortable.

"I, uh, burned them. Your shirt and underthings. There was too much blood. I should've thought…uh, Bobby Joe's shirts will fit. I'll bring one to you."

"Bobby Joe?"

"My brother," she said, before dashing out of the room.

Hell, she had a brother? Where was he? And why was Jenna stuck doing the work of three men on this farm, when she had a brother? He'd seen her come in after a hard day, her brows furrowed, her skin burnished from the sun's heat, her eyes weary with fatigue. She'd come at night to tend him, trying to pretend that she wasn't dog-tired. Being cheerful and positive of his recovery. But he knew what she'd sacrificed to take care of him.

"Here, Blue," she said, coming back into the room with no real intention of meeting his eyes. She handed him the shirt and backed away. "I'll have breakfast ready soon. Eggs and bacon with biscuits.''

It was the same food she'd been offering since he was able to eat anything solid. "I'll help."

She whirled around and her gaze fastened to his, pleading. "No need. You should go back to bed."

He stood and put on the shirt. "I'm gonna help," he said firmly. He'd been in her care far too long. He needed to do something with his hands, his time. He wasn't one to allow others to do for him yet how he knew that fact he hadn't a clue. "I can't do much, but I'll be damned to spend another day in that bed, doing nothing."

She watched his fingers work the buttons of her brother's shirt and then lifted her eyes to his. "You're alive, Blue," she said softly. "And that's all that matters."

Oh, damn. He'd upset her, making it seem her fault for keeping him down in that bed for two weeks. She'd done nothing much really, except save his sorry life. She'd come in late at night to tend him. She'd check on him, sometimes in the predawn hours, when she should have been sleeping herself. She'd sacrificed her time and energy to make him comfortable. And he was punishing her for it.

He approached her, watching her eyes flutter nervously, like a butterfly ready to wing away. Slowly, carefully, he put his hand to her cheek and let the softness seep into his skin. "I'm sorry. I haven't even thanked you for saving my life."

Her lips quivered, from fear or from something else, he didn't quite know. "What else would I do, Blue?" Her eyes, not so guarded now, shone bright and filled with a shimmering glow.

He backed away, suddenly realizing the full impact of what his touch evoked from her. The look on her face told all. Jenna had real feelings for him. Feelings he didn't have, or couldn't remember. Feelings he wasn't sure he was capable of sharing. Everything inside his head was gray and clouded like a threatening thunderstorm. Nothing was sky-blue clear. Not one blasted thing.

"Where's your brother?" he asked, pouring her a mug of coffee, attempting to let that unguarded moment slip away. He grabbed a knife to slice off bacon for the griddle she was preparing.

"Bobby Joe? Gone. He comes home from time to time. It's been more than a year since I've seen him."

"Why isn't he here, working the farm? Helping you?"

He noticed Jenna beat the eggs faster and harder while she shook her head. "He's not one for farming. I share my crops with Ben and his wife. We're partners now. We manage."

"Still, your brother, he should be—"

She turned to face him then with a defensive lift

of her chin. "I don't like talking about Bobby Joe, Blue. You know that."

"I do?"

"Yes, well…I mean, you should know from the letters."

"Oh? You're talking about the letters I don't remember?"

Her face fell instantly and he hated putting that look there. Jenna, it seemed, needed him to remember his past as much as he did. They were strangers in nearly every sense, until his memory returned.

"I'm sorry, Blue. This can't be easy on you. But, it's just that we shared so much and now, it's as though you're a, a—"

"Stranger?" He said the word she'd been reluctant to admit.

"Yes, a stranger."

"Maybe I am, Jenna. Maybe I'm not Blue Montgomery at all."

Jenna's eyes danced then and her face lit with joy. The transformation was instant and quite remarkable. It made him want to smile. "Of course you're Blue. How'd you think you got that name? I've never seen a body with more blue in their eyes. They struck me when I first met you years ago. Nobody's got eyes that color, Blue. Nobody but you."

"And then there's the Bible with my name in it, right?" he asked, wanting so much to be Blue

Montgomery for Jenna. Wanting to remember everything.

"Right," she said.

And he sat down to share the morning meal with the woman he was supposed to love, the woman he came here to marry, pushing aside the doubt that shoved its way through his gut.

Jenna sat that night alone on the porch, looking out over the land ready to be cultivated and planted and felt a pang of pride in her farm. Twin Oaks was *her* farm. Not Bobby Joe's. He hadn't put in so much as one short day's work on this farm since her daddy died some years back. Bobby Joe had no rights where Twin Oaks was concerned. None. With the help of Ben and Rosalinda, she'd worked the land, toiled until her back ached and her hair hung down damp from sweat to make this land prosper. She had crops of corn and soybeans growing, hogs in the pen, more than two dozen chickens, a tough Percheron plow horse and a big beautiful milk cow named Larabeth. Soon, the land would be ready to nurture their main crop of wheat. It wasn't much as far as farms go, but they made do and one day, Twin Oaks would prosper again.

"It's my farm, Bobby Joe," she whispered into the still night. "You have no claim." The farm was hers by rights. She wouldn't think about it again. Heavens, she hadn't given her brother a thought in months, thankfully. She'd been able to put what he'd done in the past, where it belonged. She wanted to look forward to a future. With Blue. She wanted to see her life filled with children, thriving on this farm. All she'd wanted now, all she'd yearned for, was a family to call her own. She'd dreamed of nothing else, besides a healthy crop, of course.

Her mama and papa had been taken from her early in her life. And as painful as it was true, Bobby Joe wasn't much of a brother. Her only relation had disappointed and betrayed her more times than she could count. And his most recent act of betrayal had been the last straw.

He'd gambled the farm and lost, causing Jenna nothing but heartache. How many times had she prayed for Bobby Joe's soul? She wished and hoped he'd change his philandering ways. She'd like nothing better than to have a brother who shared the same love of the land as she. What relief she'd feel to have someone sharing in the decision-making. To know that no matter what freak of nature or manner of fate occurred, that they'd find their way.

And now, she'd hoped that she'd find that solace with Blue Montgomery. Things hadn't turned out as planned with him. It wasn't his fault he'd been shot and left for dead. It wasn't his fault he couldn't remember the loving words he'd sent to her, the comfort he'd lent, the offer he'd made to make Twin Oaks what it once was. No, it wasn't his fault he couldn't remember those things. Oh, how she wished he could.

And then a thought struck and Jenna giggled aloud. How silly of her not to have thought of it before this. How silly, indeed. "Jenna, you've gone and lost half your mind over Blue Montgomery," she sang out happily.

Why, maybe Blue only needed a nudge, something familiar to help him regain his memory. Maybe all Blue needed was to see firsthand the letters he'd sent her.

Jenna was up off the old rocker on the porch faster than a wily jackrabbit and dashed to her room, her mind spinning with hope-filled thoughts. She bent down and dug out a small hand-carved burl-wood chest. It had been her mama's and it was Jenna's most prized possession. That Blue's letters were stored in there made it all the more exceptional.

With great care, she lifted the packet of those twenty-seven letters, wrapped lovingly with bright yellow ribbon and brought them close to her heart. She recalled all of the times she'd pull a letter out of the stack randomly, like picking a flower from a full bouquet, and read the words that brought her so much joy. It was her way, to ease the toil of the day, to gift herself with Blue's thoughts until another letter would arrive from him.

Jenna smiled with satisfaction. How could Blue,

after reading his own words, not remember her? Or the feelings they shared? This would work, she was sure of it.

When Jenna reached Blue's door, she held back. While he was recuperating, she'd made herself at home in his room, free to enter and exit as she pleased. But now that he was up and around, she'd grant him his privacy. Lord above, after seeing him this morning, looking virile and manly, without a covering to his chest, she was certain barging in on him wouldn't be wise for a young female who was deeply and hopelessly in love.

No, not wise, she thought as heat traveled the length of her. Soon, Blue would be her husband. And the thought nearly stole her breath. Although she'd tended him and seen most of his body, covering up the male parts that needed covering, it had been different this morning in the kitchen. More intimate, and more appealing. Blue was a fine specimen. All male, rugged and handsome with rough stubble on his face that he'd be wanting to shave off soon. She'd known his heart through his letters, but seeing him this morning had made her nervous. A good kind of nervous, she mused. She wanted to know his body.

Jenna's heart raced thinking about lying with him. She was sure that she wanted all the intimacies that went along with being married. If only Blue would remember.

She knocked on his door.

The door thrust open quickly and Blue stood there, watching her, a half smile playing on his lips. "Come to give me a bath?"

Startled by his quick response and by his question, Jenna drew back. Good heavens, he looked handsome, with those intense blue eyes fixing on her. And good heavens again, he looked dangerous tonight, but not the kind of danger that put fear in her heart. This danger was different, exciting. "No, I uh, I came to…" She glanced down to the letters she held tightly to her chest wondering now if he'd think her foolish. "I, uh, thought if you read these, you'd remember," she said and thrust the cherished packet into his hands.

"Remember?" He lifted the letters up and gave them only a cursory glance before the heat of his gaze returned to her.

"Me. Us. The letters might jar your memory."

He laughed then, a good solid laugh that brought a smile to her lips. "What's funny?"

"Letters won't make a man remember a woman, sugar."

"No?" Baffled Jenna could only stare up at him. What did he mean? Being on a remote farm, miles away from town, and little reason to venture there, Jenna had little experience with men in general, but even less experience with the way Blue was looking at her now. Her heartbeats sped up though and she knew one thing, all right. Blue Montgomery made her insides quake.

He shook his head. "A man remembers a woman in different ways."

"But we only met once, when we were children."

"Don't matter none, Jenna." He stared at her lips and stepped closer, coming out of the doorway. "There's ways a woman can jar a man's memory. Fact is, I've been thinking plenty about it."

Jenna took a swallow. "You have?"

"Oh, yeah." Blue reached out and touched her cheek and before she knew it, that same hand wrapped around her neck, drawing her close. "Plenty."

His eyes searched hers for one instant before his lips came down on her softly, brushing his mouth over hers with exquisite tenderness. Nothing in her life had ever felt more right, more perfect. The taste of Blue Montgomery left her breathless, in a thrilling sort of way. Jenna let out a soft moan, which seemed to please him. He took hold of her hand and wrapped it around his neck, coaching her and leaving no room for doubt what he wanted— her complete participation.

Jenna kissed him back with everything she felt inside. Sinful, wicked sensations edged into her thoughts as Blue took what she offered greedily, making her fully aware without question that he was a man with needs. He dragged her closer and kissed her again and again until Jenna's lips were bruised and her body raged.

And just like that, he backed off, breaking the seal of their lips, shaking his head. "That was...too good," he said with regret in his voice.

Trembling inside, Jenna prayed it didn't show. She'd never felt so wonderful in her life...or so scared. Yes, it was good, she admitted silently, wondering why he'd stopped kissing her. "Did you," she began, biting her swollen lip, "did you remember anything?"

Oh, yeah, he thought. He remembered something. He wasn't a man who knew how to handle sweet innocent women. He knew it had been a long time since he'd held one in his arms and wanted so badly, the way he wanted Jenna. But damn it all, he didn't *remember* her. More than anything, he'd wished he had. And if he hadn't been daydreaming just then before Jenna knocked, about what it would be like to have her in his arms, loving him, right there on that bed, he would never have taken her the way he had.

Like he had a right to.

He smiled at her, a deep grin meant to soothe her feathers, should they be ruffled. "I think I'll try your way, Jenna." He brought the letters clenched in his fist up for her view. "I'll read them."

With that, he closed the door, shutting Jenna out.

* * *

Jenna balanced the plow, steadying the handles with both hands as the Percheron made a slow yet efficient trek through the wheat field. "That's it, Mac," she said to the old but reliable draft horse. She had half an acre to plow today and was only an hour into her task when Blue strode up, his face grim.

"What are you doing?" he asked, none too gently.

Jenna's heart sped up at the sight of him. Every time they had occasion to talk, to be near, her reaction was always the same, a mixed-up sort of feeling that made mush to her insides. Ever since that kiss. She had trouble forgetting it and spent many a night recalling the sensations over and over in her mind.

That had been exactly five days ago, and still the memory was as vivid and clear as the Oklahoma sky on a cloudless spring day. "I'm plowing the field, Blue," she said, breathless, both from the chore and the man pointing his sharp nose at her.

"That ain't woman's work," he said, then added, "Where's the men?"

Using her sleeve, Jenna took a moment to wipe sweat from her brow. Under regular conditions, no, it wasn't woman's work, but this wasn't the first time she'd taken on the chore. With an entire wheat field to plow this spring, what choice did she have? The fields wouldn't plow themselves and she had minimal help. "Ben's gone until tomorrow evening. He took Rosalinda to Goose Creek. It's a day's ride from here. The others are working the top end of the field."

"What's so special in Goose Creek?"

Joy filled her heart. Ben's purchase today would make life a bit easier around here come planting time. And it symbolized something even more important.

Progress. She'd scraped together enough money from selling off surplus eggs and butter in Goodwill to finally purchase something to help the farm prosper. "He's buying us a seeder, Blue. You know what that means, no more broadcasting the seeds. We'll get the planting done faster and more efficiently."

"A seeder?" He cast her a dubious look. He must think her odd, a woman getting excited about the purchase of farm equipment. She expected most women only got their feathers up if their man bought them a shiny new bauble or two.

He took hold of her hands then, removing her overly large gloves and lifted up her palms to see calluses developing. She was sure it wasn't a pretty sight. He twisted his lips. "Move aside, Jenna. And show me what to do with this thing."

"No, Blue. It's too soon for you." Jenna understood a man's pride, but he was still recovering from his injuries. And it wasn't as if he hadn't been helping. He'd insisted on chopping firewood, raking out the barn and mending fences around the farm.

"I'm through standing by, watching everybody else around here get to their chores." He fit his hands into the gloves.

"You've been helping," she offered in his defense. She couldn't bear for him to think of himself as useless. He'd done everything his healing body would allow up until this point. It was all anybody could ask.

He snorted. "Slopping the hogs ain't real work, Jenna. Now move aside." His big body nudged her out of the way gently and he took hold of the handles. He shot her a quick look, his eyes beckoning.

"Just keep the furrows straight as you can. Mac knows what to do. And plow deep enough to make for a good root bed."

He nodded then sent his gaze over the unplowed land. "Don't wait supper for me."

Jenna put a hand to his arm. "You come in before sundown, Blue. Nobody's ever plowed a whole field in one day." She said this with amusement and his quick easy smile nearly knocked her off her feet.

Jenna walked away, stepping carefully over the land already tilled. She turned for a moment, watching Blue struggle with the plow until he mastered it. He'd rolled up his sleeves and she noted thick muscles straining as he held the plow firmly.

She'd never tire of looking at him, her Blue, not for the next fifty years or so.

The memories will come back to him, she thought willfully. He was a farmer from Kansas. Surely, he would remember how to farm the land. But he'd been wealthy at one time and probably hadn't cultivated the soil himself. Then the war came and he fought for the South, only to come home to find his farm destroyed and his home in ashes. Shortly after, he had lost his parents, but he'd stayed on, trying to rebuild, until the day he decided to come to Twin Oaks to marry her. And although Blue still had no memory, he was here at Twin Oaks, recuperating and working the land, just as they both had planned.

Jenna whistled a gay tune all the way back to the house, glancing at the perfect sky, imagining tall golden fields of newly-grown wheat...with Blue Montgomery standing proudly by her side.

He sank down onto the mattress, his body a mass of solid aches. Farming wasn't woman's work and he wasn't at all sure it was man's work, either. The tedious monotony of plowing the land wasn't mind-enriching labor. He scratched his head, wondering how a man who was supposed to be a farmer could find disdain in creating a healthy crop with nearly his bare hands. He should be rejoicing, shouldn't he, at the labor he was born and bred to do?

He lifted his palms up and noted hard calluses where there had been none before. "Blue Montgomery or whoever you are," he said aloud, "you don't know a thing about farming."

He wasn't ready for bed. Fact is, every night he'd started reading one of the letters he'd sent to Jenna, not quite making it halfway through the entire contents. He found it hard reading about himself and what he'd been through, wondering if these events had really occurred *to him.*

Stretching out on the bed, he gave a little groan. Hell, he was hurting. His body rebelled against stiff joints, sun-drenched skin and torn-up muscles that cried for relief. With a little twist, he turned up the kerosene lamp on his bedstand and picked up another letter. He'd promised Jenna to read them all, and he would. This time he'd read it to the end. The next letter in the batch began:

My dearest Jenna,

I do hope this letter finds you well. I think of you there at Twin Oaks often. How brave a woman you are to keep the farm from ruination after your parents passed on. I know it must be difficult and often wish I could be there with you to lend a hand and comfort you. As for your brother, Bobby Joe, well, I will not speak of him in a bad way, other than to say he should be ashamed of himself abandoning you for his gambling ways. He should be there taking on the brunt of the work, making up to you for the evil he'd sent your way. He's not a man I admire, Jenna. Forgive me.

And as for Montgomery Farm, all I can say is that I have tried to keep the farm operating, but the soil is plainly worn out. I've planted hay and buckwheat where the soil is the most tired in a dire effort for rotation, but you know, sweet Jenna, a farm cannot thrive without its main crop and the grain crops have been poor for three years now. Weeds are hard to keep down and there isn't the time or laborers to keep the crop from failing yet once again. For the love of the family name I shall continue to try, but I do not hold out much hope.

I look forward to another of your letters as they are the solace and console I need to sustain my days. You have become a balm to my heart, sweet Jenna.

Always,
Blue Montgomery

He folded the letter, carefully replacing it back into its place in the stack and tying up the ribbon. Jenna treasured these letters; but so far, nothing had sparked even the slightest memory in him. He felt as though he was barging in on another's thoughts. Yet, he was learning something about himself and more importantly, about Jenna.

Something had happened between Jenna and her brother. There was reference to it in the letter, but Jenna didn't have cause to discuss it with him. The light had gone out of Jenna's eyes when last they discussed Bobby Joe Duncan and he knew then he wouldn't ask again. When Jenna was ready to trust him with the truth, if that day ever came, then he'd listen.

It didn't set well that her brother had hurt Jenna. Tender feelings surged forth; a protectiveness that was fierce in nature seeped into his senses. He didn't know what to do with these feelings, but he damn well knew if Bobby Joe Duncan showed his face here, there'd be hell to pay.

Jenna had saved his life. He'd not allow anyone to hurt her again. The feelings overwhelmed him and he stood abruptly and paced the room. Noises caught his attention and he glanced out the window. Light from a slice of the moon put a dim glow onto the barnyard below. He thought he saw movement in the shadows. The barn door opened and from his viewpoint on the second floor, once again movement caught his eye.

He buttoned up his shirt and put his boots on with two quick effective tugs then headed downstairs. As he approached the barn door, he listened intently.

"That's a good mama. You've got five little babes here, Button. And aren't they cute!"

Jenna?

He popped his head inside, being drawn to the sound of her cooing voice, and was instantly struck by the sight of her. Wearing a robe of white cotton he'd only caught glimpses of before, with her long golden hair down about her shoulders and framing her face, Jenna turned to him with wide eyes. Two dimples popped out like twin diamonds on a face that positively beamed with joy. The robe split open, revealing a thin chemise underneath and everything male inside him went tight.

"Blue, look here," she said softly, the lilt in her voice calling to him. "Button's had her a litter. Aren't they the sweetest things you've ever laid eyes on?"

He glanced down at the five scrawny wet kittens and nodded. But his mind was on Jenna and how *she* was just about the sweetest thing he'd ever laid eyes on.

Images of Jenna coming to lie with him in his bed, wearing that soft thin strip of cotton and nothing else, danced in his head. He couldn't block the image, not when she was standing there, smiling up at him with such elation. Oh, how he wished he were Blue Montgomery. How he wanted to be. And why shouldn't he believe it and take what Jenna offered? Why not accept the love she had to give and marry her? Why not just spend his days blissfully happy with a courageous, lovely woman who had shown him all that she was, all that she could give him, with just one passionate kiss?

"There's a chill in the air," he said and turned to close the barn door.

"Leave it open," she said firmly, a hint of desperation in her tone.

"You're cold, Jenna."

"Please, Blue. Don't close the door." Her eyes met his searching, as if he should know something that she wouldn't voice.

One last glance at the bodice of Jenna's chemise told him, yes indeed there was a chill in the air. He inhaled sharply and forced his focus to the new litter as he strolled over. "They look like rats, all damp and bony like that."

Jenna bent down to stroke Button, who was busy at the moment nursing the five newcomers. "They do not, Blue Montgomery. They are just darling. Don't you listen to him, Button. He's just being silly."

He smiled and bent down next to Jenna. Stroking the new mama's head, he amended his first impression. "Okay, so maybe they are a little bit cute."

She laughed and the sound filled the barn like a melodious song. "Nothing like new babes to make a mama proud. Right, Button? One day, I'll know the feeling."

She froze then and he saw a deep red flush come to her face.

"You want children, Jenna?"

"I, uh…I do," she admitted, but kept her atten-

tion on the kittens. "I shouldn't have said that."
She drew down on her lip.

"Why not? If it's the truth."

"Of course it's the truth. It's just that until your
memory returns, it's a bit awkward speaking of
such things."

He stood, then reached down to take Jenna's
hand, lifting her to her feet. They stood inches
apart. He studied her eyes, noting confusion there.
"And what if I never get my memory back, Jenna?
What then?"

"I don't...know."

"We can't go on thinking I'll remember something. I don't recall what we shared. Not one bit."
He softened his tone. "We have to face the fact
that I might never remember you."

Jenna shut her eyes, her pain nearly tangible. He
sensed she was a woman who experienced each of
her sentiments with strong emotion, this one causing her, arguably, the most injury. "I thought by
now you might."

"Yes, by now, I should have had some recollections of who and what I am. But it's been
weeks. I've read the letters, Jenna, and that hasn't
helped, either. The way I see it, we should start
out fresh and new. Just like those scrappy little
kittens over there. I have no past, Jenna, but together, we might have a future. Do you want
that?"

He wanted this woman. He had since the first

time he'd opened his sore eyes and saw her tending his wounds. This woman who smelled magnolia sweet and looked pretty as a picture even with dirt smudging her face and those locks of wheat-colored hair in messy disarray.

He wanted to keep the joy on her face. He wanted to take the burden of running the farm off her slender shoulders. He wanted to love the land the way she did.

And most of all, he wanted to love her…in his bed and out. He wanted to love her in all ways that mattered. It nearly shocked him to the bone to feel this way, since he didn't have a real good handle on his emotions. How could he, when he barely knew the man that he was? But he knew one thing. He wanted Jenna Duncan.

"What's your middle name?" he asked.

"W-What?" Both dimples popped out again when she chuckled.

"Just tell me, Jenna. I need your full name."

"Leah."

"Well then," he said, giving her hand a quick squeeze. Lord help him if he was making a mistake, but his gut told him, if nothing else, that Jenna was the right woman for him. "Jenna Leah Duncan, will you marry me?"

"No."

Chapter Three

"Pardon me?" he said, nearly choking on the words. "Did you say no?"

She nodded, casting him a look of regret.

Well, he hadn't expected this. No, sir. Hell, he wanted Jenna Duncan and that desire was strong, but marrying her had been all her idea. He figured he owed her. She'd saved his life and nurtured him back to health.

Living under the same roof, just steps away from her bedroom, he believed it was just a matter of time before he got her into his bed, but Jenna was a decent woman who claimed she wanted marriage. And he'd talked himself into obliging her. Now, he wasn't all too sure what the woman had in mind.

"Mind telling me why?"

Jenna stepped away from him and pulled her robe closed. Perhaps if the darn thing had been closed up tight all along, he wouldn't have gotten this fool notion in his head.

"I can't marry you, just yet."

"Just yet?" What in tarnation did that mean?

"No, Blue," she said, shaking her head. "I mean, I want to, more than anything. I want a life with you. I want," she whispered, color rising on her cheeks, "I want babies and a family to call my own. But I'm willing to wait, Blue. Just a little longer."

"Why, Jenna? Why wait?"

He saw her shudder and wanted to go to her, but decided it was best to let her say her piece. "I want you to know what we shared together, to feel it deep in your heart, like how it is in mine. I want your love, Blue. Can you say that you love me?"

He took in a deep breath and moved closer. Meeting her hope-filled eyes, he knew he couldn't lie to her. He barely knew her. He had no recollections of the love that had a man leaving his own home, traveling hundreds of miles to be with her. He might not ever recall, but he was willing to start over, if she'd been of the same mind. "Ah, Jenna."

Jenna bruised her lips with worry. "I can't explain the why of it, but I've waited for so long. A lifetime, Blue. You'll get your memory back soon. I've been praying for it. And it'll come like a lightning flash, just like that. And then you'll know."

"I'll know?"

"What we meant to each other. You'll know the love we shared. Do you think you could give me a little more time?"

Time, he had. He could grant her time. There was such a sweet look on her face now that he'd do just about anything to keep it there. Jenna wanted his love. There was no doubt in his mind, she was an innocent, a woman who'd never known a man intimately before. It was only right for her to want the bond of love before she gave herself to a man. To him. He hoped he would remember. He hoped he was the man she wanted him to be. "How long?"

Her smile jolted straight into his heart. "Not too long. Just until the fields are all plowed up and planted."

"And if my memory doesn't return, then what?"

A look of yearning stole over her face. Shyly, she answered, "Then if you ask again, I'll accept."

He nodded. "I can be patient. I'll wait. It's settled, then." He took her hand. "Let's go. We need to get some sleep."

They left Button to her kittens, closed the barn door and headed back to the house. They walked up the stairs together, holding hands as he led her to her bedroom door. With a deep sigh, he bid her good-night.

"Good night, Blue." Reaching up on her toes,

she brushed her lips to his briefly, before turning the knob and entering.

He stood outside her door a long time, staring at it as if the dang thing held all the answers he sought. But no answers were forthcoming, only more questions.

His memory would return, she'd said, like a flash of lightning. Should he dare hope that Jenna was right?

Jenna felt his eyes on her this morning. She made herself busy mixing flour for biscuits and slicing bacon for the griddle. But she knew he watched her with the intensity of a wolf stalking his prey. He had hungry eyes. And they were trained on her. "Would you like more coffee?" she asked, turning to face those eyes.

"I'll get it," he said, standing up and reaching for the pot on the cookstove. After pouring two mugs, he sidled up next to her. "Anything I can do?"

Her immediate answer was usually no, but he stood so close she could smell his scent. Earth, man and lye soap made a dizzying combination. She needed to keep them both busy. "Would you put out the plates? Eggs will be ready soon."

They'd had many a meal together. The routine should be comfortable by now, but there was something underlying, something simmering between them that made Jenna anxious. In all her imaginings, she couldn't have thought up a more appealing man. He scared her, thrilled her and lent her comfort all at the same time. Blue Montgomery was all and more than she'd ever dreamed of. She knew in her heart, once married, their joining would be like a firestorm. And the flames wouldn't burn out for years to come.

"Owwwww!" Jenna missed the handle of the griddle and scorched her finger on the heated metal. The piercing burn brought tears to her eyes. She fanned her hand to help extinguish the fierce heat.

Blue was there instantly. "Jenna," he said, taking her hand and perusing her fingertip.

"I wasn't thinking," she blurted out, but it was what she *had* been thinking that caused her complete lack of concentration.

"Let's get it in some water."

He held her hand and poured water into a bowl with the other. "Here, sit down."

"It's nothing to fuss over," she said, trying to withdraw her hand. He didn't let go. Instead, he pulled out her chair and made her sit. He took a seat beside her.

"Burns can scar if you don't take care right off." He set her finger inside the bowl and held it there.

"The eggs will overcook."

"They're fine, sugar. I'll get to them in a minute."

"I'm not used to being fussed over."

Blue stroked her hand soothingly, his thumb making circles on her skin and stirring up a different kind of heat. "You should be, Jenna. You should be fussed over," he said with velvety softness.

Her eyes met his tentatively. "I'm not that sort of woman."

He laughed. "All women are that 'sort' of woman."

Jenna denied that in her heart. She was a simple farm girl. Blue had always understood that about her. It was her love of the land that had drawn them together in the first place. "I plow fields. I get just as dirty as you and Ben."

He continued to stroke her hand. "I like seeing smudges on your face."

Her good hand flew up to her cheeks as mortification set in. "Where?"

Jenna had never cared about her appearance too much before. Who was she to impress? Larabeth, her brown-eyed milk cow? Or Mac, her dependable plow horse? But life was different now. Blue was here, her Blue.

He chuckled again. "Not now. Your face is just fine."

Relieved, Jenna smiled with him. "I think my finger is all right now. The burning's stopped."

"Let me check," he said, lifting her hand up and drawing it close, then closer, until her finger was at his lips. His tongue came out and he tasted the moistness there, sending a shock to Jenna's insides.

Gently, he moved her finger over his cool lips and blew on it. She closed her eyes, relishing the pleasure. And when he dipped her finger into his mouth and suckled, a slow sizzling warmth heated in her belly. "Ohhh."

His chair scraped back and he stood, dragging her up with him. He took her into his arms, pressing her against him. He groaned low in his chest, like a man in pain, before clamping his lips over hers.

The kiss went long and deep. Their tongues met and mated, a primal dance that Jenna had no knowledge of, but Blue was an excellent tutor and soon she found the rhythm he sought. His hands wove through her hair then traveled down her throat, touching her effortlessly with fiery passion that Jenna returned equally. His hands moved over her, down her hips, then cupped her bottom and brought them together, closer, a sensual rub of bodies that ignited something wild in her. She gasped for breath. He murmured near her ear all the things he couldn't wait to do with her, all the ways he would pleasure her.

She listened, her breaths coming ragged and fast. Then he kissed her one last time and moved aside, leaving her there, stunned and edgy with desire. She watched him roll up his sleeves, put on Bobby

Joe's hat and head for the door. "Seems I'm not such a patient man after all, Jenna."

Jenna stood rooted to the spot, her body trembling, humming out a silent resonating tune created by Blue's heat and passion. Her scorched finger went to her lips and she closed her eyes, allowing the sweet memory of being in his arms to seep in, burning her as deeply as the fire had moments ago.

He'd said it and he'd been right in his thinking. Blue Montgomery wasn't a patient man.

That's one valuable lesson they'd both learned well today.

Jenna caught a glimpse of Ben and Rosalinda riding up in the wagon. She dropped the rolling pin onto the table, deciding the pecan pie could wait. Wiping her hands on her apron, she dashed out of the house and ran over to them before Ben could climb down. "Did you get it?" she asked, knowing full well he had. It was sitting in the back of the wagon.

"Yep, that's it, Miss Jenna." He turned to help Rosalinda down and together they went to the back of the wagon.

Jenna stared at the piece of machinery that would save time and allow more planting to be done. Two large wheels to the side of the driver's seat with a large double bucket to hold the seed in the back made up the bulk of the seeder. Two small wheels for balance just under the seeding device assured a steady ride. Once hitched up to Mac, planting would take no time at all.

"It's not new. Got us a used one, the last one they had. It saved us a chunk of money, too," Ben said.

"Long as it works, Ben."

"Works fine, I tested it."

Jenna grinned. "Thank you for getting it."

He nodded.

"How was your trip, Rosalinda? Did you like going into town?"

"*Sí,* yes. It is a big town. So much bigger than Goodwill." Rosalinda's brother had been a vaquero on the same Texas cattle ranch that Ben had worked. Ben and Rosalinda fell in love, marrying young. When the ranch faltered, they decided to move to Oklahoma and earn a living farming the land instead. They'd been with her family for over eighteen years, raised two children, one of whom still worked for Twin Oaks. All through the years the loving couple had been Jenna's most trusted friends. "I bought pretty fabric for new dresses. One for you and one for me. Such beautiful material, you will see."

"Oh, thank you, Rosalinda, but where will I wear such a nice dress?" She wore most of her clothes in the fields working the land. Her threadbare dresses had all but lost their vibrancy and life. Many had holes and grass stains that couldn't be repaired any longer. She made sure they were clean. Her mama had drilled it into her about the virtues of cleanliness and all, but she didn't think she'd have use for anything new and pretty.

"Perhaps for your new man," Rosalinda said, her dark eyes twinkling.

Heat rushed up Jenna's face and she glanced at Ben.

"I'll get the seeder down. You two ladies have yourself a nice talk now." He winked at his wife and she grinned.

"But you must be hungry and thirsty, Ben. Come inside. I'll fix you both something to eat."

He shook his head. "No, I'm fine for now. I saw your man in the fields. Thought I'd see how he's doing. I'll be back later. You feed my wife, though. She's always hungry."

"Ben!" Rosalinda feigned embarrassment. Her dark eyes rolled. "He pokes fun, no?"

"Yes, that he does. Come on, I've started on a pie, but I've got cheese and bread and fresh coffee ready now."

Ben kissed his wife's cheek. "See you later, Rosie."

Jenna walked into the house with her older friend, her mind spinning in circles. She supposed Blue Montgomery was "her man," but she wasn't used to others thinking of him that way. "Sit down, Rosalinda, and tell me all about your trip."

Rosalinda took a seat and shook her head. "That

will come later. I want to hear of this man you call
Blue.''

Jenna sank down in a chair. How could she explain about Blue? All of her hopes for the future
were tied into him, wrapped tight in the letters
they'd shared, the hearts that had so unexpectedly
come together. They hadn't seen each other since
childhood, yet they'd fallen in love with words
written and dreams shared. Blue was everything
she'd wanted in a man, and more, it seemed, now
that they were actually reacquainted. She'd be truly
overjoyed at her good fortune if only his memory
would return. ''Oh, he's…he's—''

''Much handsome, yes?''

''Oh, yes, yes. But he doesn't remember me or
the love we shared through our letters.''

''He is here. Working the land, Jenna. He must
care for you.''

Jenna smiled, a tentative lifting of her lips. *Yes,
he is here.* That thought comforted her, to know
he worked the land beside her and that they'd be
together to witness the wheat rise up toward the
sun one day soon. ''He asked me to marry him,''
she confided.

Rosalinda's dark eyebrows shot up. ''And when
is the wedding?''

Jenna chuckled. To Rosalinda, life was simple.
You loved, you married, you had children. But for
Jenna, it was different. She was a stranger to Blue
until his memory returned.

Jenna stood then and cut chunks of cheese. She brought out bread she'd baked yesterday to the table, unfolding the napkin and setting out thick slices. She poured coffee for Rosalinda, then answered her. "I've asked him to wait. It wouldn't be fair to him...or to me. We are like strangers."

Rosalinda waved away Jenna's explanation. "You love him, no? He is a good man. You are a good woman. Together you make many babies. I will be a grandmother."

Jenna had been plagued with doubt since Blue had asked her to marry him. Had she made a mistake in refusing his proposal? "Rosalinda, is it so wrong to want him to remember me?"

"Ah, so that is it. No, *querida,* it is not wrong, but perhaps not so wise. We must not wait all of our life for something that will not come."

Rosalinda was right. Blue might never remember her, although Jenna sensed so strongly that he would regain his memory. And it would be soon. She had to cling to that hope. For years now, she'd had her heart set on Blue Montgomery, on the time he'd come to her with love in his heart for her and only her. Jenna wanted so much to be loved, truly loved, by this man. "We agreed to wait until the planting's done."

"Then you will marry him?"

"Oh, yes, then I will marry him."

"And you will make lots of babies." Rosalinda's satisfied smile brought moisture to Jenna's eyes. Children would fill up her house with joy and laughter. Jenna couldn't wait for that. She wanted Blue's children more than anything. If her prayers were answered, Jenna would have the family she'd always hoped for. "Yes. We both want lots of children. Blue loves children as much as I do."

"A man who loves children is worth much," Rosalinda added, with an approving nod. "You will marry and have your family, Jenna."

Jenna nodded in agreement. "Yes."

Because whether his memory returned or not, Jenna wasn't about to lose Blue Montgomery.

Three days later, dark threatening clouds bunched together, a congregation of dismal gray that blackened the sky and put dread in Jenna's heart. Wind kicked up, blowing hard enough to make the shutters on the house rattle noisily. Jenna left her garden, deciding the herbs she was about to pick would have to wait. Storms meant trouble and this one promised to be wicked. She ran to the barn and thrust the door open.

Thankfully, either Ben or Blue had groomed and settled Mac in his stall. Larabeth, the big old milk cow, looked peaceful enough. Jenna made sure there was enough feed for both, handing reliable Mac a handful of oats, just as a loud clap of thunder blasted throughout the sky.

Jenna trembled. *Storms meant trouble.* She closed her eyes, blocking out memories, of fears

Jenna needed to put to rest. But the sounds and the smell of wet earth always brought it back.

She rushed to the door and ran smack into Blue. She tried to get past him to the safety of the house, but with a quick jerk of his arm, he grabbed her. "Whoa, slow down, Jenna. It's coming down hard out there."

She blinked and blinked again, coming out of her daze. Blue was drenched. Rivers of water ran down the brim of his hat. His clothes clung to his body.

"I gotta get into the house." *Where it's safe.*

"It's best we stay in here, sugar. Until the rain lets up."

"No, no! Not in here, Blue. I don't like storms." She didn't want to stay in the barn. Not with the rain coming down in sheets and night falling. "Take me back to the house," she pleaded. "Please."

Blue's expression changed instantly and she knew she could trust him. "Okay, Jenna. Okay. We'll get you into the house."

Thunder boomed overhead. She leapt into his arms.

Blue lifted her, casting her a questioning look, but he didn't ask. She'd be forever grateful for that. Shutting the door, he took off running. They were hit with hard rain. Blue bent over her, trying his level best to keep her from the brunt of it. But Jenna didn't mind the rain, the wind or the cold.

She was out of the barn. She could breathe again. That was all that mattered.

Once inside the house, he carried her up the stairs and deposited her inside her bedroom. "Get out of those wet clothes. I'll make sure the windows are closed up tight."

Jenna nodded, her mind numb.

He slanted her a stern look. "When you've dried off some, meet me downstairs, Jenna. We're gonna have us a talk."

Again, Jenna nodded. She moved slowly about the room, peeling off her wet clothes. She changed into a cotton skirt, tucking a shirt in, and glanced at herself in the cheval mirror. She looked a sight.

It wouldn't do.

Jenna sat down on her bed, untangled her hair with her fingers, then brushed the long tresses until they were nearly dry.

Much better, she thought. Well, an improvement, at least. Jenna ambled downstairs. She heard noises in the kitchen, but didn't join Blue there. Instead, she walked into the parlor and stared out the window.

Once a body was safe and warm inside, rain could be a beautiful thing. It cleaned the air and wiped away thick dust that layered the land. It nurtured new growth, put color on the earth, helped sustain all living things. Yes, rain *could* be something beautiful, sweeping away all the ugliness in the world, allowing for a new day, allowing for a fresh start.

Jenna took a deep breath. Her sigh was audible and profound. She sensed Blue come up from behind, felt his solid warmth. He wrapped his arms around her waist and drew her back against his chest. Jenna knew it wasn't an act of lust this time, but more an act of friendship. She rested back against him, taking in his comfort, the strength he offered.

"What's got you so scared, Jenna?"

She shrugged, "I don't like storms. Ever since I was a little girl, I'd curl up in bed and cover myself with my quilt, but after Mama and Papa passed, I couldn't do that anymore. I couldn't pretend away the storm. I had responsibilities...the animals, the house. I managed until the last big storm."

"What happened then?"

Jenna hesitated. Aside from Ben and Rosalinda, she hadn't spoken of this to anyone. Blue had known because she'd written to him about it, but he didn't remember anything that had happened to her. Yet, she sensed his compassion now and his need to know. She wouldn't deny him.

Wrapped in his arms, she leaned more heavily against him. With a resigned sigh, Jenna began. "It was about a year ago. There was a storm just like this one, pounding down on the roof, the wind whipping everything about. I worried over the animals, so I took off running and made my way to the barn. I had to latch it closed so that the wind wouldn't rip open the doors. Instantly, I knew I wasn't alone. There was a man inside my barn…a stranger with small eyes and a wicked smile. I screamed when I saw him, but he rushed over to me and covered my mouth, telling me to shut up.''

Blue went tight. She felt the muscles on his arms clench around her. ''Did he hurt you?''

''No, but he would have. I believe he would have really hurt me. He was angry and asked me if he was at Twin Oaks. I told him, yes, this was Twin Oaks Farm. I'd never seen a man get so riled up, so fast. His language wasn't fit for delicate ears, Blue. I'd never in my life heard such foul words. Then he stuck a paper in my face. It was a deed to Twin Oaks. He said he won the farm in a bet from Bobby Joe Duncan.''

''Your brother bet away the farm?''

Jenna stiffened. ''He did. I couldn't believe my brother would dare do something so cruel. He'd bet our farm and sent a vile man to me to collect his due.''

''Jenna, what kind of brother—''

''He's the worst kind of gambler, Blue. Bobby Joe's been no good most of his life, but I never thought he'd ever do such a terrible thing. If only—'' She stopped, biting her lip.

''If only what?''

''If only you could remember. You had such

kind words, Blue. Your letters helped me get through that terrible time.''

"I wish I could remember, sugar. Truly."

"I know you do."

"So, if he won the deed to the farm, then how come he didn't claim it?''

"The deed wasn't real. Ben and I hold the deed to Twin Oaks now. We made sure of that early on, when my brother took up his gambling ways. He had no claim on our land. But he'd lied to this gambler, told him Twin Oaks was a lucrative ranch. The gambler was expecting horses and cattle, not unplowed land and cornrows. He was plainly furious when I told him the deed was a fake. He wanted to wring Bobby Joe's neck. I was agreeing with him on that. But then the man got an evil look in his eye, said he might as well take it out on Bobby Joe's sister, instead. I backed away, as far as I could, but the man came at me.

"I was trembling so hard, my teeth clattered and my legs were ready to crumble. A big boom of thunder distracted the gambler and I reached for the Winchester on the wall. I knew it wasn't loaded, but he didn't. I aimed it straight at his heart and told him to get out, to leave and never come back. I remember being so scared but I held that rifle straight and kept my voice steady. When he laughed, a sinful sound that wasn't really a laugh at all, I could only stare at him. He said he wasn't no damn dirty sodbuster and didn't want my broken-down farm. When he got to the barn door, he turned, and told me he might just come back one day, so I should keep my doors locked.''

"Damn. Who the hell was he, Jenna?"

"I never found out his name. When I was sure he was off my property, I ran to my room. I was spitting mad at Bobby Joe. Everything inside me went black with anger. I slumped down on my bed and…wept. It was so strange, I felt such anger boiling up inside me, but all I could do was cry. I cried loud and hard, and then the sobs came in silence until every tear I had in me was shed. There was nothing left. My bones felt like mush and my heart ached with such great pain. I recall feeling so small, so inadequate and so very alone. I'm tired of being alone, Blue.''

Blue tightened his hold on her. His warmth lent her the solace she needed now. ''Jenna, you were betrayed by someone who should have been by your side. Hell, if I ever get my hands on your brother…'' He let the words trail off then he turned Jenna in his arms. ''That's why you were so frightened in the barn tonight.''

Slowly, she nodded.

"That man won't come back. There's nothing for him here. There's nothing for you to fear. But if I'm wrong and he does come back, I'll be right here, with you.''

"Oh, Blue.'' There was such understanding in the depths of his eyes and so much more. They looked at each other a long time, until Blue finally took her into his arms. She clung mightily to him, feeling his strength, his kindness and for the first time in a long time, Jenna's fears were put to rest.

Blue spoke in a voice filled with emotion. ''I'm going to marry you, Jenna. As soon as the storm lets up. I don't want to wait another day.''

Chapter Four

It took three full days for the storm to pass. But Jenna assured Blue that was all right, because it had given her time to get ready for the trip to Goose Creek for their wedding. Ben had gone to Goodwill, when the storm had simmered down some, to telegraph the preacher in Goose Creek and make all the necessary arrangements. Jenna seemed pleased.

He still had doubts.

The void inside him was strong. He had no past. He didn't know what kind of man he was. Would he make a good husband? Would he be faithful and kind and caring? Would he provide for Jenna sufficiently or would he tire of the farm, finding the monotony too tedious? All manner of doubts crept inside him. The only thing he knew for certain was that he wanted Jenna Duncan and if it took marrying her to have her, to make her happy, he'd do it.

With the wagon all packed up, he turned when Jenna came bustling out of the house. "You ready, sugar?"

She looked beautiful. Rosalinda had insisted on sewing up a new dress for her, soft pink with ribbons and ivory lace. The dress fit her form perfectly. And Jenna had left her hair down just the way he liked it best, flowing in waves down around her shoulders. So pretty, with golden threads blending softly just like the wheat she cherished so much. His chest filled with pride. And with longing. Soon, he'd know her intimately and the need was powerful. He had trouble thinking of much else these past three days but their wedding night.

"I'm ready," she said, her smile bringing those dimples to life.

"Do not go so fast." Rosalinda came up quickly, breathing heavy from her fast stride. Ben was steps behind. "We have a gift for you, Jenna."

Rosalinda smiled warmly and handed Jenna a bouquet of flowers. The arrangement was filled with all of Jenna's favorites and decorating the center was one large white magnolia. Jenna's face beamed with joy as she clung to the fragrant bouquet. "Oh, these are beautiful."

"They match the beauty in your eyes, Jenna. You go and be happy with your man." He heard her whisper, "You make lots of babies."

Jenna's face flushed with rosy color and a little nervous chuckle escaped.

Making babies with Jenna. He couldn't wait. The sooner they got onto the wagon, the sooner they'd get to Goose Creek to make it all legal. And then came the baby-making time. His body had been tested to its limits lately. And the thought of finally claiming Jenna as his put notions in his head that weren't fit for a morning ride.

Ben strode over to him, handing him an envelope. He stared at it, wondering what Ben had in mind.

"For the weddin'," Ben said. "This is money left over from the seeder. Rosalinda and me, we thought a nice dinner and a stay in one of them fine hotels for the night would make a nice gift."

He hesitated, his pride getting in the way. He had no money of his own, not a dime to his name. He'd wanted to do something special for Jenna. This was her wedding day. She deserved so much more than he could give her. He'd planned on selling his long coat to make do in Goose Creek, but Ben had hinted that he'd need that coat. Winters in Goodwill could be brutal. He couldn't argue with that and now Ben faced him, his gray eyes filled with encouragement.

"Take it, for Jenna." Ben passed him a look only another male would understand. He spoke quietly, "She deserves a nice weddin'."

He accepted the offered envelope then, shaking

Ben's hand briskly, thanking him. Jenna did deserve a nice wedding and he'd see to her happiness from now on. He'd provide for her and take the burden of running the farm out of her hands. As soon as he learned about farming, that is.

He glanced at Ben once again, vowing that he'd make it up to him, too...to all of them. They'd been good friends.

Shortly after, they took off, leaving Twin Oaks in the dust. He sat back in the seat of the wagon, listening to Jenna's enthusiasm. Once she'd accepted his proposal, she'd begun making all kinds of plans for the farm. How much more acreage they could plant now. And with him working alongside of the others, their profits would go up. She wanted to enlarge the henhouse so they could buy more chickens. She wanted to breed the hogs and maybe one day raise some sheep. She had all sorts of new things stirring around in her head.

He liked listening to her. He liked seeing her happy. She was a woman a man could stay with forever. For the first time since he'd been bleeding out by that pond and left for dead, he thought that somehow his luck had changed.

He was a man with no past. But now, thanks to Jenna, he had a future. He liked that about her, too.

"You enjoying the meal, Mrs. Montgomery?" he asked, watching Jenna push food around in her plate. They'd gotten to Goose Creek two hours

ago, met with Reverend Archer and in the space
of one hour were married. It was a quiet, simple
ceremony and that suited him just fine. He was a
married man now, sitting across from his new bride
in the Honey Belle Hotel, eating dinner in the din-
ing room.

He kept glancing at Jenna's face. She sure
seemed happy. She'd been talkative on the way
into town, but now she sat quietly, forking her food
slowly and smiling shyly, relishing the meal and
taking it all in. She deserved to be waited on, he
thought earnestly, deserved the best in life. If he
could, he'd try to give her that.

But for now, he couldn't wait for the meal to be
over. She'd ordered steak and hot mashed potatoes
with some fancy gravy and more vegetables piled
on a plate than he'd seen growing on some farms.
She had a ways to go on the food. But their hotel
room was not fifty paces away, up the stairs, then
a turn to the left, the hotel clerk had said.

It was all he could think about.

Getting naked with Jenna. Making love to her.
Making her his in the eyes of the law and of the
Lord.

Hell, he just wanted to get to it.

"It's going take getting used to," she said, stopping the fork from going into her mouth.

"Huh?"

"Being Mrs. Montgomery. Of course it's all

I've really wanted for years now. But still, it sounds sorta funny hearing you say it.''

She took the bite that had been on her fork and he let go the breath that he'd been holding.

"If it makes you feel any better, I'm having a time getting used to being *Mr.* Montgomery. And that's been my name since birth.''

"It'll come, Blue. One day, you'll remember.''

"I'm not planning on it happening soon. Seems it would've happened by now. Why, I'd bet the last of the money in my pocket that I don't get my memory back at all this year.''

Jenna froze, her face going white as snow.

"What? What'd I say?''

"You wouldn't, would you, Blue? You wouldn't gamble away your last dollar? You wouldn't *gamble* at all, would you?''

Where had that come from? Blue didn't even know why he'd said it, but he should've been more considerate of Jenna's feelings, knowing how she hated gamblers. Knowing *why* she hated gamblers. He called himself every sort of fool for speaking without thinking first. Fact is, he wasn't thinking about anything other than getting his beautiful new bride upstairs. He took her hand. "No, it's just a saying, is all. I wouldn't bet on anything and I'm sorry to have put that look on your face.''

They'd promised each other that they'd never speak of Bobby Joe and what he'd done to her again. It was over and done with and he admon-

ished himself for not realizing how his offhand re-
mark would affect her.

She smiled and began eating again. "Oh, I'm
sorry for taking offense, Blue. It's silly of me. I
know you hate gamblers as much as I do. You said
so…in your letters. They are useless men who
don't know how to earn an honest living, that's
what you said."

"Mmmm," he replied, not really hearing Jenna.
He found the loosened lace that secured her bodice
more interesting. One pull and the whole darn
thing would come down.

"I'm through," she said finally, pushing her
plate away. "I just couldn't eat another bite."

Relief swamped him. Now they could get to the
baby-making part of the wedding night. He grinned
and called the waiter over, ready to pay up.

"Sir, would you and the missus care for dessert?
We have a wide array of fine pastries, cherry cobbler, blueberry cream tarts and puddings in several
flavors?"

"No," he said firmly.

"Yes," she said at the same time.

The ache in his groin intensified. He ran a hand
down his face.

The waiter offered cordially, "Shall I bring in
the dessert tray, madam?"

"Yes, yes. That would be lovely," Jenna said.
"Blue, don't you care for dessert?"

Blue gritted his teeth and shook his head. *She*

was all he planned on having for dessert. "I'm fine, Jenna. You go on and have whatever you like."

She smiled as the waiter returned with the tray filled with delectables. "Oh, they all look so delicious. It may take a while for me to decide."

After she finished dessert and coffee, Jenna gazed up at her husband. He had those hungry eyes again, which frightened her a bit, but at the same time thrilled her. She wanted to know him in all ways and tonight she knew she would. He stood quietly, took her hand and led her up the stairs to their hotel room. With a click of the latch, she found herself alone with her new husband in a room Jenna might have only dreamed about. She moved about the room, taking it all in. Frilly curtains of lemon yellow covered the windows and flowery wallpaper decorated the walls. To one side, a curtained partition hid a large porcelain bathtub and on the other side, centered on an oblong mahogany table, a cut-crystal vase held cheerful yellow daisies. When she braved a glance at the rather large sleigh bed all fluffy with quilts and pillows, she took a hard swallow. "It's lovely," she managed, turning to him.

"The best room in the hotel, Jenna. You deserve the best."

"Oh, Blue."

He came to her then, taking her hands, then

drawing her into his arms. His steadfast embrace soothed her nerves. He whispered softly, "I'm your husband now, Jenna. You're my wife. Don't be afraid. I won't hurt you, I promise."

Jenna gazed up into his eyes and witnessed his sincerity. She knew then she could do what he asked. She could set aside her fears for Blue. Jenna Duncan Montgomery finally felt at peace. She cast her new husband a smile.

He kissed her then, a long, drawn-out, sweet kiss that spoke of trust and caring. Jenna relaxed. This was what she'd dreamed of, what she'd wanted for so long. "I love you, Blue."

He smiled, a crooked cocky lifting of his lips that melted her bones. He kissed her again and again, this time with passion, and she returned his kisses heartily. On a deep guttural groan, he pulled her against him, his hands roaming freely, touching and caressing everywhere. She felt the pull of ribbon and her dress parted down her shoulders. He helped ride the sleeves down and then brought his mouth to her breasts.

She moaned from pleasure and joy and denied him nothing. Within minutes, she was standing in a pool of her clothes, petticoats and dress discarded easily. He lifted her then and carried her to the bed. Gently, he lay her down and removed the last of her protection. Her chemise met with the rest of her garments on the floor.

Those hungry blue eyes were on her again, studying her with an expression of delight.

"Beautiful, Jenna." He stroked a hand through her hair, releasing pins and arranging the locks against the pillow. "Remember when I told you what I wanted to do with you once we were married?"

She nodded. How could she forget such erotic things? They'd swirled around in her mind for days on end, making her lose precious sleep at times. She'd wondered about what he'd said, what he'd actually meant. She'd thought and thought, trying to figure out just how it would all work. And tonight, she would find out. She would give herself completely to Blue, placing her heart in his hands, her trust in him entirely.

"Let me?"

She gulped down. Tonight, she'd find out what she'd always wondered. Tonight, Blue would claim her as his wife. She would be his, and he would be hers for all of their days. Her dream was coming true. "Yes," she whispered.

He kissed her again and brought his hand down past her belly, finding her soft woman's center. He stroked her lightly and she moaned from the delicious sensations that slight touch evoked. "Oh, my."

His touch elevated her senses. She felt everything threefold, and these new feelings were much more startling than Jenna had ever imagined. Blue stroked her body with careful finesse, a bold yet tender caressing that left Jenna positively breathless. He played her body like a fine instrument, gliding, tracing, strumming her until her breaths became ragged and her heart thumped nearly out of her chest. He touched her everywhere, his eyes dark with appreciation and desire. He spoke softly, gentle whispers belying the wildfire he was surely creating. His lips found her breasts, his hands, her hair and when he groaned, the deep rich sound made every nerve in her body tingle.

Blue rose from the bed and undressed before her. His gaze latched onto hers, beckoning her and daring her to watch. Boldly she stared as her new husband peeled away his clothes and the reality struck her like a bolt of lightning. Blue was hers, all bronzed skin and solid strength. His magnificence should have frightened her, but how could it? She'd never witnessed such beauty in anyone before. She'd never known a man could be so rough and hard in one way and so impossibly beautiful in another.

He came to her then, pressing himself down onto the bed. He kissed her until her lips bruised sweetly, and then he was above her, his hungry eyes on her with heat and desire. And as they joined, flames burst forth, first with slight pain, then with something far more staggering in its wonder. Blue was careful with her, coaxing her, caressing her, holding back his own passion so that she might find her way. And Blue seemed to know the exact moment when she had. Together, as one, they climbed to the highest peak, stunning Jenna with its intensity. Both cried out, two souls joining, the blazing fire blasting one last time before simmering to a slow sizzle of heat.

Blue took her in his arms and held her. No words were necessary now. Nothing they could say would match what they'd both experienced. Jenna closed her eyes, content and sated, with Blue Montgomery by her side.

Just like she'd always dreamed.

He left her lazy and rumpled in their bed and went downstairs to order bathwater for her later on. With the bit of money left in his pockets, he decided to buy Jenna a wedding gift. Something real nice, something fancy that she'd never think of buying for herself.

Jenna deserved the best.

She'd probably sleep for another hour at least. After the night they'd spent making love, she'd probably like to sleep all day. He would have loved that as well. Waking up with Jenna in his arms had been nothing short of wonderful. He'd been awed by Jenna's beauty, taken by the gift of her body, the way she'd placed her faith in him. He'd been gentle with her, as gentle as his hungered body would allow. He'd promised not to hurt her and he hadn't. For that, he was grateful. He'd held back for as long as he could, making sure she'd been properly readied.

But he hadn't expected her passion to run as deep as his. He hadn't expected her responses to shatter him the way that they had. She'd been more than he'd hoped and now they were bonded together forever. They'd have their days together, and then their nights. He had a whole lot planned for those nights. A wide grin split his face thinking, memory or not, today he was about the luckiest man alive.

He strode down the street, heading for the mercantile. Voices from the alley between the barbershop and the telegraph office caught his attention. He glanced down the narrow path. Three men had a young man pinned up against the wall. They were beating him senseless.

He shot a quick look up and down the street, noting the sheriff's office was too far away. The man would be dead before he raced back with the law. Instinct had him heading down that alley. "Hey!" he shouted, hoping a witness would be enough to scare the men off. That had been his first mistake. All three men turned, casting him hard jaded looks. These men weren't about to be scared off.

"Mind your business. Get out!" One man shouted. He appeared to be the leader, brawny in build and evil to look at.

Blue glanced at the young man's swollen face,

bloodied and bruised. Whatever their argument, three against one just wasn't fair odds. Without thought, he bounced into the fray, pulling one man off the victim and knocking a fist into another.

The men couldn't help notice him now.

He found himself reaching for his gun, a holster that wasn't there. He had no time to think on that, on what that meant. The young man, no longer pinned up against the wall, got into it as well, making the odds much better. Two against three was a bit more justified, even if the young victim hadn't much spirit left in him.

He noticed the brawny man who'd shouted at him reaching for his gun. On sheer gut instinct, Blue quickly hoisted a gun out of another assailant's holster. Taking aim, and realizing the other man wasn't about to hesitate, he fired a shot, winging the man in the shoulder. The gun the man held flipped out of his hand.

"Damn, you shot me," he cried, his good hand coming up to the wound. Blood oozed out through his fingers.

Blue held the gun steady on all three, as bits and pieces of memory returned quickly like *lightning flashes*. Images burst through in waves, until his head spun. The gun, the shooting. He saw himself in another situation, standing in a saloon. It had been three against one then, too. And that time he had been the *one*. He'd shot a man and he knew that man was dead.

"Hey, I know you!" One of the three offenders shouted. "We all thought you was dead."

"What?" he asked.

"You, why you're—"

He didn't let the man get the words out. He didn't have to. He knew who he was. Suddenly. He knew *what* he was. Memories poured in, fast, like darting animals across a field, but he had no time for them now. He spoke his own name as dread seeped into his gut. "Cash Callahan."

"That's right! We heard you was beaten and robbed, you and another man, yanked right off that stagecoach. Left for dead."

Cash recalled some of that now. The images were blackened and faded, but starting to come through. And the realization hit him hard, the implications far too confusing for him to sort through at this time.

"Thanks, Mr. Callahan." The young beaten man came up to him, holding his jaw, but not looking too worse for wear. He'd be all right in a few days.

Cash couldn't see past the images fogging his mind, but he knew he had to. This situation wasn't resolved yet. He held three men at gunpoint, one of whom was bleeding.

"I didn't like the odds," he said to the young victim. And suddenly he knew why that was so important to him. Suddenly, he knew that playing the odds had been his life.

''What happened here?'' He pointed the gun at the three men looking for answers. It dawned on him how easily he held the gun, how right it felt in his hand.

''Willy cheated us at cards last night. We came to get our money.''

''Did not,'' Willy denied. ''I won that money fair and square. You folks were drinking too much to know a king-high straight from a pair of deuces.''

The four men began arguing, raising voices, making accusations.

''Hold it!'' he shouted above their ranting. ''We're gonna let the sheriff decide.'' With the tip of the gun, he nudged them out of the alley.

''Ahh, do we have to?'' One of the assailants whined.

''Sure do. I don't trust you all to settle this on your own, and we got a man here bleeding. He needs to see a doctor.''

Two hours later, after giving a statement to the sheriff, Cash waited by the wagon for Jenna, still reeling from his revelation. His insides churned, the bitter reminder of who he was couldn't be ignored. Though Cash found it hard facing the truth about himself, about the life he had led, he knew he had no choice but to open his mind and allow all those memories to flow in. And they did flow, hundreds of images coming to mind, and each one reminding him that he wasn't the man Jenna wanted. He wasn't Blue Montgomery, farmer. He wasn't the man who Jenna had admired, who'd struggled hard on a family farm, until soft words and hope-filled pages in those letters, had him venturing to a new life with a sweet, loving woman.

No, he was Cash Callahan, notorious gambler. Each day of his young life had been about one sole thing, survival. He'd been cast out so many times he'd lost count. He'd been alone, a youngster on his own and had to make do with the devices the Lord had given him. He'd developed a knack for gambling. Some said it was a gift. He'd struggled hard to survive in an often cruel, calculating world, starting early in life, fighting to gain a reputation until he'd finally come into his own. Up until this point, he hadn't had harsh thoughts about the life he'd been forced to choose. He'd done what he'd had to do to sustain his life. But now, it was different. Now, he had a wife, who wasn't really his wife. And he had to tell her who he was.

In one bleak moment, Cash would shatter all of Jenna's dreams. Her heart would break in two. The news would crush her, no doubt. And if his being a gambler didn't destroy her, then learning the hard truth about what happened to the real Blue Montgomery certainly would.

Cash had been responsible for his death.

Jenna approached the wagon, a rosy glow shining on her face. Hell, Cash had put that look on her face. Just hours ago, he'd had the same contented look. But now, Jenna would know no happiness. He'd wipe away that glow and bring her nothing but pain and heartache.

"Blue, you look pale." Her expression faltered, her dimples disappearing, replaced by sincere concern.

He helped her up into the wagon and took a seat next to her. He wanted out of Goose Creek, real quick.

"Is something the matter?" she asked, when he didn't respond.

All he could do was shake his head.

Hell, every damn thing was the matter. He had to find a way to break the news to her. He had to explain who he was. But he decided telling her here and now would be too hard for Jenna. The truth of it would rattle her too much. She needed to be home, among friends. They'd lend her the comfort he couldn't give her. Once they reached Twin Oaks he'd tell her. He'd muster the courage and explain to her all that he could. She wouldn't understand, of course, she wouldn't take it well. She'd hate him and he wouldn't blame her. At the moment, he hated himself.

Halfway home, Jenna put a hand on his arm. "Blue, you're scaring me. You haven't said one word. Did I do something to upset you?"

She'd given him a slice of heaven, that's what she'd done. Last night they shared something magical, something he'd never forget. Jenna had given herself to him completely, placing her faith and trust in him. Cash had never known a woman like Jenna. He'd never touched a decent woman. The hell of it was, he didn't deserve her concern. He didn't deserve *her*.

But in truth, she hadn't really given herself to *him*, but to the man she believed him to be, the man she'd fallen in love with. Cash Callahan was a stranger to her and he'd unknowingly taken her innocence. "No, sugar, you haven't upset me. I've got a lot on my mind, is all."

He left it at that. Every so often he'd glance at Jenna's face and see the worry there. She'd nibble on her lip, or frown, then catch herself, attempting to appear cheerful, but Cash knew she was just pretending. He hated that she fretted so, but it couldn't really be helped. He couldn't pretend to be someone he wasn't. Not even for Jenna.

He heaved a deep weary sigh when they reached the gates of Twin Oaks. This had been his home for weeks. Jenna had taken him in, saved his life and nursed him back from the dead. He'd been content here, with Jenna by his side, and if his memory hadn't returned, they would have begun their new life together as husband and wife. But that wasn't to be.

He owed her the truth.

He turned to her then, taking her hand and placing a kiss there. The last one they would share.

"Jenna, you're a special woman. I think I'm half in love with you, but you have to know the truth."

"Oh, Blue," she said with a wistful sigh, "you love me?"

Cash's gut clenched at the sweet, hope-filled sound of Jenna's voice. He had half a mind not to tell her, not to crush all of her hopes. Never in his life had he faced such a difficult dilemma. But could he go on pretending that he was Blue Montgomery? Could he fake being a farmer, to keep a smile on Jenna's face? And what if she learned the truth in another way? The harm done with those lies would devastate her even more. No, he had to tell her. He had to speak the truth.

"That's just it, Jenna. I have no right to you. I'm not Blue Montgomery. I'm not your Blue."

Chapter Five

Jenna sat impatiently on the parlor sofa waiting for Blue, or the man she *thought* was Blue, to return from unhitching the wagon. She couldn't believe this was happening. He had to be mistaken. The man she just married had to be Blue Montgomery. There was no other explanation. Yet her palms were moist with sweat, her heart raced overly so and her mind went hazy, miserably trying to rehash events that pointed to Blue not being Blue at all.

Could it possibly be?

The door opened slowly and Blue entered, his gaze locking with hers. What she found in those deep penetrating eyes truly frightened her.

"Jenna," he said quietly.

She followed his movements, the long purposeful strides she'd come to know as Blue's. He sat beside her. His nearness brought her comfort, but when she gazed into his troubled eyes again, all that ease disappeared.

"I have to try to explain." He reached back to rub the back of his neck, but tension still marred his face. She'd never seen him appear so shaken and perplexed. Jenna's heart took a steep tumble yet she had no choice but to sit there, waiting, fearful of what that explanation might be. "It's not a pretty story, I'm afraid."

"You...remembered then?"

"Yes, I know who I am. It came to me...like a lightning flash, Jenna. Just like you'd said." He smiled quickly then his face went somber. "My name is Cash Callahan."

Jenna squeezed her eyes closed. Tears stung the backs of her lids, but she wouldn't allow them. Not yet. She tilted her head and glanced at him warily, unable to believe that this man, whom she had nursed back to life, this man that she had married, this man to whom she'd given her body, was a stranger to her. It was all too impossible, too painful.

Cash Callahan. The name seemed so foreign to her. "G-Go on."

He took a deep breath and spoke softly. "I was on my way to Twin Oaks. As you know, the stagecoach was attacked. There were only two of us left on our journey. The others had gotten off at the last town."

"You were coming here?" Puzzled, Jenna's

brows knitted together. What call would a stranger have to come to Twin Oaks?

"Yes, Jenna. I was coming here."

"Why?"

He ran a hand down his face and let out a slow uneasy sigh. "I had business here."

She shot her head up. She didn't know this man, and that fact played heavy in her heart, since she'd married him, lain with him, oh…this wasn't at all how it was supposed to be, but who was he, really? "What kind of business?"

"I'll get to that later. You see, the attackers were after me, and well, because the other gentleman on the stage looked so much like me, they weren't quite sure which one I was. After they killed the stagecoach driver, they shot and beat us both. I recall thinking it so strange when I first got on the stage to see a man who nearly mirrored my own image. Same height, same hair color, but mostly it was the eyes. They were as deep and blue as mine." He took a sharp breath and continued. "They robbed us and left us for dead, but the other man still had breath in his lungs. I recall him crawling over to me, giving me his Bible and telling me to find Jenna Duncan. He wanted me to tell you…he loved you. Those were his last words."

Tears spilled down Jenna's face. She couldn't believe what she was hearing. She couldn't believe the real Blue Montgomery was dead. She'd nursed him back to life, hadn't she? She'd been so sure, so certain, the man sitting here on her sofa had been her Blue. Her heart ached, the pain knifing through with powerful force. Yet, she fought the disbelief. She fought it, because it was all beginning to make sense, somehow. "That was my Blue? The real Blue Montgomery?"

He reached for her hand, but pulled back before they actually touched, his blue eyes narrowing, going dark and filling with regret. Jenna was grateful he hadn't taken her hand. She didn't want his touch. She didn't want to be reminded of the night they'd shared when she'd believed him to be her Blue.

Dear Lord. How could this be? What cruel manner of fate had done this to her? She didn't want to hear this awful truth. She only wished she could go back to yesterday when her life was simple. When she had her whole future ahead of her.

"Yes, I believe he was Blue Montgomery."

"Ohhh." Sobs escaped and Jenna couldn't look at this man, this stranger. She wept for the man she would never know. She wept for Blue Montgomery. Jenna couldn't fathom her life without Blue. They'd had so many plans; the promise of many healthy children, of land thriving with wheat and of a life filled with true and binding love. Blue had been her world. He'd been kind and compassionate, a man Jenna had admired. His words healed her when she'd been down. They'd lifted her up and had given her hope again. That she would never know him, never lay eyes on him, never share another word with him, brought her the deepest kind of sorrow and regret. "L-Lord, r-rest his soul," she managed after a time.

Then Jenna cried for herself.

She cried for destroyed dreams. She cried for the years of wanting, yearning, waiting. She cried for the loneliness that would surely be her life now. She cried and cried and finally, once her tears were shed, reason took over.

Jenna wiped her tears on her sleeve, too distraught to worry about the stricken look on the man's face beside her. She had so many questions running through her mind now. She shoved her heartache aside for a moment, to get the answers she needed. "I don't understand. Why didn't I find him when I found you?"

"He died there, by the stagecoach, as did the driver, but I didn't have strength to bury them. I left the area, fearing the attackers might come back and see that I was barely alive. I crawled on my hands and knees, bleeding and not knowing if the breath I was taking would be my last. I don't recall how long or how far I was able to go, but I searched for help. I think I would have died that day by Turner's Pond if you hadn't found me right then."

"Oh," she said, realizing that this man was not at fault. He'd been through a horrible ordeal and nearly died. She had been the one insisting he was her Blue. Yet who was Cash Callahan and what business did he have with Twin Oaks?

"I did the Christian thing. I would have taken you in, no matter who you were."

"I know that, Jenna. You're a special woman—"

"Don't," she said, halting his kind words. She couldn't bear to hear them right now. Unfair resentment settled in her belly that this man had survived when Blue hadn't. She wasn't proud of this feeling, yet she hadn't the strength to fight it, either. She couldn't forget that they'd spent the night together, that she'd given her body to a stranger. She didn't want to hear any more of his soothing words. Words wouldn't change a thing.

"You saved my life, Jenna. I will be grateful for that until the day I die."

Blue was dead, but she'd managed to save this man's life. Whoever he was. It was time she found out. "You said you had business here, at Twin Oaks."

"Yes," he said, glancing at her warily, before lifting up from the sofa. "Wait here a minute."

Puzzled, Jenna stayed seated, wondering what this man, this Cash Callahan was up to. A minute later, he came back into the room with his long wool coat. With a small knife he produced from his pocket, he began ripping away the back inner seam of the garment. Stunned, Jenna could only watch.

Once the seam was opened considerably, he reached inside and pulled out a piece of paper. "This was my business, Jenna," he said with such regret that Jenna's heart lurched.

"W-What? What is that?"

He unfolded the small paper and placed it on the sofa between them. Jenna looked down and gasped. "It's a deed to Twin Oaks!"

He nodded. "It's a fake deed, Jenna. I know that now."

Yes, it surely was a fake deed. Just like the one she'd seen once before when a stranger came onto her property, angrily threatening her. If this man carried a deed to Twin Oaks, then how did he get it? Jenna's mind considered the possibilities, yet she refused to acknowledge the one truth that would destroy her completely.

Cash Callahan folded the paper back up and shoved it into his shirt pocket. He ran his hands through his hair then, on a hesitant pause, softened his eyes to her. Jenna sat ramrod straight waiting for his explanation, praying this was all a big mistake.

"I met your brother, Bobby Joe, at a gambling hall in north Texas. Can't even remember the town now. There have been so many. He wagered Twin Oaks for a large sum of money. Of course, he'd duped me into thinking it was a cattle ranch. I was coming here to check over my newest acquisition when the Wendell cousins caught up with me. You see, Jenna, I'm a gambler. It's the only life I've ever known.''

"No!" Jenna's mind muddied up. This couldn't be true. Bobby Joe wouldn't have done this again. Her brother wouldn't have sent this man, this Cash Callahan, out here to claim her farm. The implications were pulling her apart. Her brother had betrayed her again, but this time, she hadn't been the only one to suffer. Blue was dead because of it. And this man, this horrible gambler, whom she'd saved, then married, then bedded, oh, she couldn't even face that fact as yet, but this man and her deceitful brother had been the cause of it all. "No," she mumbled, her body sagging, defeated. She'd been duped once again.

"I'm sorry, Jenna. It's true."

Jenna lowered her lids, unable to bear the reality another second. She prayed for it all to go away. Like a bad dream, she'd awaken to find this man, this gambler gone. Blue would be by her side and he'd be smiling, taking her into his arms, speaking loving words to her. They'd set out to plow their fields and make a life together. Jenna wished it so. She desperately wanted to wake up from this nightmare.

"Jenna."

The voice so familiar, yet strange to her now, broke into her hopeful thoughts. She just wanted him to go away. "You came here to take my farm away from me."

''No.''

''You traveled quite some distance. You had the deed.''

''I thought I won it fair and square.''

Jenna put her head down. She ached with bone weary pain.

''I wouldn't have claimed the land. I wouldn't have taken the farm you love. Once I'd learned the truth, I would have left. I'd never harm you, Jenna. You have to believe that.''

''You're a gambler. Why would I believe anything you said?''

''Because...you know me.''

Jenna laughed with grinding bitterness. She'd known one too many gamblers in her day, and all of them had brought her nothing but grief. ''No, I don't know you at all.''

With a determined look, he stated, ''I've lived here for weeks. Hell, Jenna, you're my wife now.''

Jenna shot up from the sofa and whirled around to face him. ''No, I'm not. I married *Blue Montgomery.* You're nothing like him. You never could be. I'm not your *wife.*''

But when he stood, towering over her, his close proximity was too much to take so she moved away, to the opposite end of the small parlor. She had to face the sorry fact that she'd lain with this man. She'd been betrayed by her brother, then bedded by a stranger.

So much for her foolish notions of love and family. Jenna had had so little of both in her lifetime, how could she have held out hope that she'd attain either?

"Jenna, please listen. We can make this right."

Jenna shook her head briskly. "No, nothing could make this right." Heartache settled inside, a permanent part of her now, robbing her of any future joy. She knew now it would remain there, always, a reminder of a young girl's silly thoughts of love, of wishful dreams that would never come true. "You used me, just like Bobby Joe, just like that other man, coming here ready to take away my farm. There is no way to make this right."

"Jenna, listen to reason here. I was nearly dead when you brought me in. Men who wanted revenge had bushwhacked me on that stage. I didn't recall any of it. I didn't remember."

"And they killed Blue because of you." Jenna would never get over that. She viewed Cash Callahan with narrowed eyes, seeing him only as a low-bellied poisonous snake. Snakes sucked the life out of people. Gamblers did the same. She had no use for any of them. "What'd you do? Why were they after you?"

"I shot a man dead."

Jenna gasped and backed away from Cash. His gut clenched, but he couldn't say that he blamed her. The look on her face, the fear on her body, stuck like a knife in his heart. Regardless, he had to make her see the truth. "I caught him cheating at cards and he pulled a gun. He was ready to kill me. It was him or me, Jenna. I had no choice.''

''There's always a choice,'' she said in a whisper.

''I defended myself, just like you did that day the gambler came here to take claim of your farm.''

''He was nothing but a gambler...like you.''

''I wouldn't have taken your farm even if the deed had been real. You have to believe that.''

Jenna held back a well of tears, shaking her head. He could see her whole body trembling. ''There's nothing you can say to make this right. I think you should leave.''

Cash thought hard about this and came to the same conclusion. She was right. He had no place with Jenna Duncan. He would always be the man Jenna would regard as having stolen her innocence and taken away her future. He'd been duped and betrayed by her brother, just as she had, but he couldn't fight her hatred of gamblers. That much was painfully clear. Her mind was set.

Life with her had been a dream for a man with no past. But Cash recalled his past now, and he knew he wasn't fit for a woman like Jenna. He knew he could never keep her, never stay here on this farm and make her happy. It wasn't even an option.

From the time he was ten years old, all Cash had ever known was gambling. It was what he did, who he was. He'd been given a glimpse of a life he might have had, if his own life had been different, but Cash wasn't fool enough to believe he could change. He knew only one thing, only one way to survive. And he knew what was best for Jenna. "I'll leave in the morning, Jenna. I didn't mean for any of this to happen, but it did and I'm sorry you were hurt."

"I want you out of this house," Jenna demanded. "Now."

"I'll sleep in the barn. I'll be gone at first light." Hell, he'd leave now, if it meant taking that scowl off Jenna's face, if it meant removing her pain and the hurt he'd caused. But he had to speak to Ben. He had to make sure Ben and Rosalinda knew the truth. He had to make sure they would take special care of Jenna now. She was going to need them to get through this.

Cash dipped into his long coat once more. There was something else in there, a stash of cash for emergencies. Cash hadn't existed all these years on his own without a back-up plan. He'd always known how to survive.

He rolled up the money and handed it to Jenna. "Take this, for the farm. It'll see you through the winter."

Jenna's look of disgust nearly destroyed him. Memories of his earlier days, when townsfolk gazed upon with the very same sentiments, flooded in, reminding him of a time when he'd been regarded as dirty and foul, an unwanted youth who had been cast out from decent society.

"I don't want gambling money." She shoved it away with all of her slight might. "Just leave, Mr. Callahan. And never come back."

Jenna hadn't awoken from her bad dream, as she'd prayed. The nightmare was all too real. She curled up in her bed that night, her head propped by a pillow, staring up at the ceiling, lifeless. There were no more tears to shed, no greater pain than she'd suffered today. She didn't know what purpose her life held. She was tired, so tired of fighting. If it wasn't for Ben and Rosalinda, she'd be all alone in this world.

How could she face the day, the sun shining bright bringing hope, when all Jenna felt now was darkness and despair? She'd not shed another tear, yet she bled inside for the children she wouldn't have, for the family life she'd craved. All she'd wanted in life was to find love.

She had Ben and Rosalinda's kind, loving support and thank heavens for them. They'd been like family to her. And their son Antonio, the eager young boy who was rapidly becoming a man before her eyes, had been like a brother.

Jenna knew they wouldn't judge her, but how could she possibly face them? She'd been so sure, so absolutely certain the man she'd saved had been her Blue. She'd married the man, bedded him. Oh, Lord!

"Jenna Leah Duncan, you are a fool."

She closed her eyes then and prayed for sleep. Her body needed rest, having been drained from a tumultuous two days of highs and lows. Finding love, getting married, then to have it all brutally taken away in such a short span of time, had done damage to her mind, her heart and her body. But Jenna had responsibilities she couldn't ignore. Twin Oaks was all she had left.

"Sleep, Jenna. Sleep."

Tomorrow would be no different than any other day.

She had a field to plow.

A loud knocking at her door startled her awake. Jenna sat up, hopeful, until the events of yesterday rushed heartlessly into her mind, pulling her down into a dark void. She rubbed her eyes, assembling her thoughts. They were at best clouded and hazy yet.

"Miss Jenna. Are you awake in there?"

"Uh, yes. Just a minute, Ben." Jenna inhaled slowly, not quite ready to face the day.

"Just checking. It's almost noontime. Rosalinda and me, we was worried about you."

Noon? Heavens, Jenna never slept late. She rose up from her bed and donned her robe. Wrapping the ties around her waist, she secured the material and spoke behind the closed door. "I'll be down in a minute, Ben. Give me time to get dressed."

"No rush, Miss Jenna. I'll wait on you down in the kitchen."

Not ten minutes later, Jenna stood in her kitchen doorway. Ben was pouring coffee and Rosalinda had just set out a dish of spicy tamales, Jenna's favorite. The older couple turned to face her with looks of sympathy in their eyes. The sweet gesture of support put a sting in Jenna's swollen eyes.

"Ah, *querida,* come sit down. Let Rosalinda fill your belly with her tamales, no? Come, come." Rosalinda approached, taking Jenna's arm tenderly and guiding her to a seat at the table. "Sit. You must eat."

Jenna's stomach felt queasy. She had no appetite, but she couldn't hurt Rosalinda's feelings by refusing. The woman had gone to a lot of trouble. "These look…delicious." She gazed down at the plate set before her and her stomach lurched.

"Coffee?" Ben said, coming over and pouring her a cup before she could answer. Jenna noted Ben's quick glance at his wife. They both sat down at the table.

Jenna lifted her fork and took a small bite. Hungry or not, no one made tamales like Rosalinda. "Thank you both, but this isn't necessary."

"*Sí, sí,* Jenna. We must talk."

Ben took over then, his voice more cautious than

Jenna had ever heard. "We know the story, Jenna."

Jenna nodded. She'd figured as much. Ben and Rosalinda rarely came for a visit so early in the day. This was one of the busiest times on the farm. Plowing came first, then the planting. Jenna assumed Cash Callahan had spoken to them, explaining the reason he'd just been run off their property. Why else would her two dearest friends have come by to check on her? "Then you know that I married a stranger." She lowered her head.

"Do not put blame on yourself!" Rosalinda's outrage brought Jenna's head up and she witnessed stormy fire in the woman's eyes. "You did not know."

Ben took Jenna's hand. His rough blistered palm comforted her some, the familiar work-roughened hand of a man who loved the land, who worked hard for his family. That's all Jenna had wanted for herself—a man who would work alongside of her, till and plant the soil, then rejoice when the crop was healthy. "Mr. Callahan came to me this morning. He told me the entire story. If it means anything to you, I believe he is sorrowful. He did not mean to cause you harm, Miss Jenna."

"He's a gambler." It was almost more than she could bear. To think, that she had given her body to that man, had placed all of her faith and hope in him.

"Yep, he told me that. But Miss Jenna, he

couldn't recall anything. I don't think he would have harmed you. I don't think that man would have taken anything off this farm."

"But he did take from the farm. He took…my hope. My future."

Ben squeezed her hand, his gray eyes crinkling a bit, but there was encouragement in his tone. Dear sweet Ben. He was one man who would never let her down. "Nah, he did no such thing. You have your land. The crops will come in. You have the animals."

"And us, *mi corazon*," Rosalinda added. "You have us." Ben nodded in agreement.

Jenna tried to smile, hoping she succeeded. She loved these people, but she had dared to hope for more. She had hoped to marry, to raise a family and share a life with a man who had the same desires. "I know how lucky I am to have you both. I love you."

Ben's face reddened. "We love you, too," he said, looking a bit uncomfortable. Ben wasn't a man who spoke of such things normally. His admission only endeared him to her more.

"Is he gone?" Jenna glanced out the kitchen window, looking toward the barn. She couldn't even smile when she saw Button stretching her sleek body, a small respite away from her demanding kittens. No, she'd had only one thought, to be rid of the gambler.

"I took him into Goodwill this morning. The

man offered to pay me a tidy sum, but I didn't want money. I just was wishing things would've worked out better. I do believe he was thinking the same."

"*Sí*. He had the most beautiful bride. It is not easy to give up such a wonderful woman," Rosalinda said, with the slowest shake of her head.

Her friend was filled with romantic notions. At one time, Jenna had been no different, but she'd learned a bitter lesson recently, one she'd never forget. No more would she be so gullible, so trusting. That Jenna Duncan was dead and buried along with all of her hopes. "I was never his woman, Rosa. I never could be. I'm just relieved he's out of my life. Now, I've got to get to the fields."

She lifted up and Ben's steady hand went to her shoulder, lowering her back down.

"Not today, Miss Jenna. Today, you rest. Eat this meal my wife has cooked up for you. You look tired. You sleep the day away."

"Don't be silly, Ben. I have chores to do."

"They'll wait. You just stay put and take old Ben's advice."

"Later, I will bring you something especial. We will have more tamales then, no?" Rosalinda cast her a sympathetic smile. Jenna was inclined to agree with her, just to keep that smile on her face. She hated that her friends worried over her.

"Oh, all right. Thank you both," Jenna said, a bit disoriented. All she knew was working her land

and in the past doing just that brought her a full measure of peace and solace. Yet today her heart wasn't in it. She didn't feel like doing much of anything. Nothing held appeal. There was an unfathomable void within her, an emptiness that might never be filled again.

The life Jenna had yearned for had been cruelly ripped away. How would she manage to go on? She had nothing left to look forward to and she wondered how long she'd be able to endure such powerful loneliness.

Chapter Six

Cash rode into town, grimy and road-weary, ready for a hot bath and a shave. This had been his third stop in as many weeks. He'd been making his way south, heading down toward Fort Worth, leaving Oklahoma in the dust. The only time he wasn't thinking about Jenna was when he was holding a dead-to-rights winning hand. And even then, thoughts of her would slip in enough to stymie his concentration.

Cash hadn't been winning. Fact was, he'd been on a sorry losing streak for weeks now, ever since leaving Twin Oaks. Hell, he should consider himself fortunate that a woman with a good and kind heart saw fit to cheat death and nurse him back to health. She'd done that, brought him back to the living. And that's what seemed to put Cash's mind in a commotion. She'd given him a taste of what his life could be like, a small bite of something so powerful and pure, that it nearly hurt going down.

But just as fast as that lightning flash Jenna had predicted, Cash had lost it all.

He'd lost Jenna.

He couldn't be the man she wanted. Hell, if she knew the half of it, of the life he'd lived, of the methods he'd had to resort to in the name of survival, she probably wouldn't have even bothered with him that day at Turner's Pond. She would have left him for the buzzards.

Now he couldn't win a hand if he was holding four aces amid a table of drunken greenhorns on payday. But his luck would change. It always did. If Cash knew anything, it was how to survive.

So after a lukewarm bath and a pretty close shave, he strode into The Palace Saloon, waved to Chuck the barman, and headed straight into the gaming room.

"Hey, Cash," Louella called out, hustling her buxom body over to him. The fiery redhead was a welcome sight for a man whose luck was running low. If Cash needed anything right now, it was an old and cherished friend.

"Louella."

"Good to see you're back. Now, take everything off. I'm an impatient woman."

Cash stopped to a dead halt and chuckled. "You have a way with words, Louella."

"Yeah, well. No sweet-talking me out of it, I want to see you with everything off. Now."

Cash shook his head, marveling at how Louella

got away with her demands in such a rowdy town. Blackwater, Texas wasn't known for its church choir. But Louella ran her business the way she saw fit, and if a body didn't agree, she and her six-foot-tall barman were happy to escort them out the door.

With a finger, Cash flicked the catch on his gun belt and unbuckled it.

Louella smiled, her light brown eyes twinkling as she grabbed the belt from his hand. "I'll take the knife in your boot, too."

"Ah, Lou. You've got to leave a man with some pride."

"Pride, as you call it, took my man from me, right here in this very room not five years back. You know the rules, handsome. I've got to have all your weapons."

Cash frowned and leaned over to pull the knife out. "Here, satisfied?"

"Honey, I ain't been satisfied for going on five years." She winked. "What can I get you?"

"The usual, Lou, and bring the bottle."

"My, my, the whole bottle? You don't ever drink hard when you're gambling at my place." Louella gave him a stern look. "Except when you're troubled."

"You gonna stop mothering me, Lou? Or do I have to take my business elsewhere?"

Louella laughed. Her loud boisterous voice boomed across the gaming room. She stood with hands on curvy hips, giving him a sly look. "There ain't anywhere else in this dirt poor town to gamble, Cash. What's got into you, boy? Want me to send over one of the girls to make you feel better? You always seemed to like Belinda."

Cash shook his head. The last thing he needed was a woman. Cash had had enough woman trouble to last him five lifetimes. Jenna Duncan had pretty much ruined him for all women. Not a one would compare to her in his mind. "Not now, Lou. Right now, I need a bottle and a game. There is a game going, isn't there?"

Louella gestured to the corner table in the back of the room. Cash recognized a few of the men. He'd had the privilege of emptying their pockets a time or two in the past. "It ain't much, just a few locals passing the time. Higher stakes come later tonight."

"It'll do."

Cash walked over to the table, pulled out a cane-backed chair and sat down. "Afternoon."

They nodded, too deep in thought to greet him properly. Cash knew instantly they were sitting ducks, ripe and ready to pluck. He could read each one of their expressions. It was a knack he'd acquired in his youth. He didn't quite know how he'd done it but the fact remained, he knew how to read his opponents. All he had to do was concentrate.

And not think about Jenna Duncan.

Thirty minutes later, with a stack of chips keeping his side of the table warm, Cash raised the ante. "Twenty dollars to stay in."

He was met with lifted eyebrows, then one by one, the men folded, tossing their cards down. Cash hid his grin. Hell, all he was holding was a pair of threes.

"Game looks about over, Bobby Joe, but you come back tonight."

It wasn't Louella's voice that startled him, but the name she'd used. Cash turned his head to find Louella entering the room with Jenna's rattlesnake of a brother. Cash stood, his blood pumping hard and fast through his veins.

Bobby Joe turned white as a spinster's sheet and took off running, nearly knocking Louella down in the process.

Cash wasted no time. He shot out of The Palace, willing his legs to move faster, pressing hard and gaining on Bobby Joe. Vile thoughts of what he was going to do to him when he did finally catch up spurred his anger and fueled his body.

Next thing he knew, he was rolling around in the dirt with Bobby Joe right smack in the middle of the street. Cash managed to straddle the man, pinning him down and pushing his face against the ground. He reached for his gun and met with a handful of hip. Damn that Louella. She'd taken his weapon. Cash hissed out violently, "I should kill you right here."

With a yank, Cash pulled the man upright. A

crowd had formed on the sidewalk. Wagons stopped in their tracks. Cash cursed and shoved Bobby Joe to the edge of the mercantile building. With his back to the wall, Bobby Joe had nowhere to run.

"Hold on!" Bobby Joe shouted. "You got no call to kill me."

"No? I figure death comes to someone who cheats a man, but I ain't gonna hold that against you. It's what you did to your sister that you're gonna pay for. You don't even know the damage you've done."

Bobby Joe's wary eyes studied him. He pushed his hair off his face. "Jenna can take care of herself. She always could."

Cash gritted his teeth. He'd like nothing better than to shove a fist in his face in the hopes of knocking some sense into him. Jenna's brother had no notion how much his betrayal had hurt her and would probably continue to hurt her for a long, long time. "Maybe that's because she never had a choice. *You* never gave her a choice. She ever tell you what almost happened to her one year ago, when you lied through your teeth and cheated another man of his due? That man went over to Twin Oaks, ready to take your cheating out on her."

"Nothing happened. Jenna told me."

"She did, did she? I bet you don't know the half of it. Your sister's got more good in her than a handful of angels. You don't deserve to claim the same name.''

"She only cares about that shabby farm."

Cash gripped the man's shirt collar and pulled him so they were nose to nose. "That farm is all she has. You ever pull that fake deed stunt again or cause your sister one more bit of harm and I will kill you. I'll find you and I'll kill you. You got that?''

He released Bobby Joe quickly and the man's body hit the back wall. "I don't know what's got you so riled. Seems to me, you got no cause for revenge.''

"What?"

"I been back there. Just last week. I talked to Ben. I know all about you and my sister.''

Cash's anger gave way to softer feelings, thinking of Jenna at Twin Oaks, on the farm she loved with her whole heart. "Then you know the trouble you caused.''

"I know one thing, all right. I know you got no call to blame me. Seems you got the best end of the deal. Hell, my sister ain't never lain with a man before. It didn't take you long to bed her. I bet she gave you a real good time.''

Cash's fist found Bobby Joe's face. Blood oozed out of his mouth and nose when the man landed on the ground. Jenna didn't deserve the anguish this man had caused her. Cash wouldn't allow one bad word about her, not one. Brother or not, Cash would see to it that Bobby Joe looked upon Jenna with respect. Cash was ready to pounce, to teach him a thing or two when Louella's loud voice stopped him. "Cash!"

"Stay out of it, Lou."

Louella grabbed hold of his arm. She pleaded with him, her voice steady and her grasp firm. "You're about ready to kill him. I can see it in your eyes. Now back off. As it is, you probably broke his nose and he's gonna be eating on his back teeth for a long time."

Cash stared at Bobby Joe, lying there, his face a bloody mess. It wasn't enough. It might never be enough. Bobby Joe would never right the wrong he'd done to Jenna, but Cash would see to it he'd never hurt her again. "I should kill you."

With his sleeve, Bobby Joe wiped away blood on his mouth. "You'll be dead before you can do that."

"What'd you say?" Cash stepped closer to see the certainty in Bobby Joe's eyes.

"The Wendells know you're alive. You ain't exactly been hiding out. They're mad as hell they killed the wrong man. They're gonna come after you again. How long before they find out you took yourself a wife?"

Cash's face twisted. Damn. He hadn't thought of that. His mind hadn't been right since he left Twin Oaks weeks ago. He'd been wallowing in self-recrimination, thinking about Jenna, spending days drifting and nights, sleep-deprived. "If you told them about Jenna—"

"They got their own ways of finding out. Seems they got some kin in Goose Creek area. Only a matter of time before they find out about her."

Cash's gut tied into knots. If the Wendells knew about Jenna, they might go after her, just to get to him. A thousand thoughts passed through his mind, but he kept coming up with the same conclusion. Jenna could be in danger. The Wendells were ruthless. No telling what they might do, if they knew about her. "You keep your mouth shut about your sister."

Bobby Joe lifted his bloody chin and became defensive. "I ain't gonna send them her way, if that's what you mean. She's my kin."

Cash narrowed his eyes, unsure whether to believe the scoundrel. Bobby Joe was a liar, plain and simple. That this man and Jenna were blood relations seemed completely unfathomable. "You didn't mind sending that gambler to her at the farm."

"Didn't think he'd do her any harm."

"Lucky for you, he didn't," Cash warned. No telling what he would have done to Bobby Joe if one hair on Jenna's head had been injured. He probably would have killed him today, right here for the entire town to witness.

"C'mon, Cash. Let's get out of here." Louella took his arm and led him away from Bobby Joe.

Cash allowed that, because his head was spinning about the Wendells. "Go on up to your room, get yourself clean, then head back to The Palace. We'll have ourselves a talk."

Cash stopped and turned, giving Bobby Joe a cold hard look and his voice boomed like thunder when he cautioned, "Stay away from Twin Oaks. Stay away from Jenna."

"I ain't going back there. No way. Ben nearly ran me off the property anyhows. And Jenna wasn't her usual self. She didn't look too good, sorta pale and she don't eat like she used to."

Cash didn't want to hear this. He didn't want to care. It was better for Jenna if they never laid eyes on each other again. But Bobby Joe said she looked pale, she wasn't eating. It was too much for Cash. He had to know. "What's wrong with her?"

With a smug expression, Bobby Joe announced through bloodstained teeth, "If you ask me, I'd say she was in the family way."

Cash leaned his elbows heavily on the table in Louella's back room and played aimlessly with a pair of dice, rolling them again and again. He kept his focus steady on those dice, but his mind had drifted off.

"You gotta go back," Louella said with quiet determination.

"I can't." Louella didn't know all the facts. She didn't know how Jenna had kicked him off her land. She didn't know Jenna hated him just on the basis of how he earned his living. She hated gamblers. Cash couldn't go back there. It would only bring Jenna more pain.

"From what you told me, that girl could be in danger."

"If I left a trail and led the Wendells away from here, further south, she wouldn't be." Cash had been planning that in his mind since the moment Bobby Joe spouted off about Jenna. As soon as Cash had gotten wind that she might be in danger just from knowing him, he'd started formulating a plan.

"You want to spend your entire life on the run?"

"I'm not afraid to face them." He wasn't. Not if it meant keeping Jenna safe.

Louella took hold of his hand, putting a halt to his dice playing. He stared down at the snake eyes he'd just rolled. "Cash, you might never get that opportunity. The Wendells wouldn't think twice about shooting you in the back. They'd probably prefer it that way. You'd never see them coming. You wouldn't stand a chance."

Cash massaged his shoulder as he contemplated. Oddly, that familiar pain from working the farm comforted him. "She doesn't want me back there, Lou."

"That don't matter."

"She's opposed to the life I lead."

"That don't matter, either. You owe it to that girl to go back. What if her brother wasn't lying just then? What if that girl is carrying your child?"

Cash's breath caught for a moment. A child? *His* child? Hell, he knew what it was like for a child to have nothing or no one to call his own. He'd been that child, not so many years ago. He hadn't forgotten. Of course, the baby would have Jenna. And Ben and Rosalinda would be there. But Cash knew it wasn't enough. He wouldn't abandon Jenna if she were carrying a child. And what of the danger she might be in? Yet he was fighting going back.

But why? Then the reason flashed in his head as if the image had been there in the back of his mind for weeks now, ready to slap him hard with the truth.

It was the look of disgust and scorn on Jenna's sweet face when she'd found out who he was. In her eyes, nothing was more despicable than a gambler. From that moment on, she'd despised him. Cash had fought too long, struggling all of his life to attain a degree of dignity and with one look, Jenna had managed to wipe his pride away.

"You care for this girl, Cash." Louella's accurate assessment had him lifting his head to meet her light brown eyes.

He inhaled sharply. "I don't want to."

"But you do," she offered firmly, nodding her

head so that one tight red curl piled atop her head came down to bounce on her shoulder.

Cash stared at that curl for a time. Hell, he couldn't deny he had protective feelings for Jenna. He wouldn't allow himself anything more. "Yeah."

"Then you go see to her safety. You do the right thing. You know you're going back there. There ain't a bone in your body willing to desert that girl when she might need help. And from what you two shared in the past, who knows? Something good might come of it."

Cash grinned, concealing his trepidation. At least he could talk to Louella. She was the friend he'd needed right now. "Who knew you had a romantic soul, Louella? I'm going back to Twin Oaks, but don't be surprised if I'm back real quick. She might take one look at me and toss me off her property."

"You see to it that she doesn't. You owe that girl your life. You go back there, Cash, and make sure she's safe."

Cash knew he'd have to think long and hard to figure a way for Jenna to accept him back on the farm. Hell, he had to protect her, even if it meant sleeping in the wheat fields, watching out for the Wendells. One way or another, Cash was going to see to Jenna's safety, and he knew for damn sure, she wasn't going to like it. Not one dang bit.

* * *

Three days later, Cash turned in his saddle, not surprised to see the dog he'd fed in Blackwater still riding his coat tails. "Ain't you tired of following me yet, Scrappy?"

The mangy dog, thin as a string bean, had been beholden to Cash since he'd offered him table scraps from the diner. Cash hadn't the heart to turn the dog out, seeing him hungry and alone. He pretty much knew he'd gain a friend for life if he fed the darn animal, but that wasn't enough to thwart his intentions. He couldn't let the dog starve. The desperate longing in that mutt's eyes reminded him of a place Cash never wanted to be again. So now, he had a companion. Hell, he'd make a good watchdog, if nothing else. "We're just about there, Scrappy. Won't be long now."

A short time later, Cash rose up from his saddle and peered down the hill, witnessing workers busy plowing the field at Twin Oaks. He'd rode his mare hard, once the idea had settled in his head, hoping to get to Jenna before any danger might occur.

Relief swamped him when things appeared normal. Ben's son Antonio was tilling the soil on the east end of the property. There, they would plant oats. The crop rotation was meant to keep the soil fertile and where the soil was too tired, the field would remain fallow; nothing would be planted until next year. As he scanned over the land, it appeared to Cash that they'd accomplished some, but had much more to do since he'd left. Soon the wheat seeds would have to be planted.

He pushed his mare forward and after a time, he caught sight of Ben, working on a faulty axle by the barn. Cash's luck was holding out. He'd wanted to speak to Ben first, before he approached Jenna.

Cash sat high in the saddle and was ready to dismount when he was met with Ben's wary stare. "You want something, stranger?"

"It's me, Ben. Cash Callahan."

Ben squinted, blocking sunlight and stepping away from the axle. "Didn't recognize you in them fancy duds. And that mare of yours looks like a mighty fine piece of horseflesh."

Cash had forgotten that the folks at Twin Oaks hadn't seen him in anything but work clothes. He realized all too late that his suit coat, new Stetson hat and shiny boots would only remind Jenna of the way Cash made his living. He appeared every bit the gambler in his duds. And his horse was the best money could buy. Cash knew a good horse when he saw one, and apparently, so did Ben. "I suppose you got a problem with me?"

"Nah, I got nothing against you personally. But I do got a problem with you coming back here. Miss Jenna ain't gonna like it."

Cash dismounted. He preferred speaking to a man on level ground. Cash could never be accused of talking down to a man. Scrappy, ever loyal, stood right by his side. "I know. But listen, Ben, I came back here for a good reason. Hear me out first before judging me."

"I suppose I could do that."

They took a seat on the back end of the wagon Ben had been working on. After a few minutes, Cash appealed to the older man's sense of fairness after explaining all about the Wendells and the trouble they could cause Jenna. "Well? Will you help me?"

Ben scratched his chin, thinking hard. "You say Miss Jenna could be in real danger?"

"Yes, it's real. The Wendells are merciless. I don't trust them. If they find out the ties I had to Jenna, they'll come here looking for her. I've thought on it and me coming back here seems the best way to keep her safe."

"I'm here," Ben said, a bit defensively.

"Yes, you are. And I'm sure you look after her the best you can. But you don't sleep here. You have your own place. And that leaves Jenna all alone at night."

Ben's eyes grew wide and the older man's ire sparked. "Now, wait a minute. You ain't gonna be *sleeping* here, neither. I don't even have to tell you, Miss Jenna won't allow it."

"Ben, even if Jenna would have me, I won't go near her. You got my promise."

"You thinking she's not good enough?"

Cash twisted his mouth. He knew a no-win situation when he saw it. The old guy had a stubborn streak when it came to protecting Jenna, but Cash admired Ben's loyalty to her. "More like I'm not good enough for her."

"I might agree with that," Ben said, but there was no malice in his voice. Actually, it seemed Ben was teasing. Hard to know what went on in that old man's mind.

"But I'll be here, on the grounds. I'll sleep outside or in the barn. I'll be watching out. Just until the danger has passed."

"Miss Jenna ain't gonna like this. She won't want your protection."

"She won't know I'm protecting her. I don't want her to fret about the Wendells or the danger she might be in. She's had a rough time lately. I don't want to add to it.

"I'm hoping to convince her to let me stay on until the planting's done. I owe her, Ben. With my life. And that's the truth. You folks could use another hand on this farm. I'm hoping to convince Jenna of that."

"It's doubtful she'll be agreeing," Ben said with a shake of his head.

"That's where you come in. I'm betting that you want to see Jenna safe. I'm here to do that. I'll watch out for her, I swear to you. If you could help make her see that you need me here, at least until the planting is done—"

"Well, I don't know." Ben scratched his head,

a look of indecision on his face. "Jenna has her own mind. You'd best talk to her about it. And…" the old man said, after a moment of contemplation "…and I'll put a bug in her ear, but I'm making no promises."

"Thanks, I appreciate it."

"Fact is, we could use another hand around here."

"That's how I see it, too. How…how is Jenna?"

Cash held his breath waiting for the old man's answer. Ben took his time, darting a glance at the house, then at the rusty axle he was fixing. "Well, now, I won't lie. She's been better. Like I said, this is between the two of you. You'd best see for yourself. Go on. Get over to the house. I got work to do up on that barn roof, patching some holes, and I'm losing daylight."

"Right. I'm going." Sudden unexpected fear climbed up Cash's spine. He'd faced many an unholy situation in his time and had come through without a scratch, but somehow, meeting Jenna head-on scared the dickens out of him. One part of him couldn't wait to see her and the other feared her reaction to seeing him again. He wasn't a fool. He knew she'd not greet him with a hearty welcome.

Yet he was here to see to her safety. He owed her that. He'd have to find a way to stay on. He'd use every power of persuasion he could muster to make Jenna see that he was needed here.

After he'd left Twin Oaks, he'd felt as though he'd abandoned her as well as Ben and Rosalinda. He'd been a help to them on the farm. He'd seen how much work they'd had to do, knew his being here had made a difference.

Cash headed for the house and worries set in. What if Jenna was sick from carrying his child? What if she was in a bad way? Cash wouldn't leave her, no matter how much she argued the point.

"Stay here," he commanded to the mangy dog. Scrappy planted his bottom down, his tail doing a half swish, as if the animal couldn't decide if staying put was a good thing or not. Cash didn't take time to unsaddle his mare, Queen, but he did unload one parcel she'd graciously carried on her back from Blackwater. He lifted the package and knocked softly on the front door. When Jenna didn't answer, Cash walked around to the back door and knocked again. "Jenna."

No answer again.

Cash turned the knob and quietly let himself in, shoving aside thoughts of Jenna's reaction when she found him inside her house. He had good reason to be here. "Jenna," he called out again.

Cash made his way inside the parlor and stopped up short when he caught sight of Jenna Leah Duncan, sprawled out lazily on the sofa, fast asleep. One of Button's kittens, the orange-and-white lump of fur Jenna had aptly named Pumpkin, slept curled up right next to her, just under her chin.

Cash stepped back ready to leave the room, but he found himself drawn in by something he didn't want to put a name to, by something he didn't want to fight. He set the parcel down then lowered himself onto an old wooden rocker that had seen the last of its rocking days, and waited.

Chapter Seven

A wisp of soft fur tickled her nose. Jenna's lips curled up as she inhaled the sweet scent of her contented kitten. She came to slowly, relishing the peace of waking in the late afternoon. She'd been overly tired lately. She refused to think on it as melancholy, yet by day's end, Jenna just didn't have much fight left in her.

A flash, a subtle movement across the room, caught her attention as she squinted against the drowning sunshine. She saw a man, sitting in her rocker. Blinking, Jenna whispered, ''Blue?''

He rose and came toward her, lowering himself down on his haunches. ''No, Jenna. Not Blue. It's me, Cash Callahan.''

Jenna met his gaze, peering into those incredibly deep-river blue eyes. She shot straight up on the sofa, displacing the befuddled kitten, and stared into his face, blinking yet again. ''Mr. Callahan?

W-What are you doing back here?'' Jenna grabbed up Pumpkin and held her tight to her chest.

Cash rose and backed away, giving her the space she needed. "I had to come back, Jenna."

Stunned, Jenna's mind clouded. Her heart pounded. She never thought she'd lay eyes on this man ever again. She'd all but thrown him off her property, weeks ago. What possible reason would he have to return? She didn't want him here. She'd been desperately trying to forget him. "I don't see any reason for that, Mr. Callahan."

"Jenna, my name is Cash," he offered softly.

She lifted her shoulders, shaking her head, forced to remember how he'd used that gentle tone in the past. It was the last thing she'd wanted to recall, his tenderness when they'd lain together. "You're a stranger to me."

"Jenna, we can't pretend we haven't been—"

"Don't!" Jenna put up a hand to stop him from saying more and to stop the memories from filling her mind as well. "A true gentleman wouldn't remind a lady of such inappropriate matters."

"Inappropriate? Jenna, we *were* married. At least, we both thought so at the time."

Heat spread to Jenna's cheeks. She'd been trying to block out those images, but they were doggedly persistent in her mind. She'd been dreaming of him, of Cash, and remembering the one night they'd shared as man and wife. But in the morning she'd dredge up all the reasons to hate him, to blame him for her misfortune, to loathe the way he made a living. Oddly, those thoughts brought her no peace, as she had hoped. They'd done more to confound and confuse her. Jenna had never been one to harbor hate.

"Please," she pleaded, "just tell me why you're here."

He sat down on the opposite end of the parlor sofa and ran a hand down his face. "Jenna, you saved my life. Nobody has ever done for me, what you had. Nobody has ever cared enough."

Jenna didn't want to know what kind of life he'd led before coming to Twin Oaks. She didn't want his gratitude. Yet amazingly she stayed calm while he sat there on the sofa, saying his piece. "I thought you were someone else," she whispered.

"You would have saved me, even if you knew who I was. I know you, Jenna. You would have."

Jenna shrugged, realizing he was probably right. She wasn't one to leave a man bleeding, nearly dead on the side of the road, if she had a chance to save him. But that didn't mean that she had to like him. It didn't mean he had a right to come back here. "You've already thanked me. And as I recall, I asked you to leave Twin Oaks. So why are you here?"

Cash stood up, walked over to the window and glanced out, looking upon the fields for a time, before turning to her. "I owe you a debt I might never be able to repay, Jenna. But I want to try.

You had so many plans for the farm, when you thought we were, well…'' He stopped talking and frowned. ''Anyway, you could use another worker. I'm asking you to let me stay on, at least until the planting is done. I want to help out here. I owe you that much.''

Jenna bounded up from the sofa, her heart filled with despair. Did he think that would make up for all the heartache she'd endured? Did he think she'd just welcome him back here? Did he think she'd want to see him each day, when with every moment she'd be reminded of all that she had lost? ''No.''

''Jenna, hear me out,'' he said, his eyes going dark with determination. He set his hands on his hips, ready to do battle, it appeared.

Jenna knew how to be just as determined. She assumed the same stance. ''No.''

''You need more help on the farm. You can't afford to hire anyone.''

''That's true. My answer is still no. I'll thank you to leave, Mr. Callahan.''

Jenna made her way to the front door, opening it, her dismissal clear. But then a low anguished shout from the barn startled her, shoving instant fear down her throat. ''It's Ben,'' she screamed, running out the door. She heard Cash's footsteps right behind her.

''Ben!'' She came upon him, lying across a rusty axle, his body in an awful twist. A ripped pant leg oozed deep red blood and a gash about the size of a short hemp rope, one inch thick and nearly a foot long, almost reached his knee. "Oh, no!" Jenna gasped as overwhelming fear plagued her when she witnessed Ben's ashen face.

"He must have fallen from the roof. Looks as though he fell right onto this axle," Cash said, pointing to the bloody piece of metal, then moving Jenna aside to bend over him. "He's out cold."

"You mean he's not…"

Cash shook his head. "No, he's not dead, Jenna. He's banged up bad, knocked out from the fall, but he's breathing. Quick, get me some cloths and rip them up. And a bucket of fresh water. We'll clean him up and stop the bleeding, then I'll bring him into the house."

Jenna dashed into the house gathering up the necessary supplies, praying Cash was right about Ben's accident. He had to survive. Jenna couldn't imagine losing another loved one on this farm. She couldn't fathom Rosalinda without Ben by her side.

"Here," she said, handing Cash the cloths and setting down the bucket of water. She worked alongside of him as he bathed the wound on Ben's leg. Jenna kept a cool wet cloth to his Ben's head, gently wiping at his thick graying hair. She stayed close by him, speaking softly, calling his name, hoping for him to awaken. "Please, Ben, please. Wake up."

Cash didn't take his eyes off the gash, soaking up as much blood as the cloth would allow. With head bent to the task, he spoke with certainty. "He's going to be fine, sugar. Don't you fret. As soon as I wrap his leg real good, we'll get him into the house. Go on in and get some blankets. We'll put him on the sofa."

"But—" Jenna wanted to ask how he knew Ben would be fine. She wanted assurances. Sick with worry, Jenna's stomach clenched.

Cash cast her a quick confident look that put her somewhat at ease. "Go on, Jenna. I'll bring Ben inside in a few minutes."

Two hours later, Jenna wrung her hands and paced the floor. Stomping her boots wouldn't help. Yelling at the top of her lungs wouldn't help, either. Once again, fate seemed to step in where Cash Callahan was concerned. He was back on her farm and there wasn't a darn thing Jenna could do about it.

Ben had come to an hour ago, waking up madder than a penned-up stallion. Upset that he'd fallen and gotten injured, Ben had cursed up a storm. But Jenna's heart went out to him, knowing what great pain he suffered. Shortly after, Rosalinda had rushed in, crying pitifully.

Jenna had been grateful that he'd awakened and that he'd most likely make a full recovery in time. But now, as he lay resting on her sofa, his leg propped up with a pillow to keep the seeping down and Rosalinda praying silently over her prayer beads, Jenna had to face facts. Ben's leg wouldn't be healing up for weeks. He'd probably have to be taken to Goose Creek to have that injury checked out by the doctor there.

And just minutes ago, Cash Callahan had offered them his help on the farm, deliberately ignoring the dagger-like glances Jenna had cast his way. Ben had looked to Rosalinda and she'd nodded in agreement. Both of her dear friends had made their decision without consulting her. And now Cash Callahan was preparing the wagon to take Ben home. The gambler barged back into her life without care or thought of her feelings from a misguided sense of duty. He claimed he owed her, but all she wanted from him was for him to leave. Ben and Rosalinda didn't see it that way.

"I don't want him here," Jenna said, folding her arms across her middle. How could they think that she would?

"It is for the best, *querida*," Rosalinda said softly, seeking to comfort her. "You will see." A bright light gleamed in Rosalinda's eyes. "It is like a miracle that Mr. Callahan came to the farm when he did, is it not? I believe God sent him here. He will be of great help. Already he has taken care of Ben and now he fixes the wagon to take us back home. He offers to do Ben's labor on the farm,

Jenna. We could not refuse. He is needed here now.''

Jenna didn't want him here. Heaven knew, she truly didn't want him here. Her mind rebelled, as did her heart. But Jenna couldn't argue. Ben's decision would have to stand. She shoved aside her trepidation and tried to look at this situation rationally.

Rosalinda was right, of course. Without Ben, the planting surely wouldn't get done in time. She had no call now to prevent Cash from working the farm. But she didn't believe that his coming here was a miracle. No, it seemed bad things happened when he was around. Why, if he hadn't shown up today, Ben probably wouldn't have taken that fall. Irrational as that seemed, Jenna truly believed it. Now, for Rosalinda's peace of mind and for Ben's general welfare, she had no choice but to allow him back on the farm. But he didn't have to live here, did he? ''Where will he stay?''

Both Rosalinda and Ben chorused at once. ''Here.''

Ben beseeched her with a small, loving smile. ''There ain't room in our place, and Rosie's gonna have a time of it, taking care of me while I'm laid up.''

Rosalinda smiled warmly at her husband. ''I do not mind taking care of you. But I do not have room in our small house for another.''

Jenna bit down on her lip as dread set in contemplating once again living with the man, only now she saw him for whom he was, a gambler, and not the man she'd vowed to love. She saw him as the man who had taken everything from her, in the name of one sorry bet.

Cash entered then, looking toward Ben. "Wagon's all ready. You think you can make the trip, Ben?"

Ben turned to her "My leg aches like the devil. You got any whiskey, Miss Jenna?"

"It's in the small cabinet by the back door," Cash responded instantly, a brutal reminder that he'd been familiar with all aspects of Jenna's house. He'd been familiar with other things as well. Intimately familiar. Jenna had trouble forgetting that. "I'll get it," he added, before leaving the room.

Rosalinda darted a glance at Ben. He cast her a brief smile, a daring feat seeing as he'd been knocked out cold a few hours ago. "That man's got good in him."

"Because he's serving you whiskey?" Jenna asked with disbelief. Had both of her friends forgotten what Cash Callahan had done?

"No, *querida,*" Rosalinda intervened, "it is because he came back here. He is willing to help us."

"I have a lot to thank him for, myself," Ben said, nodding in agreement with his wife. "He did a mighty good job of patching me up."

"He's a gambler. Don't count on him staying

long." Jenna knew in her heart, Cash Callahan wouldn't last long on the farm. He wasn't a farmer. He didn't have the same love of the land as they did. He'd be gone before she blinked twice. Perhaps, she shouldn't worry about him living here since he'd probably take off first chance he got.

"A man's word should count for something, Miss Jenna," Ben said, his voice growing weak. He really needed to get home to rest, Jenna thought. "And I believe he's good to his word."

Jenna doubted that, but for Ben and Rosalinda's sake, she'd take Cash Callahan in. After all, he had helped save Ben, knowing just what to do and how to do it. Jenna wouldn't deny him that.

But she also wouldn't be a darn bit surprised if she woke up one morning to find him long gone.

Cash entered Jenna's house later that night. He'd helped get Ben situated in his bed, and made sure Rosalinda had everything she needed to tend the ailing man, before he returned.

He'd been sorry about Ben's accident, but because of it, Cash had gotten what he'd wanted—for Jenna to allow him to work the farm. He could protect her now, just in case the Wendells came here looking for him. He'd be ready. He wouldn't let down his guard and, most important of all, Jenna would be safe.

Cash had almost forgotten the package he brought with him today. He entered the parlor and bent by the rocker to pick it up. On impulse, Cash had made a stop in Goose Creek to pick up a present for Jenna. Whether she accepted it or not, Cash had been compelled to buy her something real nice. Hell, she deserved so much more than he could ever give her. He owed her his life. He owed her *her life.* Because of Bobby Joe's trickery, many lives had been destroyed. And if the gift he'd purchased brought Jenna even the smallest measure of joy, then it would be well worth it.

Jenna appeared in the doorway, her arms tightly folded around her middle, her body slumping. Clearly the events of the day had worn on her nerves. "Did you get Ben home okay?"

Cash nodded. "He's going to be all right, Jenna. That gash is deep though. Antonio is taking him to Goose Creek tomorrow to see the doctor. I rewrapped his leg, hoping to keep the bleeding down. It's about all we can do for now."

Jenna worried her lip then spoke gently, "Thank you for taking care of Ben."

It was the first time Jenna's voice had softened to him. Maybe in time, she'd come around. Cash didn't want to do her any harm. He had to make her see that. "Listen, I know you don't want me here—"

"That much is very true," she interrupted.

A frown pulled at his lips. She wasn't going to make this easy. "But now that I am, I'm going to help out as much as I can. I'll do Ben's work, starting tomorrow. But it's been a long day for us both. I'll bed down in the barn and let you get some rest, if that's all right?''

"Yes, that's all right.'' She wasn't too happy about any of this, but Cash knew Jenna was plumb out of options. For Ben's sake, she couldn't refuse his working here. Perhaps giving her the parcel would go a ways to getting her to come around.

"Oh, and here,'' he said, handing her the package. "This is for you.''

Jenna's light-blond brows lifted. "For me?'' She appeared stunned, as though she'd never received a gift before. She took the package from his hands, casting him wary glances. "I don't understand.''

"Go ahead. Open it, Jenna.''

Jenna sat down on the sofa and placed the package on her lap. With tentative fingers, she undid the thin string tie and the package folds opened slightly. Spreading the folds open all the way, Jenna stared down at the contents. "Oh, my.''

Her fingers grazed over the soft material of the dress. "This is beautiful.''

"Take it out,'' Cash encouraged, hoping she'd accept his gift. He'd spent some time with Miss Millie at the emporium trying to find just the right one.

Jenna lifted the dress, the golden color nearly a perfect match to her long unruly hair. "It's store-bought,'' she said in awe.

Cash stepped closer, gratified by the look of

pleasure on Jenna's face. She'd probably never owned a dress that hadn't been sewn on this farm. "It should fit. When I saw the color, it reminded me of you." Golden, like ripened wheat fields. "I went by my recollections of your size."

Jenna's head shot up and her pale complexion turned rosy red. Cash cleared his throat. What could he say? A man didn't forget the taste and feel of a woman like Jenna Duncan. He knew her size right down to her tiny delicate ankles.

She dropped the dress down, regret filling her eyes. With a chill in her voice, she said, "I can't accept this."

"Why not?"

"You bought this with gambling money."

"Jenna, you saved my life. A man has a right to say thank-you for that. It's a proper gift for a proper lady."

She began refolding the dress, setting it back in its wrap. "Using gambling money isn't my idea of a proper anything."

Cash spoke with quiet regard. "Gambling's all I've ever known, Jenna. It put food on my plate and a roof over my head since I was just a boy. I can't help it, any more than you can help being a farmer. I didn't have much choice. But if that dress can bring you an ounce of joy, then please accept it. You deserve something nice."

Jenna nodded, her eyes downcast. She wouldn't fight him on this, but she also refused to understand. She had a real blind side when it came to gambling. Damn, she peered at the dress with such longing that Cash knew she truly wanted it.

"It's really very lovely," she said finally.

"Then keep it. You don't have to wear it. But keep the dress up in your room. Even if just to look at."

Jenna studied the garment, her gaze travelling over each detail, each pearl button, each golden stitch. The kitten jumped playfully on the dress, and Jenna shooed her away. "I don't...think I should."

Cash kept his patience. "It won't hurt anything if you just tuck it away in your room, Jenna."

She lifted her eyes to him, the fight all but gone from her. She'd had quite a wearisome day, he assumed, by the sound of her long drawn-out sigh. "Fine, then, Mr. Callahan."

Mr. Callahan? Cash couldn't abide her stiff formality and he hoped to change that real soon. But at least she accepted the dress. That would have to be enough for now, he decided.

A short time later, Jenna headed to the barn carrying a thick wool blanket and a basket. Standing just inside the doorway, she peered inside. A lantern burned dim light into the loft. "Mr. Callahan?"

"I'm up here," he called out and Jenna saw his face appear at the edge of the loft.

"I brought you a blanket and some food. It's nothing much, since I didn't cook today. There's some bread and cheese and Rosalinda's pecan pie."

A wide grin split his face. "You got pie?"

"I'll just leave the basket. You can return it in the morning." Jenna set both the basket and the blanket down, anxious to leave. The less time spent with him the better.

"Wait! I'm coming down."

Jenna paused. She didn't want to be alone in the barn with Cash Callahan, yet to leave so abruptly would only make her seem foolish. She'd only come to offer him a plate of food. Short moments later, Jenna stood face to face with him. "Is there something else?"

Cash lifted the basket and peered inside, his eyes going wide like a young boy finding a hidden treasure. "Haven't had a decent meal in days. Been eating hard tack and beans mostly. Me and Scrappy."

"Scrappy?"

"My dog. Sort of followed me from town and the darn mutt won't leave my side. Didn't you catch a glimpse of him today?"

"Uh, no. I wasn't paying much mind to anything but Ben." Jenna glanced up and saw the thin, unkempt black-and-white dog wag his tail from above. "Looks like he could use a good meal, too."

"He'll fatten up on the farm. He ain't particular. He'll eat anything he catches."

"Really? What do you suppose he'll catch on the farm?" Jenna had visions of a rat and mouse slayer. True, Button was the farm's foremost predator in that regard, but what on earth would a dog be able to catch?

Cash's lips curled up. "Anything I throw his way."

An unexpected chuckle bubbled up and Jenna shook her head with amusement. Despite her not wanting him here, Cash Callahan could make her laugh.

"He'll make a real good watchdog."

"Right," Jenna said, holding back a smile now. "I noticed the way he nearly pounced on me when I came in."

"Yeah," Cash said, rubbing his chin thoughtfully, "I noticed that, too." He lifted his head toward the loft. "You just go back to sleep, old boy. We'll work on your watchdog skills tomorrow." Cash smiled. "Appreciate the food, Jenna."

"It's nothing special. There'll be a hot meal for you in the morning."

Cash nodded, gesturing to the barn with a sweep of his hand. "Should I take my meals in here?"

Jenna flinched. "Oh, um—" She hadn't thought that far ahead. She didn't have to condemn the man to eating with the barn animals. It was enough he was sleeping with them. "No, I'll have a meal waiting for you in the kitchen. I'll unlatch the door in the morning.''

"That sounds fine to me." Cash smiled wide, his dark blue eyes a bright gleam in the dimly lit barn.

"Well then, Mr.—"

He placed a finger to her lips. "It's Cash."

She squeezed her eyes shut. His touch, the soft yet rough texture of his skin on hers, brought back memories of the night they'd shared, of how his fingers had traced the outline of her lips, before his mouth had come down over hers. When she opened her eyes, his finger was gone and Cash had taken up the blanket and basket, ready to climb the ladder leading to the hayloft.

"Sleep tight," he said as he clutched the rung of the ladder.

Jenna prayed that she would. She had a long day ahead of her tomorrow and dreaming about Cash Callahan was simply out of the question. Her good memories of him warred in her head with the bad ones, creating unsettling and uneasy thoughts. Yet, she had no choice but to accept him for the time being. He was here, not by her choice, but by Ben and Rosalinda's bidding. Jenna would have to learn to live with that, and with him.

"Good night...then."

He paused on the third step, but didn't turn around. Softly, he uttered, "Thanks for the meal."

She watched him until he was knee-deep in hay then dashed out the barn door.

Cash woke before the sun made its way up, hearing the sound of the barn door creak open. He reached for his gun then crawled over to the edge of the loft, covering himself with hay. Gazing over the rim, he watched with amazement as Jenna stroked the old milk cow, Larabeth, softly, using soothing words to coerce her into a contented state.

Then she sat down on a tiny stool and proceeded to milk her. Cash heard the tink, tink, tink as milk entered the pail.

Button walked up and rubbed her silky body against Jenna's leg. "You're only cuddling me 'cause you want something, don't you?"

Button removed herself, sitting a few feet away in a regal feline pose. She eyed Jenna with controlled anticipation, her sharp gaze never wavering as she sat waiting. Jenna laughed quietly, the sound a small whisper of delight. "Okay, okay, Miss Button, mistress of the barn. Is this what you want?"

Jenna aimed the teat and squeezed. Milk squirted out and hit Button right on the nose and mouth. The cat eagerly lapped up the milk and waited for more.

"Two more squirts. That's all I have time for, you sweet mama kitty." She aimed and didn't disappoint the cat, the milk blasting forth onto Button's face.

Cash laughed aloud, startling Jenna. She stiffened, as though she'd forgotten he'd been sleeping there. "It's just me, Jenna." He climbed down from the hayloft and stood beside her. "That's quite a trick."

Jenna relaxed her stance and Cash made a note not to startle her again. It would take some getting used to, he supposed, for Jenna to remember he was a temporary resident on her property now. "Button loves it. It's like a game with her. Did I wake you? I almost forgot—"

"No, you didn't wake me." Cash, dressed in only an undergarment and his work trousers, shook his head. "But do you always rise so early?"

"I like to get an early start."

Cash stretched, his arms lifting and pulling the muscles taut. Jenna averted her gaze and resumed the milking.

"You could sleep longer if you let me do that," Cash said, thinking aloud.

"I get enough sleep," Jenna responded, matter-of-factly.

Cash studied her from the back, the lift of her shoulders and the curve of her hips. She was a strong woman, but again, he wondered if she carried his child. "You look tired, Jenna. An extra bit of time in bed could do you good. I'm here in the barn anyway. I could learn how to milk the cow."

"It's not as easy as you think," she offered and

Cash got the distinct impression Jenna didn't think he was up to the challenge.

"It doesn't look hard at all."

"Larabeth is used to me. There's trust between us."

"Tarnation, is that all? Why, I bet I could have that old milk cow filling that pail faster than a jack-rabbit stealing into a lettuce patch."

Jenna's back went ramrod stiff. "There'll be no betting on this farm."

Cash suppressed a chuckle, putting a somber tone in his voice. "Okay, I *believe* I wouldn't have a bit of trouble milking old Larabeth here. Want to show me how?"

Jenna gazed down into the half-full pail. "I'm about through for now. Best if we try again later tonight. That's if you really want to learn?"

Cash nodded. "I do."

"Fine, then. I'll meet you in here after supper tonight and we'll see how you do." Jenna lifted the pail and shoved the stool into the corner. "I'll have your breakfast ready in an hour."

"What should I do until then?"

"Feed the animals, muck out the barn and chop some wood. After breakfast, we'll get to the fields."

"We? Jenna, I don't think you should—"

"I'm a farmer, Mr. Callahan. It's what I do."

Jenna's raised chin and defiant tone was meant to put Cash in his place. He understood her pride, her determination. She hadn't had too many people to count on during her life. But the hell of it was, he didn't want her killing herself out in the fields. Not while he was here. Not while she might be with child.

And damn it all, if she didn't stop calling him *Mr. Callahan,* he was going to have to resort to desperate measures, like *kissing* her mouth shut.

Wouldn't that put Miss Jenna Duncan in her place?

Of course, it could also land him off of Twin Oaks completely, tossed out onto his backside.

Cash wasn't entirely sure it wasn't worth the risk.

Chapter Eight

Jenna just couldn't believe Cash Callahan wanted to learn how to milk old Larabeth. A man like him, well, he just wasn't suited for such things.

Drinking fine whiskey, eyeing the ladies and betting his money down, that's what Cash Callahan knew how to do. He was no farmer, and soon, the ravages of the day would get to him. Wouldn't be long before he'd leave. Farm work took stamina. It took persistence. It took *faith*. Without the latter, no man, woman or child would ever become a farmer. Simple forces of nature could destroy your crop, a drought, or heavy rains, or creatures, both big and small, could do enough damage to dishearten even the most stout-hearted of men.

No, Cash Callahan, with his finely embroidered three-piece suit, his fancy horse and studded saddle, would never have enough faith to stay on. He'd never…

"Jenna?"

Startled from her musings, Jenna bit her lip and turned from the cookstove. Hard thoughts had a way of entering into your heart, Mama used to say. Made you hardhearted. "I'm just about through cooking up the meal. Come in."

Cash entered with the basket from last night. On top sat a beautiful wildflower, rosy in hue and so very cheerful. "Brought your basket back," Cash said.

Jenna stared at the flower, awed by its simple beauty. "Th-thank you," she mumbled, standing there in the middle of her hot kitchen, ready to cry.

Cash stepped closer, setting the basket down on the table. "Jenna, what's wrong?"

She shook her head and turned away. "Nothing. It's just the onions. They sting my eyes."

She heard him take a deep breath, then pull out a chair. When her bout of melancholy was finally over, she turned to set down a dish of diced ham and onions, biscuits and apple butter.

"Smells good," he said then dug into the food like a man possessed. Jenna watched him devour the meal, leaving a portion of the food untouched. She poured him more coffee when he'd emptied his mug.

"Tasted even better," he said when he was through, patting his stomach and smiling. "You're a good cook, Jenna."

"I make do, is all. After a long day in the fields, even mush tastes good."

"I've had my share of mush, Jenna. And this here is good food."

"I didn't think they served anything but the best in those gambling houses."

Cash chuckled. "They don't. But there was a time in my younger days, when I'd consider anything that wasn't moving around on the plate a meal. Of course, that was some time ago."

Jenna nodded, her curiosity kindled. But she wouldn't ask.

"Aren't you eating?" Cash asked, eyeing her from top to bottom. His sudden and intense scrutiny had her turning around completely, toward the stove.

"I ate something earlier."

"What?"

She spun around then, unable to control her irritation. "What did I eat?"

Cash lifted himself from his seat. His deliberate gaze pierced her with blue fire. "Yeah, I asked you what did you have to eat?"

Flustered, Jenna responded, "Why does it matter?"

"It matters. So, are you gonna tell me?"

"I had a biscuit and some milk," she said firmly. Why did the man feel compelled to question her so?

"That's all?"

"Yes, that's all," she answered, raising her voice.

"Well, shoot. That ain't enough to feed a bird, Jenna. Why in hell aren't you eating? I recall a time when you'd eat a portion and a half without blinking an eye. What's got into you? You're losing weight and you look tired all the time."

"That's none of your business, Mr. Callahan!" The nerve of the man, Jenna thought angrily. He had no right inquiring about anything having to do with her. And she certainly didn't appreciate that he'd even bothered to notice her lack of appetite and the dark marks of fatigue under her eyes.

"Sure it is. It's my business if you're…sick."

"I'm not sick!"

"Well, you look sick."

"Thank you for that." She held back tears.

"Ah, Jenna. I didn't mean it that way. You're as beautiful as ever. Just tell me what's wrong."

Jenna whirled around and braced herself against the counter. She couldn't face him. Couldn't look him in the eye and tell him the truth. She *was* sick, heartsick.

She'd lost everything because of Cash Callahan. She had nothing to look forward to—no joy, no future, no family to call her own. So what if she wasn't eating or sleeping well? Why did he care? And what good would it do to admit that to him? She had a farm to run, crops to plant. That's all that sustained her now. She doubted that a man like Cash Callahan would even understand a young girl's foolhardy dreams.

"I'll clean up here and meet you in the field. We have more than two acres to plow this week."

Cash grunted something she didn't understand then stormed out the door with his plate in his hand. Jenna peered out the window just in time to catch him tossing the last portion of his meal to Scrappy. The dog didn't let even a morsel touch the earth. With tail wagging and a bounce in his step, the loyal animal followed behind Cash's long purposeful strides until Jenna lost sight of them in the fields.

She turned away from the window, her gaze settling on the basket and the pretty wildflower that Cash had brought to her. She walked over to it and fingered the petals slowly, enjoying the silky texture, breathing in the subtle scent.

You're as beautiful as ever.

"I don't understand you, Cash Callahan," she murmured quietly. She wished he'd never come to Twin Oaks. She wished he'd leave, the sooner the better.

"Wonder what you'd say to me now, Mama. You raised yourself a hardhearted daughter. That's for darn sure."

By midafternoon, Cash had seen more of the Lord's worm-laden earth than he could have ever imagined. He'd come out and plowed with a vengeance, angrier with Jenna than he'd ever been. Damn, a man had a right to know if a woman carried his child, didn't he? But he couldn't come right out and ask her. Instead, he hoped for signs; and this morning, Jenna's lack of appetite gave him reason to wonder. She'd been eating poorly lately. Cash didn't know much about the subject, but if Jenna carried his child, would she have more of an appetite, since she was feeding two, or less of one, since the pregnancy might make her ill?

The hell of it was, he just didn't know.

And just as his stomach grumbled, Jenna appeared, coming up from behind carrying a thin quilt and a tall jug. "Ready for the noon meal?" she asked, her face flushed. The rise of color looked good on her, a distinct contrast to her sallow appearance of late. Cash wondered if her rosy appearance had more to do with her irritation at him than any newfound bit of good health.

"I was planning on working until suppertime."

"You can't work straight on through. You need to take a break. I brought sun tea. You must be thirsty by now."

Cash wiped his face with his sleeve. She handed him the jug. "I could use a drink. Thanks, Jenna."

"Give Mac a rest and you come and sit down on this quilt." She unfolded the quilt then uncovered a plate of food that had been tucked inside. Cash helped her set the quilt down right there on the soil he'd just plowed. The only shade trees on the property were back at the homestead.

Cash sat down, stretching out his long legs and

glanced up at Jenna. She wore her work clothes, a ragged dress that would have been considered pretty at one time, beat-up leather boots and an apron. Long strands of golden hair draped onto her face. Cash caught her making futile attempts to push the wayward locks back into her braid. "You gonna sit down with me?"

"Only if you promise not to pester me about eating or insult my appearance."

"Insult your appearance? I didn't do that." Tarnation, he'd told her she was beautiful. And it was the truth. Didn't she know that? Her raised brows told him that she probably didn't. And the sour look on her face said she wouldn't buy his explanation anyway. Cash nodded. He knew a no-win situation when he came across it. "Fine."

She sat down across from him, but stared at the field instead of looking at him. He lifted a piece of fresh bread to his mouth.

"When do you start planting?" he asked, although he pretty much knew the answer. Getting Jenna to talk was what he had in mind, and he knew she'd offer all she could about her farm.

"We can start next week or the week after, depending on how the plowing goes. We'll have most of the fields ready. Ben and Antonio have almost finished tilling the soil up at their end. There's just a few more acres, then we'll try out the new seeder. There's nothing quite so beautiful as a field waist-high of new wheat. It's a grand sight. I think we'll have a real good crop this year."

"Why so?"

"The earth here was worn out, so we let it rest. Our crop last year was small, but good. This year should be our biggest ever. We've never plowed so much land before. I think the soil is ready."

Cash nodded. Jenna knew about farming and at least she was willing to share that part of her life with him.

"Well, I'd better get to Mac. He looks ready to get moving again." Jenna rose from the quilt and headed toward the plow.

"Jenna, wait a minute." Cash jumped up quickly. "What are you planning?"

"I'm going to finish the plowing this afternoon." She squinted when a shock of sunlight broke from the clouds. "Whoops, forgot my bonnet. Let me borrow your hat." She reached up fast and lifted the straw hat from his head. "Thanks," she said mischievously, a quick but sweet smile lifting her lips. She set the hat atop her head.

Cash knew strong-arming Jenna would do no good. But he'd be damned if he was going to let her plow up the fields while he lay down on that quilt and watched.

He reached up just as fast and snatched the hat back, lifting it from her head. "Hey!"

"Jenna, you can't plow this field."

"Oh? I'll have you know I just finished trading

off with Antonio up at his end. I *can* plow this field and I will."

"No, you don't understand. I'm just now catching on. It's taken me all this time, but I think I've finally got it right. Mac and I," he offered, glancing at the large Percheron, "we've bonded. I think I finally understand the old boy. I don't want to stop now."

"Are you telling me you enjoy plowing?"

Cash rubbed the back of his neck. That lie would be too far a stretch for even Jenna to believe. "Enjoy, now that's a powerful word. I *enjoy* a lot of things, Jenna. A warm bed with a good, uh…book." He cleared his throat. "A nice hot bath." He rubbed his neck again. "A delicious meal, but I can't really say I *enjoy* plowing."

"So then, why do you want to get back to it?"

"I'm a man who likes a challenge. Farming is that, wouldn't you agree? It's something new and different. I want to learn as much as I can."

"Why's that? I mean to say, you'll be leaving soon."

He nodded, stalling for time. Jenna had him dead to rights. Then a thought struck. Perhaps it had been lingering all the while. "True and all, but it feels good working with my hands. There's a sense of something…I don't know. I can't put a name on it. It just seems…right."

Jenna nodded and he could see the spark of recognition in her eyes. Was he just telling her what she wanted to hear, or was there some truth to what Cash had just admitted? Damn, looking into Jenna's soft tawny eyes had his head spinning. He wasn't seeing straight, that was for doggone sure.

"Okay, I'll leave you to plow the field. But keep the jug and the food here, for later. I'll take the quilt back now. I'll see you for supper tonight."

"Right," he said, relieved. He watched her sashay away, her torn skirts blowing in the breeze, and Cash knew one thing. Whether she was carrying his child or not, he didn't like the thought of her working her fingers to the bone out on these fields. His own body ached with new awareness, the muscles screaming of abuse, but Cash was stronger than Jenna. She shouldn't have to work so doggone hard. And while he was here, he'd see that she didn't.

The sun had set. Jenna glanced at the meal she had waiting for Cash. It was beyond cold. She'd have to throw it back onto the stove to heat it up, if the man ever decided to come for his meal.

Half an hour ago, she'd seen him enter the barn. She figured he would take a moment to clean up before coming to the house. But he hadn't come. Jenna paced the kitchen, wondering what was going on.

On impulse, Jenna opened the back door, ready to march into that barn to see what was taking Cash so long, but something caught her attention and she gasped. There on the doorstep sat the plate she'd given him today, cleaned and hosting the most amazing flower. A wild rose. The color of each petal, soft ivory, but the truly remarkable nature of the flower was that the outline of each one of those petals boasted a hue of pale peach.

"Oh, my!" Jenna lifted the plate and took it inside. She picked up the rose, studying it, awed by its beauty, but struck even more by its very existence. "Where did you find this, Cash?"

Jenna peered outside, but darkness had descended, a gray cloudy night with an absence of stars that denied her any view at all. She was late milking Larabeth. She couldn't ignore that chore. She lit a lantern and headed for the barn. And if she happened to run into Cash, so be it.

When she entered the barn, all was dark and quiet. A quick stirring of fear rose up from her belly. "C-Cash? Are you in here?"

She heard a sound, and nearly jumped out of her skin. The low grumbling sound grew louder in pitch, then went soft again. Jenna lifted the lantern shoulder high and glanced around. All looked peaceful, and then the sound again seemed to boom across the barn. "Cash!"

He didn't answer. But Scrappy showed his face, his dark eyes barely visible up on the hayloft. He gave her a look, as if to say, why are you disturbing my peace? "Where's your master?" she whispered.

Then Jenna knew. She climbed the steps quickly and when she reached the top, it was just as she'd thought. Cash lay fast asleep on his bed of hay, his chest heaving, his slumber so labored that he snored.

She chuckled at the sight. And her heart softened a bit, ever so slightly, at the man who had been so sure he could master farming in one day that he'd nearly exhausted himself.

Jenna couldn't wait until tomorrow. If he thought plowing was a challenge, just wait until he tried milking Larabeth.

Chapter Nine

"**P**ut your hands under Larabeth's udder," Jenna instructed Cash. She sat beside him on an overturned bucket, giving him the official milking stool to sit upon. "And wiggle your fingers."

"Like magic?" Cash turned to her, puzzled.

Jenna smiled. "Some say it's the Lord's magic. But in this case, Larabeth doesn't like cold hands."

She grasped Cash's hands, feeling for warmth, but instantly she knew it was a mistake to hold him. They sat so close, their bodies nearly touching that when Jenna inhaled, the scent of man, of earth, hay and fresh soap, assailed her. She hadn't forgotten his scent. She hadn't forgotten many things about the man who had claimed her innocence. His hands felt warm enough, but it was the burn of his gaze that seared Jenna just then. She dropped his hands. "No need to wiggle," she said lamely.

He stared deep into her eyes then after a moment, he asked, "Now what?"

"Now, take hold of her here. It's all right, Larabeth," she said to the cow, stroking her gently. "It's going to feel a bit different, but you'll do okay." Jenna nodded for him to proceed then bit back a grin when Cash hesitated.

"Just hold her here and pull?" He appeared skeptical.

"Yes, right there. Make sure to get all the milk in the pail now."

Cash shot her a look and Jenna did grin then.

"Here goes." Cash grabbed hold and squeezed too hard. Larabeth jerked. Her tail lashed out like a long curling whip, smacking Cash upside the head. He leaned into Jenna, his body falling against hers. Both lost their balance and toppled off their seats. Next thing Jenna knew, Cash Callahan was beside her on the ground, half on top of her, nestled in a bed of hay.

They took one look at each other and burst out laughing.

Jenna had never seen Cash laugh so heartily. Tears actually filled his eyes, and it was long moments until his laughter simmered down.

Cash leaned over her, his eyes still twinkling, but there was concern in his voice. "I didn't hurt you, did I?"

"No," she whispered up at him.

"Can't say as much for Larabeth."

"You didn't hurt her Cash, she was just startled."

"I'm usually more gentle with the ladies," he said candidly. His gaze softened, the blue twinkle only a tender gleam now. "I was with you, wasn't I, Jenna?"

Jenna's mind raced. She looked up at Cash, a man she didn't really know. A gambler. A man who had married her, bedded her and had shown her a thing or two about passion. But he was still a stranger to her, someone who would leave soon. Yet her answer seemed important to him. And she couldn't deny him the truth. She squeezed her eyes shut. "Yes, you were gentle."

Cash plucked a few strands of straw from her hair, his fingers threading through her braid lightly. Jenna gazed up at him, fearful. Not of him, but of what his touch evoked within her. She didn't cringe, didn't pull away so when he lifted himself to stand upright, Jenna's heart took an unexpected fall.

He reached down to take her hand and tugged her up. She found herself standing inches from him. "My lesson is most definitely over for today. Poor Larabeth, I believe we've confused the old girl, but I'd like to try again tomorrow."

"Tomorrow is fine." Jenna nodded and began removing remnants of hay from her dress, fully aware that Cash watched her every move.

"Have you tried on the dress, Jenna?"

For a moment, she didn't comprehend his question. Then she remembered the lovely garment he'd brought to her, the one she'd stowed away in her chest. Suddenly, she wished the subject were back on Larabeth and milking techniques. "No, no I haven't."

"I'd like to see it on you. Just once."

It wasn't quite a plea or a command, but his request fell somewhere in between.

"I, uh, I've been so darn busy." She swatted a fly then returned the stool to the upright position. Cash did the same with the bucket. The milk pail he handed to her.

"Soon as I master milking Larabeth, you'll have more time, Jenna. Then maybe you'll try the dress on for me."

For me. He made it sound so personal, so intimate. As though she'd be parading around in a fancy gown just for him. Jenna didn't know how to respond. She didn't understand what she was feeling. Cash Callahan confused her and made her edgy.

"I have to get breakfast."

Cash inhaled sharply, the way he did when he was displeased. "All right. I'll do some chores outside then see you in a bit."

When Cash was out the barn door, Jenna set about milking Larabeth, soothing her with a song. But her mind wasn't on milking. It was on unforeseen wild roses, pretty new dresses and a man hellbent on stirring up Jenna's emotions.

* * *

Cash patted Scrappy's head. "What's the matter, boy? You've been licking that paw all morning. Nearly kept me up half the night with that slopping sound you make."

The dog lifted sorry eyes his way.

"You got an ailment there?" Cash was careful inspecting the dog's paw. He didn't see any thorns or sharp splinters that would give the dog reason to favor the paw, yet the animal continued licking. "Your bones are getting creaky, I'll bet. Don't you fret about that, happens to the best of us."

He gave the dog one last stroke behind the ears then headed for breakfast.

When he entered the house through the back door, Jenna stood with her back to him, preparing the morning meal. He peered over her shoulder, his nostrils picking up an appetizing aroma. "Flapjacks?"

"With maple syrup and strawberry preserves." Jenna flipped a browned flattened cake over with her spatula. "Coffee's almost ready."

"I'll get it," Cash said, lifting the pot from the stove to pour two mugs. He took them to the table and sat down, noting that Jenna had set out a vase, cracked in several places, but probably one of the finest pieces that she owned. The wildflower and rose he'd given her adorned the vase, surrounded by greenery he recognized from a shrub just outside the front door. The arrangement made a cheerful display and Cash wondered if Jenna was beginning to put the past behind her. She was too young and beautiful to give up hope for a happy future.

"Think Larabeth will forgive me?" Cash asked, his mood suddenly light.

He could see Jenna's silent laugh from behind. "We'll see tomorrow, won't we?"

"She nearly knocked my brains out today. Wonder what other tricks she has ready for me."

"I don't know. You know what they say about a woman's scorn."

She set three large flapjacks onto his plate and added the same amount to hers. It looked like her appetite was picking up. Cash sipped his coffee, ready to dig into his meal, but the inquisitive look in Jenna's eyes stopped him.

She stared at him, then at the flowers on the table between them. "They're lovely."

Cash swallowed. "I suppose."

She turned to him. "Why'd you give them to me?"

He shrugged. He didn't want to get into this. "I thought you'd like them."

"I do," she rushed out, "but why did you put them on the plate when you returned it? And where did you find such a beautiful rose?"

Cash knew he couldn't lie to Jenna. He didn't want to divulge anything unsavory about his life to her, but he'd lied enough already about the reason he was living here. He owed her more. He owed her the truth. "The rose is my secret."

He shot her a quick smile. He'd found the rose bush way out beyond Turner's Pond, miles from here. He'd gone back there a few times when he had no memory, thinking if he'd seen the place where Jenna had found him, he might recall something. It was there that he'd found the bush filled with wild roses, and he'd never forgotten it. But it was Jenna's other question he really didn't want to answer. "And the other goes back a long way."

"I'm listening."

Darn her, she *was* listening. Leaning forward on the table with eyes wide, Jenna eagerly waited to hear things Cash hadn't wanted her to know.

He cleared his throat then took a sip of coffee.

Jenna sat patiently.

Staring at the flowers, he began, "My father abandoned the family when I was real young. My mother took his leaving real hard. We lived in an old shack, not much bigger than this here kitchen. There was never much to eat. My mother tried her best to keep us fed and clothed. Often we'd go on the streets, begging for food, hoping someone would take us in, or at least give us a meal. She had her pride, my mother, but she also had a young boy to feed. I know she did what she had to do to survive. And whenever anyone saw fit to feed us, my mother never returned the plate empty. She always said we ought to show our gratitude.

"I used to have a collection of rocks, shiny and unusual in ways that young boys think are special. If we couldn't find a flower, or a nice button to lay on the plate, I'd give up one of my rocks."

"And you never stopped showing your gratitude, Cash?"

He shook his head and laughed bitterly. "No. I can't seem to break the habit." Jenna's eyes filled with understanding. The look tore up his heart.

"Some habits shouldn't be broken," she said softly. "What happened to your mama, Cash?"

"She died when I was ten."

"Ten? Oh, Cash," Jenna said, her voice laced with pity. He hated the sound, wanted to wipe that sorrowful look off her face. He didn't need her pity. Hell, Jenna hadn't had an easy life, either, losing her parents, having a no-account brother and working herself into old age on this farm. She had no right pitying him. He'd struggled, sure, but he'd survived and was a stronger man because of it.

"What happened to you?" The softness in her voice twisted his gut.

He turned to her and pierced her with a hard look. "I took up gambling."

Jenna swallowed, her expression hard to read and Cash thought that would be the end of the discussion. Yet, she sat there, eyes still wide, waiting.

He took a slow breath, his mind conjuring up memories he'd like to leave in the past. "At first, it was just little things, like my best rock for some-one's lunch. I'd bet anybody who would take me up on it. I'd bet I could race them faster, throw a ball farther or steal a kiss from the prettiest girl in school.'' Cash's recollection of Betsy Cummings squealing at the top of her lungs when he'd done just that brought a smile to his face. ''That one always brought me a good price.''

''I'd bet on anything, Jenna, and I became really good at it. I'd mastered the art of gambling by the age of fifteen. And I won often because I had something the others didn't…a powerful need to survive. And I never bet on anything that wasn't a sure thing. I learned early on that greed is a fierce motivator. I'd always offer something more valu-able than my opponent was putting up. They gave little thought to what they stood to lose, until of course, they lost it.''

Jenna asked quietly, ''But couldn't you hire on at a ranch or work in town? Surely there were ways for you to earn a living besides gambling.''

''I tried that once. Didn't work out.'' Cash's memory of his life on Beau Raley's ranch was best kept to himself. He'd been just a boy then but he hadn't been able to lock that terrible time away. It was a constant reminder to Cash of who and what he was. There was no changing that fact. ''I'm no good at anything but gambling, Jenna. It's what I do.''

Jenna rose from the table, her eyes clear with

new knowledge. "Well then, I suppose it's a real good thing you'll be leaving the farm as soon as the planting's done."

Cash stood to face her, meeting those clear eyes directly. "As soon as the planting's done. You have my word."

Rain poured down hard. Jenna sat up in her bedroom, listening to the sound hitting the roof, the forceful knocks pounding as though ready to drive straight through. In some areas of the house it had, and Jenna had diligently placed buckets and bowls to catch the dripping water.

A blast of wind rumbled through the house and she shuddered, running her hands up and down her arms. She dashed to the window to make sure it was secured, then opened up the chest that sat at the foot of her bed. Reaching inside for a quilt to warm her, she shuffled aside the dress Cash had given her.

The garment, wrinkled slightly from being shoved inside a crowded chest, appeared just as stunning as ever. Jenna forgot about the quilt and took the dress out. On impulse, she lifted it up and pressed it to her body, fitting it against her to see just how close Cash had come to remembering her figure.

"Oh!" Jenna peered at herself in the cheval mirror, fully surprised at the perfect fit. The dress molded to her as if made especially for her and complemented the tawny hue of her eyes, the wheat color of her hair. "I don't dare put it on," she mused aloud. "I'll never want to take it off."

Jenna chuckled, her mood lifting. "That would be a sight, Jenna Duncan, *farmer,* plowing the fields in a dress fit for a princess."

Still, Jenna didn't have the heart to put the dress back into the trunk, as it would only wrinkle more. She had nothing to hang it on but the mirror, which was tall enough to accommodate the length of the gown. Two adornments at the top would suffice as holders to keep the dress from falling.

Jenna stepped back once she'd made the proper adjustments and admired her work. The dress hung grandly from her mirror. The reflection slightly visible from behind made its appearance seem all the more impressive. "It does take my breath." Then Jenna admonished herself. "Silly woman, you do have chores to do. You can't stay up here all morning, daydreaming."

But Jenna did think about Cash while she worked, about his life and the events that had landed him on her doorstep. At times, it was more thinking than she wanted to do. She was just beginning to learn about the young boy who'd been left to his own devices at an early age and of the man Cash Callahan was today. And she wasn't entirely sure if that was a good thing.

With the rain still coming down in buckets, Jenna resigned herself to her sewing, taking out a pile of socks that needed mending. But she noted the pounding on the rooftop sounded different this time. She looked up toward the ceiling as the steady tap, tap, tap sparked her curiosity. She put down her darning and rose. Then she noticed the constant annoying dripping filling two pails in her bedroom had ceased yet the rain was still coming down hard. Jenna reached for her wrapper, climbed down the stairs and ventured outside.

Cash caught sight of her from the rooftop. ''Get back inside, Jenna. It's freezing cold out here.''

Jenna only stared. Where did he get the wood to fix her roof? It wasn't firewood; these planks were long and sturdy and fully capable of plugging her leaks. She'd tried many times to use sod to fill the gaps, but nature had a way of drying it off and blowing particles away, allowing rain to soak through.

Cash looked down again and gave her a stern look. ''You're getting soaked,'' he shouted as whipping wind muted the harshness from his tone.

Before her hair plastered to her head from the downpour, Jenna ran back into the house. She threw more logs onto the fire, wielding the poker until orange-blue flames crackled with warmth. She shivered and stood close, her clothes pretty much drenched. If *she* was soaked, Cash would surely catch his death up there on her roof.

Jenna whirled around when the front door blasted open. Cash entered, standing in the doorway, sopping wet from head to toe. He removed his hat, tossing the wet thing out the door. "Did I get all the leaks?" he asked.

Jenna nodded and relief swamped her at seeing him safely in the house. She shooed him away from the door, toward the fire. "Come in and get those clothes off. You're positively soaked. I've got the fire going strong."

"No, I can't stay. I've got to fix the barn. Those leaks are getting mighty bad. The loft is drenched. There's wet straw everywhere."

Jenna shook her head. Ben had fallen from the barn roof trying to patch those holes on a clear day. If Cash went out there, with the wind whipping about like it was, no telling what might happen. "You're not getting on top of the barn today. Those leaks can wait until the storm passes."

Cash shook his head. "No, they can't. I've got to fix them now or I can't sleep in there. It's like a small river up on that loft."

"You won't sleep there tonight, Cash. You'll catch your death. You'll sleep here by the fire. Lord knows it's going to take all afternoon to get you dry. Now, take off your shirt. I'll get you a towel."

Jenna moved quickly and was back with a towel. Cash stood by the fire warming his hands when she returned. His shirt clung to his body as if it had been painted on.

She tossed him the towel, but all he did was stare at her, his gaze catching her every move.

Jenna ignored him, more concerned with getting the man dry. "Heavens," she said, coming up to his chest and undoing the top button, "you'd think you'd lost all your hearing up there on that roof."

She undid the second button, then the third, fully aware of Cash's gaze on her. And fully aware of the powerful strong chest she was exposing. She'd had knowledge of the solid strength of him, of the way his skin had felt under her fingertips, hot and silky and so very smooth. She stared at the fine hairs there, moistened and slick, and couldn't help but notice his nipples had gone hard. Cash was cold. Chilled to the bone cold. She bit her lip then lifted her eyes to meet his. "You can manage the rest. I'll get you some hot cider and then you can tell me how you got the wood to fix the roof."

He nodded, but as she turned away, he took hold of her wrist, stopping her. He spoke in her ear, his voice husky. "I don't know if I can sleep in here, with you."

It was a good thing Jenna didn't face him. His admission had thrown her, causing heat to rise up on her neck, creating sensations Jenna thought long put to rest. She swallowed, stared a the floor and shook her head. "Don't say those things, Cash."

"It's true, Jenna. I haven't forgotten. I don't believe you have, either. It was good between us. I'd be lying to say I don't want that again. I think about holding you in my arms and—''

''No! Don't. I don't want to be reminded. You're to leave as soon as Ben is capable of working the farm. There's no use in wishing for things that won't ever happen.''

Cash ripped the wet shirt from his body and tossed it on the hearth. ''You're right, Jenna. Damn it, you're right.''

She turned to dare a glance at him. He was facing the fire, his back to her now. She couldn't allow soft thoughts of Cash Callahan. He wasn't a farmer. He was only here because he felt obliged to her for saving his life. And now, because of Ben's injury, he'd be staying on a while. Jenna wouldn't fool herself into thinking it was any more than that. She wouldn't fall for Cash's charm. He was a gambler, a man who had ripped away all of her dreams. How could she forget that?

''I'll be back with the cider,'' she said softly, a hollow ache developing in her gut. The pain was familiar and all too real.

When she returned to the parlor, Cash's mood seemed to have lightened. He granted her a quick smile and Jenna swallowed hard. He'd taken off all of his clothes, leaving them to dry on the hearth. A towel was all that covered him from below his waist to his knees.

''I'll get you one of Bobby Joe's shirts.'' She handed him a mug of hot cider.

He took a slow sip and closed his eyes, as if relishing the warmth and the taste. "Don't bother. There was just the two. This one and one I washed this morning. It's hanging up outside, on the fence post."

"Oh," Jenna said, "then you'd best stay by the fire until your clothes are dry."

He nodded and took another sip of cider. "I think my bones are drying out, too." He laughed and sipped some more. "Heat feels real good."

Jenna wrung her hands, debating whether she should stay in here a while or leave him alone. She wasn't looking forward to an evening alone but Cash was near naked by that fire and so very appealing.

"You've got no reason to fear me, Jenna." He'd spoken as if he could read her thoughts.

"I'm not afraid of you."

He arched a brow, the blue in his eyes gleaming. "Aren't you?"

"No, I'm not." She had her pride, after all. She wasn't going to give him the satisfaction of knowing she'd been doubtful of her own intentions.

"Okay, then. Sit down and talk to me."

Jenna made a move to sit on the sofa, but Cash shook his head. "Not there. Here, where it's warm. Sit here by the fire with me."

Jenna hesitated.

"You're not afraid, remember," he reminded her.

She hid a frown. "I'm not used to sitting with half-naked men in my parlor, Cash."

"Ah, well, I'm glad of that." He smiled.

Jenna relaxed a bit and sat down near him, but not so close that he would get ideas. Heavens, the man had practically announced earlier he'd like to take her to bed again. That wasn't going to happen. Jenna wouldn't allow it. And as long as she remembered who and what he was, she'd be safe from temptation.

"So how did you get the wood for the roof?" she asked, a harmless enough topic.

"I went into Goodwill today with Antonio. We had to buy some supplies. I bought enough wood to fix the stairs, too."

"*You* bought? How did you pay for it?"

"Same way as usual, sugar. With cash."

"But I don't have any cash."

"I know. I said *I* bought the supplies."

"You used your own money? I can't possibly pay you back. I don't have enough—"

Cash reached out and took her hand, squeezing gently. "I have some money. I paid for the supplies. It wasn't a loan and I don't expect you to pay me back."

"But—"

"Jenna, while I'm here, I'm a part of this farm. I'm going to do as I see fit. The roof needed repairs. You were low on supplies, so we picked some up."

Jenna cringed inside. Her pride was at stake, and foolish as it seemed, she didn't want Cash Callahan or anyone else for that matter taking pity on her and her farm. "What else did you buy?"

"Sugar, some canned goods and Arbuckle's Ariosa coffee. It's so good, Jenna. I can't wait until you taste it."

"Real coffee? I've always made my own." Her coffee often contained parched wheat or bran. Sometimes she made it with dandelion roots, but Cash had bought authentic coffee, a luxury she hadn't been able to afford for many years.

"I know, and it's good, but you've never tasted anything like Arbuckle's. You're going to love it."

Jenna shook her head. "I can't accept it."

Cash dropped her hand. "Don't start on that again, Jenna. I pay my own way. Hell, you've been feeding me and I've got a roof over my head."

"It's just a leaky roof, Cash. And you work just as hard as anyone on the farm. You don't owe me anything."

"I do, but I'm not about to argue that point. And if I decide to gift you with a few new ribbons for your hair, I'd appreciate you accepting them," he announced, his eyes dark and cold like creek waters at dusk.

"You have ribbons for me?" Her heart raced with excitement. She hadn't received many gifts in her lifetime, much less gifts from a man.

He grunted. "Pink and yellow ones."

"Really?" She smiled despite herself. "No one's given me much of anything before."

"Small wonder," he grumbled, sipping his cider, eyeing her carefully.

"What did you say?" Jenna's chin shot up.

"I said, when a man wants to do something nice for a woman, he shouldn't get grief over it."

Jenna found herself making excuses. "It's just, well, it's just that you know how I feel about your money. The way you earn it, I mean."

"If I want to spend my money on this farm to help out, then I should be able to."

"But, I'd rather you didn't."

He grunted again. "Too bad." He folded his arms across his middle, reminding Jenna of a little boy who didn't get his way.

She didn't enjoy arguing with Cash. She'd like it just fine if they could get along cordially until he left the farm. The less she had to think about him, the better off she'd be. "I made you angry," she stated.

"Hell, you're good at it."

"I don't mean to be," she said as sweetly as she could. Cash had helped her dear friend Ben, fixed her leaky roof and bought supplies she desperately needed for the farm and all she managed to do was anger him.

"Then take what I offer you, Jenna."

She didn't *want* anything from him. But she'd be a fool not to accept his gracious offerings.

"Well...okay." She drew in oxygen, breathing deeply and the words tumbled out, words she'd been conditioned to say since the time she could talk. Words she meant from the bottom of her heart. "Thank you. It was very kind."

Cash shook his head then grinned. "Jenna Duncan, you've got me spinning around in circles, you know that?"

Jenna thought he was doing the same to her, sitting there, so close, wearing nothing much of anything and buying her pretty ribbons.

Chapter Ten

Cash rose before Jenna woke up. He'd lain awake half the night, thinking about her sleeping upstairs in that big bed alone. In truth, as much as he wanted to make love to her again, and that need proved strong, he would have been just as content sleeping beside her, cradling her in his arms, keeping her warm. Yep, he would've liked that, waking up with Jenna again, breathing in her flowery woman's scent, stroking her soft skin. But Jenna had made her intentions clear and he'd honor her by keeping away.

Yet he could still show her a thing or two about Larabeth. He dressed quickly, then headed outside. He was met with early sunshine, the morning sky so bright he squinted as he made his way to the barn.

Larabeth cast him a lazy look then stared straight ahead when he drew closer. "You're play-

ing with me, lady. But we're going to be best
friends.''

Cash lifted his bedroll from a small storage
drawer against the wall and plucked up a handful
of sugar cubes he had tucked inside. "Seems I
found a gift or two for you in Goodwill, too.''

Cash placed the stool near Larabeth's middle,
set the pail under her then walked around to face
the brown-eyed bovine. He opened his hand and
the cow instantly wiped the sugar cubes clean.
"There's more for later, if you cooperate," he
said, stroking the cow's thick neck the way he'd
seen Jenna do.

"Ready? I'll be gentle this time." Cash sat
down, rubbed his hands together to warm them
then proceeded to Larabeth's udder. He pulled
down with adept fingers. The cow let out a low
moaning sound, shifted position and her flank
knocked right smack into him, yanking him off the
stool onto his back. He shook his head to clear it
and found himself directly underneath Larabeth.
He stared up at a full udder, with all of its points
aiming straight for his face. "Facing down a barrel
of a gun can't be more thrilling, Larabeth.''

Laughter from the barn door had him tossing the
pail and turning his head. Jenna stood with a hand
covering her mouth, but the look of pure joy
crossing her face gave her away.

"How long have you been there?" he asked as

he maneuvered himself away from Larabeth and stood.

"Long enough to see you bribe my cow." Again, laughter erupted. Jenna couldn't seem to stop herself.

Cash swatted hay off his trousers. "Yeah, well, she'll come around."

"I'm sure she will," Jenna offered, amused.

There was such beauty on her face. And such joy in her eyes—the healthy glow of a happy woman. If Cash could find a way to keep that look about her, he'd not hesitate.

"You going to give me another lesson in milking?"

She shook her head and sashayed over to the cow, milk pail in hand. "Just watch and learn."

She stroked Larabeth then whispered something. The animal wiggled both ears and Jenna sat down on the stool but she didn't touch Larabeth, at least not with her fingers. She began singing.

Pretty cow, oh pretty cow,
Fill the pail, if you are able,
Put sweet milk on our table,
To soak our bread, and make a cake,
And spoil the kittens, for goodness sake!
Pretty cow, oh pretty cow,
I'll pat your head and stroke your side,
Your milk is rich, I will confide.
With gentle hands, I shall guide the way,

And feed you oats and grain, each day.
Pretty cow, oh pretty cow,
Fill the pail if you are able,
Put sweet milk on our table.

"There now, I think we're ready," Jenna offered softly. She milked the contented cow, filling the pail and continuing to hum the melodious tune.

Button and Scrappy both appeared, sitting ready to get their due. Jenna didn't disappoint, she gave equal squirts to both. Humming the tune, she continued on with a chore she made seem a pleasant morning outing.

Cash's gut went tight, knotting up inside. He realized something then. Something he didn't want to admit. He'd been playing a losing hand, one he was certain he could never win.

He was falling in love with Jenna.

Cash kept his distance from Jenna for the next three days. He'd spent his time plowing the fields, working on the barn roof, and trying his best to make Larabeth come around. Larabeth wasn't having any of it. Hell, he'd never had such a time coaxing a response from a female.

"Come on, Mac," Cash urged the plow horse, "just one more row and we'll stop for the day."

The blade dug into the ground, grinding up dry soil. After the storm had passed, spring heat roasted the ground and pretty much set Cash's body temperature to near boiling. Cash wiped sweat from his brow. "Only thing more fickle than the weather is a female mind," he muttered, thinking of Larabeth and Jenna.

Cash went out back of the barn to the water barrel, cursing the hot day. Hell, he needed a good soak in a tub and if he'd thought of it sooner, he'd have made tracks to the creek, but today, washing up near the barrel was all he could manage.

Antonio rode up on his old mare, wearing a big smile, just as Cash had removed his shirt and splashed water on his face. "Cash, you've got to get Miss Jenna to come on over to our house, soon as you can."

"Why? Is there a problem with Ben?" Perplexed, Cash couldn't figure this out. Antonio's voice sounded urgent, yet he was wearing a silly grin.

"No, Papa's fine. You just tell her Mama needs her in a fast hurry. And you bring her yourself."

"Me?" Cash stuck his index finger into his chest. "Hell, you know Jenna. She's gonna ask me nothing but questions about this."

Antonio grinned even wider. "I know. That's why I ain't gonna tell you neither. You just tell her what I said. You just tell her Rosalinda needs her quick. She'll come."

Cash hesitated. So far, he'd done a good job of keeping his distance from Jenna. He'd seen to it there were no more evenings by the fire, soaking

up heat, staring into each other's eyes, and there
had been no more bouts with Larabeth, either.
Cash always woke up earlier than Jenna, tried his
best with the obstinate cow then pretended sleep
or was out of the barn before Jenna would come
in. He'd taken his meals with her then begged off
quickly to get out onto the fields, and during the
supper hour, he always claimed fatigue and hustled
off to bed.

His plan was working, too. He found time to
think about his first love, gambling. He thought
about getting back into a game, and of raising the
stakes until everyone was on edge. He thought
about reading his opponents with expertise. He
thought about the thrill of the win. And how much
he longed to get back to his own life. His gambling
life.

But he couldn't refuse Antonio. Something was
definitely up and if Rosalinda needed Jenna, then
he'd oblige and bring her to their home. "Okay,
I'll bring her. But she's gonna be a pest about it
all the way over."

Antonio laughed before riding off. Cash shook
his head hard enough to spray water out, sort of
like how Scrappy did when he got a bath, then he
entered the back door of the house to relay Antonio's message.

Jenna couldn't imagine why Rosalinda needed
her so urgently. She prayed that nothing was se-

riously wrong with Ben. She took just enough time to put away the food she'd been cooking, then dashed out of the house.

Cash stood by Queen, who was saddled and ready in front of the house. Jenna approached them, glancing up at Cash's horse. The bay mare stood tall, her pose stately, as though she really were a queen. "I don't think I can reach." But she tried a little hop to grasp the saddle horn and missed. She lost her grip and slid down the horse's flank.

Cash swooped her up in his arms before she fell to the ground. He held her gently, but his words were sharp. "You don't let anyone do anything for you, do you?"

"I do what needs to be done." Chagrined, she bit out the words defensively.

"Uh-huh," Cash said, "I've noticed."

"Are you going to hold me like this all day, or put me up on the horse?"

Cash grinned, a quick flash brightening his dark indigo eyes. "Well now, I could carry you all the way to Ben's. You weigh hardly more than a feather, but it would be faster up on Queen."

He swung her up onto his horse, then without hesitation, mounted the horse behind her. "Hold on tight."

She grabbed the saddle horn just as Cash's hand came around to her middle. "I've got you. You ready?'' he asked, but didn't wait for her response. He nudged the mare and she took off at a fast trot.

Jenna braced herself. She hadn't been this close to Cash, well, since she'd thought he was Blue Montgomery. But she felt him, his presence and the strength of him from behind. She wanted to lean back against him and relinquish all of her burdens in the power of his body. She wanted to let loose her concern over Ben and what possibly could be wrong. She wanted to let Cash take care of things, but she didn't dare, for all the reasons she summoned up at night when sleep wouldn't take her.

"I wouldn't worry too much, Jenna. Antonio didn't seem overly concerned. I doubt it's anything serious."

He'd spoken again as though he'd read her thoughts. She turned to him, her face so close to his, her heart pounding hard inside her chest. "I hope you're right."

"Bet on it."

"Cash!"

He grunted. "Oh, um, count on it," he said, nodding his head, with a twinkle in his eyes.

Jenna suppressed a smile, but she did lean back and as she allowed herself the comfort of Cash's body, his hold on her tightened a bit. For just a few minutes, she told herself, she'd indulge in the fantasy that Cash cared for her. That he was a man she could rely on, a man she could trust.

"I'm gonna be dreaming about this," he whispered into her ear, his breath a warm caress along her throat, "all night long."

She almost replied back, "Me, too."

Instead, Jenna leaned more heavily into him and was gratified when Cash brought her fully up against his chest with a deep guttural groan. Jenna knew she played with fire now, but the indulgence was too tempting, the solid feel of Cash too appealing.

They were close to Ben's house and Jenna understood these precious moments would be lost forever, so she didn't berate herself. She relished this strange, beautiful time with Cash Callahan, gambler, because soon he would be gone.

Chapter Eleven

"It's my birthday?" Jenna appeared stunned as she stood just inside Ben and Rosalinda's home.

"*Sí, querida.* We did not forget." Rosalinda grasped Jenna's hands. "Today you are twenty-one."

A look of pure joy passed between them as Jenna faced both Ben and Rosalinda. There was no mistaking it—the glow of happiness beamed on all their faces.

"Happy birthday, Miss Jenna," Antonio said, his black eyes gleaming with tenderness. He approached and placed a kiss on her cheek. Dark and bronzed, Antonio resembled his mother more than he did Ben. "We will celebrate. Mama has made you a feast."

Jenna took in the scene, her eyes misting up with tears as she glanced at the table filled with all of her favorite foods. "Oh, this is so…so—"

"We're having a party, Miss Jenna, and you're

the guest of honor tonight.'' Ben sat on a chair with his leg bandaged and propped up on a wooden crate.

Three farmhands entered, taking off their hats and smiling, their eyes wandering over to the platters of food Rosalinda had set out.

"Thank you all. I…I didn't know. I didn't remember.'' She turned to him with suspicious eyes.

Cash shook his head. "Don't look at me. I didn't know, either.'' Cash sent Rosalinda and Ben a look. "Seems like they kept both of us in the dark.''

"Well now, Cash. We, uh, know that Miss Jenna's got a way about her. If we'd have told you about it, then she would've gotten real suspicious,'' Ben said in earnest. "Might have spoiled the surprise.''

Jenna hugged both Ben and Rosalinda. "This is so thoughtful. I don't know what to say.''

"You are like my very own daughter, *mi corazon*. It is a joy to have this celebration for you. Come, let's eat,'' Rosalinda offered, gesturing with a wave of her hand. "We will take our food outside. It is very hot, no? Let's sit under the shade of the trees.''

Thirty minutes later, after filling his belly with a variety of foods from Rosalinda's famous tamales to Ben's favorite, potato pudding, Cash stood and stretched, then walked over to sit beside Ben on a bench. One of the farmhands had taken up a fiddle and the dancing had begun.

Cash peered at Jenna moving with fluid grace and agility as she and Antonio twirled around the yard, her face rosy from exhilaration, filled with joy.

Cash lit a cheroot and glanced out to the newly cultivated open field that waited patiently for the seeds it would nourish, for the climb of grain to reach heavenward and flourish. He couldn't watch Jenna another second. He couldn't see the woman who had almost been his, but for a dreadful twist of fate. He had to leave and sooner rather than later. If only he could ensure her safety.

Then he'd leave her.

And both could go back to their own way of life.

When the music stopped, he glanced at Ben. "How's the leg?"

"Coming along. I gotta thank you again, for taking care with me the other day. The doc in Goose Creek said you did a good job. He patched me up and said I'll be good as new, but looks like I'm gonna need a cane for a time. No plowing up the fields just yet, he said."

"Jenna's been fretting over you for days."

Ben smiled. "I know it. She's always been a special one. We'd like to see her happy again."

Cash nodded, tossing his cheroot down, then making sure to stomp on the flame. He had nothing to do with Jenna's happiness. Nothing. Even if he knew how to make her happy, she'd never allow it.

"You enjoying yourself?" Ben asked, shifting his weight in the chair. The movement seemed awkward and Cash noted a slash of pain cross his face.

"What's not to enjoy? Good food, good music."

"I ain't seen you dance with the birthday gal."

"I'm not one for dancing, Ben."

"Not even with Miss Jenna?"

Especially with Jenna, Cash thought. If Ben only knew the notions filling his head about what else he'd like to do with her, he wouldn't be encouraging Cash to take her into his arms.

Riding double with her on Queen tested his limits of willpower. But at least one good thing came from that ride. Cash had held Jenna around the middle and as far as he could tell, her body hadn't changed. He should feel more relieved that Jenna wasn't with child, but oddly, he wasn't.

"Not even with Jenna," he replied hastily. "Besides, Antonio seems to be dominating her time."

Ben arched a brow. "She's like a sister to him, Cash. I recall them two forever getting lost in the wheat way back, when they were so small the grain could cover them up. They surely enjoyed hiding from me. Thought it was real funny."

Cash laughed, picturing it in his mind. Little blond Jenna let loose in the stalks of grain, giggling and hiding, playing silly games. She belonged here on her farm. It was the only life she had ever known. And who better to share a life with than her childhood friend? "You think one day he'll stop thinking of her as a big sister?"

Ben shook his head. "No, I don't. Although Rosie and me, we'd pray for it if we thought it possible."

"Why not?"

"Antonio has a gal. Well, at least my boy has a gal in mind. Marcie Bender. Only old man Bender won't allow him to court her."

"Got any idea why that is?"

Ben rubbed his whiskers. "He says she's too young to go courting, but my guess is, he doesn't want his gal hooking up with a dirt-poor farmer. Bender owns the most prosperous farm around these parts. He's got five times the land and all the workers he needs to make a good profit."

"What about the girl? She feel the same way Antonio does?"

Ben nodded, glancing at his son, who was sipping lemonade with Jenna. "He says the father is all that's stopping them. Antonio is real upset. Hell, it burns me that Bender is keeping him from his happiness."

Cash took a deep breath, letting it out slowly. "Doesn't seem fair, does it?"

"Nope."

They stood in silence for a time then Ben asked,

"What about you? You hear anything about the men after you?"

Cash shook his head. "Not one thing."

"Do you think Miss Jenna is still in danger?"

Cash rubbed tension from his neck. It was all he had been thinking about lately. "I don't rightly know. I've got a friend I can wire to find out. It's time I do. I'm heading into Goose Creek tomorrow. I've got to know if the Wendells have moved on. Think you can send Antonio over to Jenna's to check in on her while I'm gone?"

"Sure thing. We'll take care of Miss Jenna." Ben pursed his lips, then slanted him a look. "You that anxious to move off the farm?"

Cash stared straight at Jenna. She'd stopped talking and stared back, her face flushed, her tawny eyes so bright and beautiful. "Yeah, I'm that anxious to move on."

Jenna helped Rosalinda put the food away when all the commotion had died down. The men were out by the barn talking and having a smoke. "It was a lovely surprise, Rosa," she said. "Thank you again."

Rosalinda smiled as she wrapped a dish of leftover tamales for Jenna. "I am glad you are pleased. Here, have these for tomorrow. You only have to heat them."

"Oh, heavens. I can't think about eating again. I'm just about stuffed. But tomorrow is another day. I don't doubt that Cash and I will finish these all up.''

''That is good. You are too thin, I think. So, how is it for you, *querida,* having him so close?''

Jenna shrugged and slumped into the kitchen chair. ''Cash? It's working out, I suppose. He'll be leaving soon, I'm sure.''

''How do you know?''

''I see it in his eyes, Rosa. He's restless, like all gamblers. He can't wait to leave.''

''Hmmm, maybe what you see in his eyes is not what you think.''

''I try not to *think* about him at all,'' Jenna said firmly, but the words rang false. Cash had managed to take up space in her mind since the moment he'd arrived, asking to help out on the farm. ''He's not staying and…and…I don't want him to.''

Rosalinda patted her hand. ''I see. Sit here, I have something for you.'' And when Rosalinda returned offering up a delicately crocheted mantilla, Jenna had no words. ''This is for your birthday.''

Tears stung Jenna's eyes. She examined the shiny black shawl, designed in an intricate pattern, with fingers that trembled. ''Oh, my.''

''It is not to make you cry.''

Jenna giggled, wiping moisture from her eyes. ''They are tears of happiness. This is so beautiful. And you made this?''

''*Sí,* I have been secretly working on it.''

Jenna stood and wrapped her arms around Rosalinda's shoulders. "Thank you so much."

"You will make use of it?" Rosalinda asked.

"I hope to, one day."

"Perhaps you may use it to warm a baby?" Rosalinda's dark eyebrows lifted in expectation.

Jenna's hand flew to her belly. At one point Jenna had thought it possible, but no longer. She would never have the family she'd wanted so desperately. "No, Rosa. I'm not with child."

"No? Are you certain?"

"Yes, pretty much. I will share a secret with you. I wished it so for a time. I want someone to love, and a child's love is a great thing to have. I've always dreamed of having a family. But it is not to be."

"Jenna, you do not know that. One day, perhaps."

Jenna's heart took a steep tumble. "No, I think not."

Rosa kissed her cheek. "It is in God's hands now. Have faith. You will see. It will all work out."

The ride home was uneventful. Cash spoke little and Jenna was content to enjoy the quiet of the evening. The heat of the day brought a balmy night filled with many stars. Jenna gazed up from time to time, finding shapes in the sparkling lights above.

It was a good way to pass the time; relishing the sense of peace Jenna felt tonight. The tension from earlier with Cash was all but gone. He held her loosely now and there were no endearments, no words that made her heart trip over itself.

Once they reached Twin Oaks, Cash said a cordial good-night to Jenna and she made her way into the house, hugging to her breast the lovely mantilla Rosalinda had crocheted for her. Jenna climbed the stairs and entered her dark bedroom. She lit a lantern quickly and the room took on a soft glow. Jenna sighed with delight as she placed the lovely mantilla over the golden dress and both now adorned the mirror.

I want to see it on you. Just once.

Jenna hesitated, taking a step back and thinking hard as Cash's words came back to torment her. Had she been unfair in not abiding his wishes? She could try on the dress and show him, then be done with it. But Jenna couldn't bring herself to do it.

"No. I don't dare," she whispered. The dress represented all that Jenna abhorred. Maybe it wasn't fair of her to place such a burden on something so lovely, but Jenna just couldn't bear the thought of wearing it. To do so perhaps meant that she would be giving up more than she would be gaining.

How had her life gotten so complicated?

She thought to dress for bed, but with the excitement of the day, she realized she just wasn't tired. She picked up her cat from atop the bed and cradled her in her arms. "Come on, Button. Let's go count us some more stars."

Once outside, Jenna sat on the porch chair, stroking Button's fine coat. "It's much cooler out here."

Button purred, enjoying the attention, the peace. Suddenly, Scrappy burst out from the barn, traveling fast and barreling over to her, his tail wagging, begging for the same such attention. Button screeched and flew out of Jenna's arms.

"Scrappy!" Cash called for the dog, then cursed quietly when he spotted him nearly on top of Jenna. Button had had enough. She jumped up on the porch rail and watched from her safe perch.

Cash was on the porch instantly. "Tarnation, dog. Get off of her."

Jenna scratched the dog's head, not minding his affection. "I don't mind. He's a good boy. He just wanted to give me a birthday kiss, right, Scrappy?"

Cash pursed his lips. "Is that what he's doing?"

"Yep."

Cash sat down in a chair next to her. Stroking the dog's coat, he replied, "Well then, can't say as I blame him."

Jenna smiled. Cash had charm, she was beginning to discover, and he was good with the animals except, of course, for Larabeth. She still didn't trust him.

"Can't sleep?" he asked.

"Didn't want to, yet. It's a beautiful night."

"It's cooler outside, that's for darn sure."

Jenna agreed.

Cash reached deep into his shirt pocket. "I was going to leave these for you in the morning, but since you're out here," he said, bringing forth half a dozen yellow and pink ribbons, "Happy birthday." He placed them into her hand. Soft satin caressed her skin.

"Oh, they're lovely."

"You going to keep them?" he asked, his voice bordering on defensive.

Jenna nodded. She couldn't deny a birthday present from Cash. The insult would hurt him and she'd never set out to do that. "I didn't think you'd give them to me. I thought you'd changed your mind, or maybe, had someone else to give them to."

Cash frowned. "There's no one else, Jenna. I bought the ribbons for you. It's just that I wasn't too sure you'd accept them."

"I made you angry that day, didn't I?"

Cash stared out into the night sky. "I don't know any other way to earn a living, Jenna."

"I think you *believe* that."

"I know it, for a fact."

"How can you be so sure?"

"I've tried, when I was younger. People took advantage of me."

"So now you take advantage of them?"

"No. Never. I play fair. I don't need to cheat anyone. I only bet when the odds are in my favor. That's the mark of a smart gambler."

Jenna sensed that Cash needed to say more. He leaned back in the chair, closing his eyes after making that pronouncement.

"Who took advantage of you?"

"Lots of people, Jenna. But I can start with Beau Raley. He's the rancher I told you about."

"You worked for him?" Jenna asked softly, surprised that she wanted to hear this, surprised that she wanted to help with this heavy burden.

"Not exactly. He adopted me, sort of. You see, when I was a boy, I didn't always have a place to live, but I tried to always attend school. I fed myself by betting for my schoolmates' lunches and sometimes I actually won money. But it wouldn't be too long before the authorities got wind of what I was doing, or someone's parent complained. I'd run off, going from one small town to another. It was always the same. I lied about having folks and a home to get into school. One day, my luck ran out. I got caught and instead of hauling me off to jail, they found me a place to live. They made it seem as though I was being adopted, but that was far from the truth.

"I lived on that ranch as long as I could take it. I worked hard, but it was never enough. Beau Raley, the man who took me in, was the meanest son-of-a-bitch you'd ever want to know. He beat me on a regular basis.''

Jenna flinched, the cruelty too hard to bear. "He whipped you? But you were just a boy."

"He didn't care. If you messed up on his ranch, and sometimes, even if you didn't, you paid the price."

"Oh, Cash."

"I ran away and got real mean after that. I gambled my way from town to town. It's not been an easy road at times, but it's the path I had to take. Hell, I've had to kill men, Jenna."

Jenna slammed her eyes shut. "I don't believe that."

"Believe it. It's the hard truth."

"You must have had a reason?"

"I always did, but killing is killing. Two men are dead because of me."

"H-how?" Jenna asked, fearing what she might hear, but having to know just the same.

"Always the same way, Jenna, someone cheating at cards and pulling a gun on me when I called them on it. I'm a good shot, Jenna. It's what's kept me alive. Otherwise, I might have been killed years ago."

"You were defending yourself. They gave you no choice."

"I suppose, but sometimes I lay in bed at night, and wonder if that's really true."

Cash was giving her every reason to hate gambling and gamblers, to confirm what she'd professed for years, yet Jenna couldn't completely condemn Cash. And that notion not only befuddled her mind, but frightened her as well.

"You almost died by Turner's Pond, Cash. You didn't go looking for trouble."

All too suddenly Jenna was reminded of Blue Montgomery, of how he died and all that she'd lost because of Cash Callahan. She should hate him, she *had* hated him when she first found out who he was, yet now she realized she didn't have hate in her heart for him. And she was just beginning to understand why.

"I shot a man named Wendell, and his kin came after me."

"But he drew his gun first, right?"

"It's the truth, Jenna. He was aiming to kill me. I swear it."

Jenna swallowed hard. It was almost too much to take. Yet it was Cash's life…the life of a gambler.

"I believe you." Surprisingly, she did believe him. He'd survived a terrible childhood, one that might have downed a less resourceful child.

His gaze locked onto hers then, a brief meeting filled with unspoken sorrow and tenderness. Gripping pain seized her and she wanted to reach out to him, to grant him the solace he needed, but she couldn't do it. She simply wasn't ready to forgive him. She didn't know if she ever would be.

Cash cleared his throat, breaking the moment. "I've got business in Goose Creek tomorrow. I'll be gone all day. Is there anything you need?"

Jenna's lips curved up. There were a hundred things she needed for the farm, but she'd always made do. She'd never ask Cash to spend his own money for the farm. He had no real claim here. And she wondered about the business he had in Goose Creek and if he were fixing to leave soon, but she didn't have any right asking. "I've got new ribbons for my hair, what more could I possibly need?"

Cash stared into her eyes, then nodded. "I'm leaving before sunup. You'll have to milk Larabeth for me." He winked. Then before she knew what was happening, he pulled her close, wrapped a hand around her neck, and kissed her full and quick on the mouth. Jenna barely had time to acknowledge the kiss, powerful as it was, before Cash climbed down her steps and headed to the barn, his loyal dog at his heels. "Happy birthday, sweet Jenna."

Stunned, Jenna watched him until the barn door closed, the wonderful sting of his kiss on her lips. She knew she wouldn't sleep much tonight. Her mind would rehash all that Cash had confided and her heart would go out to the young boy who had struggled to survive in a lonely world.

Jenna touched a finger to her lips, her body still tingling from Cash's potent kiss, creating vivid sensations that swelled her breasts and unsettled her stomach. She gazed at her cat, sitting like a statue on the railing. ''Well, how do you like that, Button?''

The feline granted her a lazy one-eyed wink.

Chapter Twelve

Cash reined in Queen a few miles outside of Goose Creek. He dismounted and lowered Scrappy to the ground. His dog had insisted on coming on this trip. The dog had been favoring his paw again, and Cash had to make several stops along the way while Scrappy licked the dickens out of his limb. After a time, Cash gave up and had set him atop the saddle, giving the mutt a ride for a time.

"You've got to walk the rest of the way, dog." Then he turned to face Queen. "Sorry to have to do this to you." Cash poured water onto the ground and worked up a nice mud puddle. Then he smeared the moist dirt onto his horse. "Can't ride into town with such a fine-looking animal. I've got to look the part of a sodbuster in every way. Scrappy will do fine, but you, you're too beautiful an animal. Got to make you look worse for wear."

Cash unrolled an Indian blanket and threw it over his saddle. The silver studs alone were worth more than some farms in the area. He un-holstered his six-shooter and wrapped it in his bedroll. "Can't ride into town wearing one of these neither," he said, reluctant to give up his weapon. He'd been accustomed to having it by his side lately.

Once in town, Cash headed straight for the telegraph office. He wired Louella about the whereabouts of the Wendells. If she'd heard or seen anything, she'd let him know. "I'll be back later in the day," he told the telegraph operator. With luck, he'd get a reply from her before leaving town.

He spent the better part of the day entering shops, listening in on conversations and walking the streets. He ate at the town diner, and spent time in the saloon, standing at the bar, making discreet inquiries about gamblers, games of chance and listening to hear of any descriptions coming close to those of the Wendells.

His last stop was the telegraph office. His luck was holding out. A wire from Louella in Blackwater had just come in.

He stood outside the office leaning up against the wall, staying in the shadows and read the wire. According to Louella, the Wendells were rumored to be in the area. She'd heard tales of them from her patrons. She believed them to still hold a grudge and warned him to be careful.

"Damn," he muttered. He'd hoped they would have moved on by now, forgetting about taking their revenge, yet a small part of him rejoiced. As much as he knew he should leave Twin Oaks and

Jenna, as much as he had hoped she was out of danger, he still couldn't abide leaving her. Cash didn't like no-win situations. He knew the longer he stayed on at Twin Oaks, the harder it would be to take his leave.

With Scrappy at his heels, he tied Queen to the hitching post at the mercantile and entered the store. He walked up and down the aisle, picking up a few items for the farm, a new hand shovel and gloves for Jenna when she worked in her garden. As he approached the counter, he heard the merchant bidding farewell to Mr. Bender and his daughter Marcie. The names registered instantly. Cash sidled up next to them and paid for his purchases.

Cash swept his hat from his head, turning to the young woman. "Excuse me, Miss. Are you Marcie Bender?" The pretty brown-haired girl appeared shocked and looked to her father.

"And who might you be?" Bender asked, before allowing his daughter to respond.

"I'm a friend of Antonio Markham."

The girl's head shot up. Cash smiled at her. "He says hello."

Marcie smiled shyly as her dark green eyes brightened with excitement. There was no mistaking that look. The girl was in love.

Bender frowned and ushered his daughter out the door. Cash picked up his purchases and followed behind.

"You go on to the wagon, Marcie. I'll catch up with you in a bit."

The girl nodded and strode down the street.

"Listen," Bender said, turning to Cash and pointing his finger. "My daughter is off-limits to that Markham boy, you understand?"

Cash shrugged. "I just relayed a message, is all."

"You work at that farm?"

"I'm at Twin Oaks, yeah."

"Well, then you know that farm's about to go under. They can't keep up with the competition. I'd make them an offer if I thought the land was worth a darn, but it ain't. The Duncan farm isn't going to see another profitable day."

Cash shrugged again, glancing at Scrappy. The dog lay on the sidewalk, licking his paw again. And then, instantly, Cash knew. Call it instinct, call it a good solid hunch, but Cash understood Scrappy now, and why his paw was acting up again.

Cash slanted the man a look. "The Duncan land's fruitful, but with the rain coming again, no telling when any of us are going to get the seeding done."

Bender's face twisted. "What are you talking about? I think the sun's baked your brains, son. It's hotter than the devil's kitchen out here. We ain't gonna see rain again any time soon."

Cash squinted into the burning sun and banked on his instincts. "I'd bet my horse, Queen, it's gonna rain tomorrow."

Bender gestured to Queen. "This is your horse?"

"Yep."

The man eyed him suspiciously. "She's a mite dirty, but a fine piece of horseflesh. One thing I know, it's horses. How'd you come by such an animal?"

Cash shrugged, slapping his hat against his knee. "Just got lucky one day."

Bender removed the blanket, uncovering the saddle then let out a long low whistle.

"Why, I'd be willing to bet my horse against half a dozen of your sheep and two hogs, that rain's coming tomorrow."

With a hand to his forehead, Bender peered up. There wasn't one single cloud in the sky. He eyed Queen again with unmistakable lust. "If you're serious, I'll take that bet."

Cash nodded firmly. "I'm dead serious."

Bender shook Cash's hand. "It's a bet then. I get your horse when it don't rain tomorrow."

"And I get half a dozen sheep and two of your best hogs when it does."

Bender grinned. "I'm going to enjoy riding that horse. I'll be by Twin Oaks, day after tomorrow," he announced smugly then turned to leave.

"Oh, and one more thing," Cash announced, "if it does rain, you allow Antonio Markham to court your daughter."

Bender's voice elevated. "My daughter? Now wait just a doggone minute here. My daughter's got nothing to do with this."

"Then the bet's off. 'Course, if you're so sure

it ain't going to rain, then there's not a problem, is there?"

Bender hesitated and Cash could almost read his calculating mind. He gazed up at the cloudless sky one more time as scorching heat blazed down. "Throw in the saddle and you got yourself a deal."

"Fine with me, the saddle and the horse against your livestock. One way or another, I'll be seeing you day after tomorrow."

"Fine," Bender said then walked off grinning.

Cash took a deep breath, glancing at Scrappy who had not stopped attending to his bum paw. "I'm counting on you, dog. You'd best come through."

Cash entered the barn at Twin Oaks late that night. After unsaddling Queen and combing her down, he walked over to Larabeth. "Hey there, lady cow. How's my friend?" He patted her head and stroked her flank, as he'd done for days now. The cow's ears wiggled in anticipation. Cash didn't disappoint her. He reached into his stash of sugar cubes and allowed the cow to eat a few out of his hand. "There you go, a nice treat for a nice lady." Larabeth was coming to enjoy the nightly ritual, and, Cash had to admit, so was he.

"Making a female come around is a difficult thing," he said, giving her one last pat on the head. "But I do believe it'll happen. Won't that surprise the stuffing out of Miss Jenna?"

The barn door creaked open and Cash whirled

around to find her standing in the doorway. Heaven
help him, her hair was down around her shoulders,
full and shiny as if she'd just brushed it to a golden
luster. The lantern she held put a glorious ethereal
glow on her face. She wore that white cotton robe,
the one that made her look like an angel, giving
him distinctly devilish thoughts.

"You're back," she said, her voice holding a
hint of disbelief.

"Did you think I wouldn't be?"

"No, uh, I…I—"

"You thought I'd leave without so much as a
proper farewell?"

"No, it's just that…it's late and I wasn't sure."

Cash pursed his lips and nodded, looking away
from Jenna, realizing just how much she still didn't
trust him. Did she think he'd abandon her while
Ben was still ailing? Did she think so little of him?
"I'm back," he said firmly, "and I'm not leaving
until the planting gets done, Jenna. You have my
word."

Jenna flinched, probably from his sharp tone.
Damn her, why'd she have to look so appealing?

"I'm sorry for barging in." Jenna turned to
leave, but Cash was too fast for her. He grabbed
her arm and gently turned her to face him.

"Ah, hell, Jenna. Don't leave."

"I shouldn't have come." She lifted uncertain
eyes his way.

Lord have mercy, he wanted her. He'd be forever wanting her. "I'm glad you did."

He took the lantern from her hand and lowered

it down, then pulled her close, wrapping his hands around her waist.

"You know if things were different, I would never leave you."

Jenna stopped smiling. She stared into his eyes then peered at his lips. Cash's body went tight, his need for her powerful. He bent his head and brought his mouth down, crushing her lips in a fiery kiss that rocked him to his very core. This wasn't a sweet birthday kiss, this was a kiss he only dreamed about when his mind shut down and his fantasies took hold.

Jenna moaned softly and wrapped her arms around his neck. He pressed her closer and there was no mistaking his need, the thin material of her robe no match against Cash's rigid body.

"Have mercy, Jenna." He drove his tongue into her mouth and savored the warmth and breath of her. He'd never forgotten her taste, the sweetness that melted away all the bad things in his life. She was a balm for him, a delicate willow in a patch of weeds. Cash needed her. He needed to be with her.

He brought his mouth to her throat, grazing her with kisses, licking her skin with the tip of his tongue. His hands moved up, just under her breasts, then he touched her there, over the swells. A shock shot right through him and Jenna moaned again. He moved her back until the barn door supported her weight, and rubbed his body with hers. "Jenna?"

She knew what he was asking. He could see it

in her eyes, the desire, the uncertainty, the fear. He saw it all and waited. It was her decision to make. He had nothing to offer her. They both knew that one day he'd have to leave. For Jenna, the stakes were high. Hell, for him, too. He'd leave here but his heart would never heal. Only Jenna had the power to heal him. He understood that now.

She shook her head and though Cash's body rebelled, he knew she'd made the right decision. "No, Cash. We can't."

He didn't argue. He exhaled deeply and put his forehead to hers. "I know."

"You're going to leave one day," she whispered.

"I know that, too."

"I'd better go in."

He nodded and released his hold on her to retrieve the lantern. "I'll walk you to the house."

They walked slowly toward the front porch. He longed to hold her again, to tell her how much she meant to him, yet it would serve no real purpose. Jenna could never be his.

When they reached the door, she turned to him. "I'll warm up your meal and leave it on the table."

"Don't bother, Jenna," he said. "I'm not hungry."

She nodded, biting the lip he'd just ravaged.

"Lock your doors. I'll see you in the morning."

She went inside and Cash stood there long moments, listening and waiting. He sensed Jenna behind the door, wondered why she didn't lock up. Then after a time, he heard her secure the latch.

"Good night, sugar," he mumbled as he walked away, his body still humming, still aching for her.

Suppertime came and went quickly that next night. Cash had been overly quiet. Jenna wasn't sure why that was, except that he kept glancing out the window during the meal. She wondered if he was expecting someone. She filled a tub with water and began washing the dishes. Cash helped as usual, clearing off the table, bringing plates to her and putting away the leftover food.

After the way he'd kissed her last night and nearly done other things, she didn't mind not making light conversation. Too many thoughts occupied her head, racing through again just when she was certain she'd put them aside. Her thoughts all centered on the man pacing her kitchen, staring out the window. Fatigued from lack of sleep, Jenna couldn't wait to slip into her bed and shut out the world. She'd never been a bad sleeper until Cash Callahan entered her life.

Cash's loud whoop for joy startled the "tired" right out of her. "It's raining!"

She whirled around quickly. Wide-eyed, Jenna stared at Cash. "What?"

"It's raining, sugar. Come on," he said, grabbing her hand and pulling her with him out the back door. They stood in the yard as hard drizzle poured down. Cash laughed heartily, lifting Jenna up and twirling her around in his arms.

Jenna gasped for air when he set her down. He beamed her a big smile. "Did you see it, Jenna?

The way the sky just suddenly clouded up, out of the blue?" He lifted his face skyward, jutting his arms out to catch the droplets.

"I saw it, Cash," she said, lifting her face to the clouds, too, and feeling the cool of the rain wash away days of heat and dust.

"Nothing like rain," he offered as drops continued to trek down his smiling face.

Puzzled at Cash's odd behavior, Jenna found herself smiling, too. She couldn't help herself, she'd never seen the man so doggone happy. "Cash?"

"I haven't gone crazy, sugar."

Jenna nodded, only half believing him. "Can we get out of the rain now?"

Cash glanced at her body, his thorough perusal making her breath catch, and she was suddenly aware that her dress clung to her skin like the peel of summer fruit. "Sure thing, let's get back inside."

He grabbed her hand again and they dashed back inside, Jenna giggling all the way. She hadn't played out in the rain since she was a child. Back then, a summer storm was as welcome as a full harvest and Jenna would steal precious moments away to frolic outside and cool off. Of course, it wasn't summer now and the rain could very well delay the planting.

Jenna reached for two linen cloths from a kitchen cabinet, handing one to Cash. "Here, dry off a bit."

Cash wiped his face then tossed down the cloth,

braced both hands against the door-frame and peered outside again. "How'd you feel about some sheep on the farm and a couple more hogs?"

Jenna hesitated, wondering where that had come from. Cash sure was acting strange today. "I'd love it. Unfortunately, I don't have any wealthy friends."

"Don't need any." He turned to face her. "Tomorrow I'll be bringing you half a dozen sheep and two of old man Bender's best hogs."

"Mr. Bender? What does he have to do with anything?"

"Simple. I bet him that it would rain today."

"You *bet* him?" Jenna's heart nearly stopped. Her mind raced with unwanted thoughts.

"Now, don't go getting riled, Jenna. I was only doing it for you and the farm. Remember when we were getting married—"

"Cash, don't." Jenna put up a halting hand. Hearing what he had to say made her stomach churn. She couldn't bear recalling their sham marriage or anything she might have professed during that time.

He came close, meeting her eyes. "Jenna, you wanted to improve the farm. You had all these notions. They were good notions. Half a dozen sheep. Two more hogs. That's got to make you happy."

"I'd be happy if I'd earned them the decent way."

"Jenna, gambling ain't indecent. It's people that are. There are good and bad people everywhere."

Jenna shut her eyes. She had thought that Cash

understood. She thought he'd known her feelings regarding gambling. "What did you have to wager for such a bet?"

"Queen. And my saddle."

She snapped her eyes open. "Cash, that horse and saddle must be worth far more than the livestock."

"They are. But old man Bender didn't mind taking the bet. He thought he would win."

Jenna sat down at the table, slumping her shoulders. She rubbed her temples, then exhaled slowly. Life certainly hadn't been dull with Cash Callahan. First his kisses had knocked her to her knees and now this. He had to know she'd not approve of his gambling, sheep or not. "And how did you know it would rain? You're not a rainmaker."

Cash grinned and sat down beside her. "No, but I think Scrappy is. I noticed him always licking his paw, right before it rained. He's got something creaky in his bones or something—he seems to know when the weather's going to change."

Jenna clasped her hands together on the table and sighed heavily. She looked deep into his eyes. "You really are a gambler. You haven't changed one bit."

"I am a gambler, Jenna. I never said I'd change. I know you won't believe me when I say this, but you're a gambler, too."

Jenna laughed bitterly at that preposterous notion. "That's not so."

"Oh?" Cash stood and walked to the back door, gesturing to the field. "Every time you plow and plant and work so hard you ache in all parts of your body, you're gambling. You're betting the sun's going to shine just enough, there's going to be plenty of rain to set the seeds but not too much to wash them away. You're betting the crop won't get diseased. You're betting on a prosperous harvest.''

''That's different, Cash.''

''Is it? Think about this, Jenna. That day you found me by Turner's Pond, you took my life in your hands. You gambled that you could save me. My luck was running high that day and you did save me.''

''Cash, you're muddling everything up.''

''No, I'm not. I'm speaking clearly.'' He strode over to her and sat down again, taking her hands in his. ''Don't you see, sugar? All of life is a gamble with the choices we make. You chose to work this farm, though you knew the odds were against you. You chose to take me in and save me. Hell, you're gambling right now that I won't leave before Ben heals up fine.''

Jenna stared at him for long quiet moments, contemplating, trying to sort out what Cash was saying. He'd gambled. He'd come here to work, but he'd gambled. How could Jenna allow that? How could she accept what he'd won, when the very idea made her ache inside? ''I can't accept your winnings, Cash.''

''A man can't go back on a bet,'' he said quietly. ''Jenna, look at me. *See* me. I'm not a hustler who would prey on innocent women. I wouldn't have taken that bet with Bobby Joe had I known about you. I wouldn't have ever hurt you. You say you don't know me, but you do. You refuse to admit to yourself that I'm not the sort of man who'd ever knowingly cause you pain. I wouldn't, Jenna, not ever. I've only tried to help you. I've got livestock to pick up in the morning, for you, for the farm.''

Jenna shook her head, denying his words. ''What if I asked you not to?''

Cash's mouth twisted in a frown. ''I'd honor your wishes, Jenna. But we'd be ruining Antonio's life.''

''Antonio?'' Jenna's head clouded up again. What could Antonio possibly have to do with this?

''Old man Bender's gonna let Antonio court his daughter as part of the deal.'' Cash cast her a satisfied smile. ''He was that certain he wouldn't lose—''

''That he wagered his daughter. How despicable.''

Cash scrubbed his jaw. ''Antonio sure won't think so. And I doubt Marcie will, either. They're in love.''

Jenna eyed him suspiciously. ''Why'd you do this, Cash? And don't say it's because you're a gambler.''

Cash shrugged. ''I've always found ways to get what I want. Survival, I suppose. And this time I wanted the livestock for you. You deserve it, Jenna. You've got a good farm here. Before I leave, I'd like to know that I've helped in every way that I could.''

His sincerity touched her. He'd done a good thing with Antonio. Just the other day, Antonio had confided in Jenna about his love for Marcie. He'd seemed so desolate at the time, wondering how they'd ever get a chance to see each other. And now Cash had found them a way.

''So, am I picking up livestock tomorrow?''

Jenna ran her hand through her hair, twisting the loose ends into knots. She couldn't refuse now, even if she wanted to. And after hearing all of Cash's arguments, she wasn't sure she wanted to. It wasn't easy to undo something that had festered in her mind for a long time. But perhaps, she was beginning to see. Perhaps it took a gambler to make her see. ''We don't have any place to fence the sheep.''

With a bright spark in his indigo eyes, Cash offered, ''I'll build them a small corral, soon as I can.''

Jenna eyed Cash with trepidation, wondering if she should trust him. Wondering if she could accept this offer, for just what it was…an attempt to help better the farm. Jenna sighed, deep in thought, then lifted her eyes to his.

''You're picking up livestock tomorrow.''

Chapter Thirteen

Up in her bedroom that night, Jenna slipped out of her wet clothes, removing each piece slowly as her mind wandered to Cash. She wondered if he was doing the same. Was he peeling off his wet shirt right now? Was rain clinging to those fine hairs on his chest? Was he thinking about her, about the way they'd kissed?

Images of Cash, naked on the bed, making love to her, flashed in her mind. Was it a memory of how they'd been that day in the hotel room in Goose Creek when they'd married, or was it a vision of what Jenna wanted now? Did she want to make love with Cash again? To have him hold her, caress her, lay with her, until both their bodies were spent and exhausted?

Jenna closed her eyes, but the image held true. She couldn't block it out. No longer could she deny she had feelings for Cash Callahan, gambler, a man ready to leave as soon as the fields were planted.

"Don't be a fool, Jenna," she muttered in the quiet room. The soft patter of rain on the rooftop was all that could be heard. Fresh, crisp air drifted in pleasingly, in the way it does after rain. There were no more drips leaking through the roof, thanks to Cash.

Jenna leaned against the wall wearing only her chemise, the skin on her arms puckering up from the cold, but it was as though she was immune to the discomfort. She stared at the dress Cash had given her, the beautiful golden-yellow gown that Jenna had never put on.

All of life is a gamble with the choices we make.

Cash's words tormented her. He had spoken what he believed to be the truth, but Jenna still was so unsure, so befuddled. Was he right? Was her life just as big a gamble as his? And if she determined he was right, what good could come of it? She could give him her heart, only to have him abandon her to go back to his old way of life, the life he preferred as a gambler.

Jenna walked over to the dress hanging up on her cheval mirror. She fingered the lace, the pearl-like buttons and the dainty stitches. "So delicate," she said, wondering how Cash could think her so. She was a farmer, a woman who got dirt under her fingernails every day. She had strong limbs from carrying firewood and hoeing the soil and guiding the plow. She wore torn tattered clothes, didn't know much about style or grace, yet Cash *saw* her in this dress. He'd picked it out special, just for her.

A strange sensation took hold and Jenna backed up a bit. She shivered but was unable to tear her gaze from the dress. It was as though the gown beckoned, as if calling her out, accusing her of cowardice, of fear and uncertainty. Draped there on the mirror, its beauty apparent, the dress held so much more for Jenna.

"What are you so afraid of, Jenna?" she asked herself, her teeth biting down hard on her lip as she contemplated. And then she knew.

Trust.

She was afraid to trust again.

And hope.

She couldn't dare hope to have the future she'd always dreamed about.

She'd done that. She'd poured her heart and soul into her dreams, only to have them shatter around her, like a glass vase that had slipped from her grip. She fought the urge. She fought the temptation. As much as the dress lured her with its elegant beauty, Jenna fought back, her defenses up and her mind set on her resolve. The dress and all it represented dashed from her head when Cash knocked on her door.

"Jenna, are you awake in there?"

She gasped when she heard his voice. He'd

never come to her room before. "Oh, um, yes. I'm awake." She grabbed for her robe, quickly tying the sash and making sure she was covered from neck to ankles.

He spoke from behind her door. "I'm heading out to Ben's. Just wanted you to know I'll be gone a while."

Her curiosity sparked, Jenna opened the door slowly. Cash leaned against the door frame, standing only inches from her. The appealing scent of soap and fresh rainwater assaulted her senses. Cash had changed into clean clothes. With his hair wet and slicked back from his face, the compelling blue of his eyes couldn't be missed. At times, not only the unique beguiling color but the piercing intensity as well, shocked her down deep in her bones.

"Why? Is there a problem?"

Cash peeked inside her room. Heat rose up her cheeks when she noted the direction of his gaze. He'd noticed the dress, draped upon the mirror. He spoke of it only by the arch of his brow then turned back to her. "No problem, sugar."

There was no pretending Cash wasn't studying her with interest. His gaze roamed over her body, slow and leisurely, as if he had the right to and as if he didn't mind the obvious torture he was inflicting. He studied her hair and how it fell onto her shoulders. His gaze traveled down her throat, stopped at her breasts, lingered there, then moved lower down.

Jenna clutched her robe tight.

The movement seemed to bring Cash back. He met her eyes now and smiled. Jenna's heart raced furiously.

"I'm going to tell Antonio the good news. Won't have time tomorrow. I'll be busy picking up your hogs and sheep. And when I return, I hope to build that pen I promised you. The way I figure, nothing should prevent a man and a woman from being together," he said, stopping to clear his throat. He spoke with slow deliberation, "If they… love…each…other."

Jenna swallowed hard, her mouth suddenly dry. With a lick of the tongue, Jenna moistened her lips. Cash blinked and leaned in, his reaction creating lightning-fast heat between them as he peered at her mouth. A fire erupted in Jenna, but she couldn't look away, couldn't step back. If Cash wanted to kiss her, she wouldn't refuse, but would welcome him.

Instead, and to her surprise, he blinked a second time then backed away, into the hallway and far from her reach. "I'd best be going now, before it gets too late. You be sure to lock up. I won't be long."

Jenna closed the door with a thud then leaned against it. Disappointment registered quickly, along with myriad emotions running rampant, causing havoc to Jenna's heart and head. Jenna had wanted his touch, and this time, it was Cash

who'd been the cautious one. The desire in his
eyes couldn't be missed, yet he'd been the one to
turn away.

Jenna had made her feelings known to him.
She'd denied him in the barn the other night, denied him in her heart as well. He'd finally gotten
a clear message. She wanted no part of him, no
part of a gambler, a man who'd bide his time here
until he would take his leave.

Jenna *had* wanted that from the beginning, but
now she was absolutely certain of…nothing.

Early the next morning, Cash dressed quickly
then climbed down the ladder in the loft and strode
to Larabeth. "How's my lady today?" The milk
cow cast him a look. He ran a hand along her flank
then patted her head. "You waiting on something?" he asked, teasing the big animal. Larabeth's ears wiggled, just so slightly. Cash was beginning to know her moves. He reached into his
pocket and came out with sugar cubes. "Here you
go. Maybe one day soon, you'll come to like me."

Hell, Antonio thought Cash walked on water.
Last night the young man had been elated when
Cash told him the news. Old man Bender couldn't
stop Antonio from courting his daughter. Cash felt
certain satisfaction in securing Antonio a chance at
a happy future.

Cash had always believed in fate. If something
was meant to be then it would happen. Of course,

being a gambler, he'd always tried improving the odds. Only there was no improving his odds when it came to Jenna.

She was just as stubborn as Larabeth. Females. No matter what a man did, they held tight to their beliefs. He knew he didn't deserve a woman like Jenna, but he wanted to leave here with her thinking he was a different sort of man. She didn't trust him and he wondered if he could blame her. He'd told Jenna things about his past he'd not shared with another living soul. She was right to be wary of him, perhaps, though in his heart Cash knew there wasn't a doggone thing he wouldn't do for her.

Jenna didn't want him here. She didn't like who he was. In many ways gambling defined him and was the only truth he had in his life.

Last night, every male instinct he held told him Jenna wanted him. When she'd opened the door and stood before him in that robe, Cash's body had grown tight. She looked at him tentatively, but there was so much more in her tawny eyes. He saw boldness and desire. She had wanted him to kiss her. And the good Lord knew, he'd wanted to do just that, but he'd gotten to the point with Jenna where kissing wasn't nearly enough.

He wanted to take her body and blend with her soul. He wanted to claim her, to pleasure her and cherish the child in her, while making pure sweet love to the woman. But Cash knew she would turn him away, as she'd done before. And she'd be right. So he'd resisted the urges pulling at him and let her be. But it hadn't been easy. Being alone with Jenna was proving more and more difficult. He couldn't imagine living here much longer without having her, yet the thought of leaving tore at his gut.

"I'm no farmer," he said to Mac as he guided him outside the barn. He harnessed the horse to the wagon and climbed up. "But I'm going to do my best today. Old man Bender is going to pay up. In spades."

Chapter Fourteen

The planting was going smoothly. Jenna had taken turns with Antonio and Cash and for three solid days they used what Cash named the "contraption" to seed the plowed-up earth. The seeder worked marvelously well and Jenna had never enjoyed planting time as much. She'd been out here each day, working the fields alongside of the men. The rows took shape and soon tiny sprouts would rise up from the ground, absorbing sunshine to grow into stalks of golden grain.

Jenna stumbled, feeling slightly weak-kneed, yet she managed to regain her balance before falling flat out as she walked along the edge of the last row. She peered over the farm her parents had tilled with love and named Twin Oaks. "Soon," she whispered, wiping sweat from her brow, "soon, we'll have us the greatest harvest ever."

But Jenna's limbs buckled under and she nearly went down again. The scorching sun beat down

with vigor. After the rains that brought new livestock to her farm, the heat wave they'd been ex-
periencing had resumed. Jenna knew it would pass.
It was far too early in the season for this degree
of heat to continue. But for now, the sweltering
heat pounded the earth.

Fatigue set in. Jenna's usually abundant strength
drained from her body. She ambled slowly toward
the house, her head spinning with dizziness. She
stumbled two more times, but managed to keep
upright. And once inside the house, she downed
two tall glasses of water. She hadn't strength
enough to sit down. No, Jenna needed to *lie* down.
She made a tough journey up the stairs then once
inside her bedroom flopped onto her bed.

Exhausted sleep claimed her almost immediately.

She didn't know how long she slept or what time
of day it was when pounding from below startled
her awake. She lifted her head from the pillow to
listen. The booming noise continued. Slowly, and
with care she rose to investigate.

She made it to the landing and peered down.
Cash had his head bent, intent on hammering nails
into her staircase. "C-Cash," she called out, feeling less strength in her limbs than earlier. She held
onto the banister for support. Her head throbbed
incessantly.

Cash glanced up. "Jenna, I didn't know you
were up there."

"C-could you do t-that another t-time?"

Cash stood and stared at her, his face marked with concern. "Jenna, sugar, what's wrong with you?"

"I'm…so…tired."

Then everything went black and she floated, light as a feather, into oblivion. The last thing she recalled was the sound of Cash's voice, cursing.

Cash bounded up the stairs two at a time. "Jenna! Jenna!" He let loose a string of curses until he reached her limp body. Lifting her gently, she appeared as ragged as a cloth doll. Cash held her with an arm then patted her cheek. "Jenna, sweetheart. Wake up."

Cash noted Jenna's eyes attempting to open. She struggled and only flashed them open for a second before they closed again. He bent his head down, placing an ear to her chest and sighed with relief when he felt the slow rise of her breathing.

Cash didn't know what to do. She needed help. He could saddle up Queen and race over to Ben's place, but he would never leave Jenna alone in this condition. He could bundle her up and take her over in the wagon, but as he looked at her pale face, weighed her wilting body, he knew he couldn't do that, either.

He opted for putting her into bed and trying to revive her. As he carried her in and set her down, shocking fear assailed him. He'd never known this kind of jolting anguish before.

He touched her forehead. She was hot, but not feverish. He touched many parts of her body, all feeling the same way, terribly hot. Cash brushed a kiss on her forehead. "I'll be right back."

He raced down the stairs to the kitchen, flinging open a cabinet, retrieving cloths and pouring a pitcher full of water, then headed upstairs.

Jenna hadn't made a move. She lay there on the bed, weak, exhausted and unconscious. "Sweetheart, you need to drink."

Cash lifted her, bringing a glass of water to her lips, but she hadn't the ability to drink, so he lowered her back down. Dipping his finger into the water, he moistened Jenna's lips, running his finger back and forth. Her lips were dry, almost completely blistered.

"Jenna, wake up. Please, sugar." Cash's heartbeats crashed against his chest. His words held no meaning for the woman lying unresponsively on the bed. He sank down next to her and peeled away her clothes gently.

Pouring water on a cloth, Cash washed Jenna's dehydrated body, allowing the coolness to stay and linger on her skin. He pressed the cloth to her throat, her arms, her stomach, her legs, leaving only a few private areas untouched.

He sat with her for hours, prying her lips open,

fingering droplets of water down her throat, and soaking her hot bare skin with cool water.

Day became night. Cash wouldn't sleep, but he tucked himself beside her, so that he could watch every movement she made, praying that she'd awaken. He stroked her golden hair, whispered in her ear and all the while, kept her cool and hydrated with water.

"I love you, Jenna Duncan," Cash admitted quietly. But she would never know. He'd not tell her. Cash was just now learning how difficult farm life really was. Aside from the crops failing, there were so many more unknowns. He'd brought trouble her way and the last thing this strong tenderhearted woman needed was more trouble. Jenna didn't want him here. He'd been a thorn in her side from the beginning. For her sake, as soon as he could, he'd leave.

He'd deal with the pain of that decision in his own way. He wasn't the important one here, Jenna was. With gentle arms, Cash embraced her, praying for her to recover, praying that life would be easier for her from now on and praying that the crop Jenna wished for would be the best ever.

A safe haven surrounded her. Jenna sank down deeper into the cocoon of warmth, her body relishing the comfort bestowed upon her. She heard her own sigh, a penetrating sound coming from deep within but her hazy mind wouldn't allow her to question it.

She shifted her position on the bed, turning to her other side. A strong hand on her shoulder guided her. Slowly, for the pre-dawn hours of the morning were not her favorite, she opened her eyes. She stared straight into the beautiful blue eyes of Cash Callahan.

"Morning," he said, with a smile that seemed a little forced. Lines of fatigue around the corners of his eyes told a different story. His jaw was clenched tight, and Jenna noted tension on his face.

Jenna blinked once, then twice and her mind began to clear a bit, beginning to comprehend. She was naked in bed with Cash Callahan. She searched for answers, but she couldn't recall how she had ended up in bed with him. The last thing she remembered was feeling tired and going up to her room to take a nap.

Cash held her in a loose embrace. Had they slept this way the entire night? Had it been Cash providing her the safe haven she'd dreamed about?

When Cash made a move to brush hair from her cheek she noted his bare chest. Heavens, was he naked as well? Jenna didn't have the courage to look any further down. It was bad enough he was here on her bed, and she couldn't remember why.

"Jenna, sugar, say something."

"Why are you in my bed?"

A chuckle erupted from the depths of his chest. "Not for the reason I'd prefer, sweetheart."

Confused, Jenna gazed into his eyes. "Why am I naked then, if nothing happened? *Nothing* did happen, right?"

"Well, if you'd like to call your fainting dead away from heat and exhaustion 'nothing,' then, sugar, I guess 'nothing' did happen."

"I fainted?"

"Don't you remember?"

"I remember feeling real tired and thirsty out in the fields. I couldn't wait to get a drink of water. But that didn't seem to help much, so I took a nap."

"That's right. I was working on the stairs, making a ruckus, pounding nails and you came out of your room to see me. That's when you fainted. Scared me half to death, Jenna." Cash bent in to kiss the tip of her nose. "Don't you do that again."

"I'm sorry," she murmured, still confused.

"Don't be. Wasn't your fault. The heat was too much for you. You've been working out in the sun for days now with the contraption. I should've said something, made you go into the house."

"I'm not your responsibility, Cash."

Cash grunted, not really acknowledging her comment.

"But you haven't told me why we were sleeping together."

"You needed water, so I stayed the night, trying

to get you to drink. I managed to get some drops into you and I figured if I couldn't get much water down you, I could at least cool down your skin."

Mortifying heat rose up Jenna's face. "You took off my clothes?"

"I had to, Jenna." Cash fingered a lock of her hair, rubbing it between his fingers. In a gentle tone, he added, "It's nothing I haven't seen before, Jenna. You're as beautiful as ever, but my only concern was getting you to wake up. I prayed that you would."

He *prayed?* Jenna's heart melted and she realized something amazing. Not only did she believe him, but she trusted him as well. Jenna had come to recognize her feelings for Cash, but it had never dawned on her that *he* would have feelings for *her.* Yet now, she believed he did.

"Thank you," she said, having no other words to express her gratitude.

"How do you feel?"

"I'm thirsty and hungry," she answered.

Cash bounded out of bed. Thankfully, he'd slept in his trousers. But, oh, what a specimen he made, standing over her, with his pants dipping below his navel and that strong powerful chest fully exposed.

He poured water into a glass. "Here, drink up."

Jenna took the proffered glass and downed its contents without the blink of an eye.

"Good girl. I would've cut off my right arm to

have you do that last night. What would you like
to eat?''

Jenna sat straight up, clutching the sheet to her
breasts, making sure she was fully covered, though
a small part of her rebelled. Cash had slept with
her fully nude. He'd seen all there was to see.
''You don't have to—''

''I do because, sugar, you're not getting out of
this bed today. Not once. And I want no arguments. You need a day to rest.''

Normally, Jenna would protest a complete day
in bed. She'd never had the luxury before, but her
limbs were tired and weak and her body ached. She
couldn't fathom getting up to do her daily chores.
''Okay.'' She slumped down onto her pillow.

''Okay?'' Cash was nearly beside himself with
satisfaction. ''No arguments?''

''No arguments.''

''Good. What do you want to eat?''

''Surprise me.''

''Oh, believe me, my cooking is going to be
your worst surprise.''

Jenna laughed, settling herself under the covers
and wondered what Cash would be cooking up.

Half an hour later with a plate filled with fried
potatoes and eggs and holding a glass of water,
Cash entered Jenna's bedroom. ''Here you go.''
He immediately noted two things; Jenna had
dressed in a nightgown and fallen back to sleep.

Cash smiled. "Okay, so maybe you weren't dying to eat my food," he said quietly. He placed the plate down on the bedside table and watched her sleep peacefully. She needed rest. Cash had a few chores to do and one important one came instantly to mind. He'd leave Jenna to rest and come back later to check on her. "I'll be back soon, sugar," he whispered.

Cash left the house and entered the barn. He picked up the milk pail and walked over to Larabeth. "It's time," he announced to the cow. The animal wasn't paying him much mind.

He opened the drawer that held his stash of sugar cubes. Nothing was left. Damn, when had he used up the last of the sugar? He didn't recall. With a lengthy sigh, Cash grabbed the stool, set it down, positioned the milk pail and spoke gently to Larabeth. "Looks like it's just you and me, darlin'. Jenna needs help, so I hope you plan on cooperating."

Larabeth nudged her body toward him, nearly knocking him to the ground again. "Now, Larabeth, you just got to trust me," he said softly, stroking her flank. He began humming the tune Jenna usually sang to the cow. He rubbed his hands together to warm them and began the milking.

To his surprise, Larabeth did cooperate. Milk squirted out, making clinking noises into the pail. Immediately, Button and her brood came running over to the sound, and Scrappy wasn't far behind.

Cash chuckled. ''Well, I'll be damned.'' He wished Jenna could see this, but a tall glass of milk by her bedside should be proof enough.

Cash didn't neglect the animals. Each one of the kittens got a share. Button and Scrappy, more than their fair share. Heck, Cash was in too good a mood to be stingy. Once satisfied, the animals licked their chops then lost interest.

When the pail was nearly full, Cash stopped to stand and stretch out his legs. He patted Larabeth and walked away, grinning. Hell, this was better than an Ace-high straight, Cash mused.

Cash entered Jenna's bedroom quietly. She was still asleep. He set the glass of milk down onto the table and stood over her. His own brand of fatigue set in, from worry and lack of any real sleep last night. His body fought exhaustion as long as it could, but admittedly, Cash needed to rest up some. ''What the hell,'' he said softly, removing his boots and shirt.

There was room enough on Jenna's bed and the picture she made, with hair flowing over the pillow, looking more like an angel than ever before, was too enticing. He'd sleep next to Jenna and it would be the best sleep of his life.

Cash lowered himself down and angled his body toward her. She rolled over as if she'd known he was there, and curled herself into his arms.

Holding her lightly, he closed his eyes. It wasn't long until sleep claimed him, too.

* * *

Hours later, Cash woke up as sunlight streamed into the window with heat and light. Jenna was beside him, her eyes bright but questioning.

"Sorry, sugar. I was tired, too."

Jenna nodded her understanding. "You stayed up all night, watching me."

"I did."

"Well, then. You deserve the rest."

Cash sat up, remembering the milk. He rose from the bed and handed Jenna the glass he'd brought up here. "You'd better drink up some more."

Stunned, Jenna's gaze locked onto the glass. "You…you milked her?"

Cash laughed. "Don't be so surprised."

Jenna chuckled, too. "But I am. How'd you do it?"

Cash shrugged. "The usual way."

"No, that's not what I mean."

Cash sat down on the edge of the bed. "Larabeth and I have come to some sort of understanding. I guess she trusts me now."

"Oh?"

"Yeah, she got to know me and I got to know her. Maybe that's all it takes."

"Trust is important," Jenna said, her gaze drifting off. "I want to thank you for staying the night and taking care of me."

Cash didn't want her thanks. Hell, he would

never have left her last night. She needed him. "I wasn't about to take any chances with you. You were pretty sick."

"And you did the Christian thing?"

Cash pushed his hair off his forehead, raking his hands through. "Hell, Jenna. It's more than that."

"It is?"

Cash stood and walked over to the window. He glanced down at the view below. The kittens were playing with Scrappy in the yard. How easily his dog had taken to the farm. And the fields, for all the eye could see, were ready to nourish new growth. Hogs and sheep filled the pens.

Cash recalled when he'd first gotten here, how the only thing he could see from his position on the bed were those two oak trees, their branches swaying in the breeze meeting each other by a touching of leaves. Twin Oaks.

"You know it is." Cash leaned heavily against the window frame, his back to her. "Wouldn't do much good to say the words, sugar."

After a long silent moment, Jenna spoke up, "Because you're leaving?"

"Yeah," he said, nodding as he continued to stare out the window. "Because I'm leaving."

And because he wasn't the man for Jenna.

He was no farmer.

Chapter Fifteen

"I feel fine, Rosalinda. It's been weeks since I was sick." Jenna gestured to her friend. "You and Ben have a seat. Supper will be ready soon."

"It is not necessary for you to work so hard. Let me help."

"Nonsense, I've been meaning to have you both to supper. I'm just glad Ben is feeling better."

Ben raised his cane and smiled. "Got me one heck of a cane here. Couldn't manage without it. Yeah, won't be long before I get back out to the fields."

"No! You are not ready. You must not," Rosalinda warned. "Jenna, Antonio and Cash have worked hard and the fields are almost planted. You must rest up some more."

Ben grumbled, looking at Jenna. "See how my woman babies me? She won't let me lift a finger at home."

"I agree with her, Ben. You're not ready to work again. You need to rest some more."

"Ah shoot, I know you're right, but I hate being confined."

Jenna chuckled and added. "That's why I asked you over tonight."

She set plates out on the table. She'd made a fancy meal, spending most of the day in the kitchen. Today, she had so much to be thankful for. She'd wanted to share the evening with her good friends…and Cash. He'd taken care of her, pampering her while she'd been ill. He'd cooked for her, watched over her and hadn't allowed her to do much on the farm until her strength had returned. She knew that any time now, with Ben getting better each day, Cash might decide to leave. "We'll pray for our crop and celebrate our friendship tonight. Where's Antonio?"

Both Ben and Rosalinda smiled, their eyes meeting each other with secret understanding. "With Marcie Bender," Ben offered. "He's been spending most of his evenings with her."

"Oh," Jenna said with a sigh. "I'm happy to hear that. What about Mr. Bender? Has he come around?"

"Well," Ben said, scratching his head. "I don't reckon the man liked losing that bet to Cash, not one bit. But from what Antonio tells me, he's not been putting up much of a fuss. The Benders have had my boy over to supper twice already."

The back door opened and Cash entered. All heads turned in that direction. He held a full bouquet of wild roses in his hand. "Evening."

Jenna faced him, her heart pounding hard. That had been happening lately—one look at Cash had her insides rumbling. No matter what he was doing, it was always the same. She'd see him chopping wood, or tossing a stick to Scrappy in the yard, or grooming his horse and her breath would catch.

Heavens, when would it ever stop? Certainly not right this minute, with him standing there, wearing a fresh white shirt, smelling lye-soap clean and holding out a batch of wild roses to her.

"These are the last of them. Make a real nice table decoration."

Jenna took the flowers offered and as his strong fingers brushed hers, her stomach tied up in knots. "Thank you." She glanced at the flowers, a lump forming in her throat. "T-These are lovely."

"Will you put them on the table?" When she looked up, Jenna was treated to the gleam of indigo-blue as his gaze rested solely on her. It was as though they were alone in the room, the others forgotten. Jenna stared into Cash's eyes, locked by the heat and longing she witnessed there.

Ben cleared his throat.

Jenna turned around abruptly in time to catch Rosalinda jab him in the arm.

"You two through mooning over each other?"

Jenna's face flushed with heat. Heavens, what had she been thinking? Flustered, Jenna made herself busy, setting the roses in a vase. Darn Cash anyway. The amused man had laughed at Ben's comment, when all Jenna wanted to do was sink right down through the floorboards.

After that, the meal went smoothly and Jenna relaxed a bit. They'd offered up a prayer for good weather, for the health of their loved ones and for their crop.

Jenna dished up creamy corn soup, chicken and dumplings, string beans and biscuits. For dessert she had made a peach cobbler. Everyone filled their bellies, complimenting her meal.

Just as they were taking the last bites of their dessert, Antonio came bursting through the back door, his face shining bright with happiness. "I'm getting married!"

For a moment, they all sat motionless at the table, apparently stunned by the news. Then, as realization dawned, everyone began talking at once.

"Congratulations!"

"When's the wedding?"

"How'd you pull that off, son?"

"*Dios,* Antonio. You give your mother a shock."

"Hey! One at a time," Antonio pleaded happily.

Antonio shook Cash's hand. His father gave him a big manly hug and Rosalinda's eyes misted with tears.

Jenna kissed his cheek. "I'm happy for you. Sit down and tell us all about it. Would you like a piece of cobbler?"

"No, no. I couldn't eat. I'm too excited." Antonio took a seat at the table. "I don't know where to begin. I have been in love with Marcie for a long time. I think I fell in love with her when she threw a rock at me in school. I chased her all around the schoolyard that day and haven't stopped."

"Oh, how sweet," Jenna said, but when she glanced at Rosalinda, the woman had tears flowing down her cheeks. Jenna took her hand. "He's in love, Rosa."

"*Sí, sí.* I know. Can't a mother be happy for her boy?"

Always pragmatic, Ben took a different approach. "How'd you get old man Bender to come around? He does know about this, doesn't he, Antonio?"

"Yes, Papa. He wasn't too happy about allowing Marcie to see me. He's protective of her. But Marcie had been wearing him down and then, well, thanks to Mr. Callahan and that bet he made, Bender couldn't go back on his word." Antonio turned to Cash. "I'll never forget what you did. Marcie and I, we might name our first child after you."

"*Dios!* A child? Are you to be a father so

soon?'' Rosalinda asked, the news obviously too much for her.

"Mama, no! Of course not. But we would like to have a family one day."

Jenna squeezed Rosalinda's hand. "They are young, but they will manage. Don't worry and when it is time, they will make you and Ben grandparents."

Antonio laughed. "We need a place first."

"Will you live on the Bender farm?" Ben asked and Jenna sensed him trying to keep his voice steady. Bender had all the hands he needed, whereas Antonio was an integral part of the success of Twin Oaks.

"No! My place is here. I would like to build a small house, if you will allow me."

Obviously relieved, Ben smiled. "I'll help you build it."

"So will I," Cash added. "Just tell me where and when. The three of us will have that house up real quick. When's the wedding?"

"Marcie wants to have the wedding soon. She's afraid her father will try to change our minds. He is going along with our wishes, but I think he would like to keep his daughter all to himself. He wouldn't mind if she became an old maid, as long as she lived on the farm."

Jenna's heart sank. She was three years older than Marcie. She wondered as time went on, if people would think of her as an unwanted old maid.

Cash caught her in his gaze and narrowed his eyes, questioning her. Jenna couldn't bear to look at him. She couldn't bear for him to know how distressed she felt. This should be a happy occasion and Jenna wouldn't bring everyone's joy down because of the sorrow she'd experienced. For Antonio's sake, she plastered on a big smile and glanced at Cash, but he didn't smile back.

Darn him. Maybe it was time for him to leave Twin Oaks. He was too much a reminder of all that she had lost, of the life she would never have.

And worst of all, he was too good at reading her most private thoughts.

Jenna bid farewell to her guests and as she stood in the yard waving, she sensed Cash watching her from a short distance away. She turned to go back inside the house.

"Jenna, wait."

She paused, then turned to him with a smile. "It's such good news about Antonio. I think he will be very happy."

Cash strode over to her until he was so close their boots nearly touched. He gazed into her eyes. "Don't, Jenna. Don't pretend. Not with me."

"I'm not pretending. I'm happy for Antonio."

He reached out to touch her cheek. The gentle

caress left her wanting more, so much more. "Happiness is not what I see on your face."

Cash had good instincts. She knew he couldn't be fooled, but she had little to say to him. She let out a weary sigh. "I'm tired, Cash."

Anger sparked in his eyes like a cold flash of metal, yet he spoke with tenderness. "Something upset you tonight. Tell me what it was."

Tears threatened, but Jenna held them back. They never helped and she wasn't one to give in to self-pity. "No, it's nothing."

"Jenna," Cash laced his tone with impatience, "it's *something.*"

Irritation gave way to anger, something Jenna rarely allowed. But this time, perhaps she had a right. "Yes, darn you. It's something. Okay? Happy to know I'm upset?"

"No, I'm not happy about it. I just want to help."

Her fury building, spurred by a situation out of her control, Jenna planted her hands on her hips. Wry amusement elevated her voice. "You, of all people, *can't* help me."

"Why not?" he asked, nearly shouting.

"Because…because I want what Marcie and Antonio have, that's why not! I want someone to share my life with, my farm. I want a family. I've prayed and prayed for a family of my own. Don't you see? I'll be that old maid Antonio spoke about, an unwanted and unloved woman, who'll never have a child, never know the joy of being a mother.''

Well, that sure dumbfounded him. Cash opened his mouth to speak, blinked his eyes then clamped his mouth closed. He looked away, off in the distance, a tick working at his jaw. When he turned back to respond, Jenna stormed off, heading for the house. She didn't want to hear anything Cash Callahan had to say.

It was too hard, feeling as she did. One minute she was hoping for his kisses, the next hoping he would leave the farm. She reminded herself over and over that he wasn't for her. She knew as soon as he could, he'd go back to gambling. That's who Cash Callahan was, after all. A gambler.

Jenna wouldn't forget that again.

Three days later, Cash lay in his makeshift bed up in the loft staring at the ceiling. He tossed and turned in a futile attempt to fall asleep. When that didn't work, he let out an oath, picked up his boot and tossed it. It landed near two sleepy kittens, barely missing them. With bewildered expressions, they jumped high in the air, the hair on their backs raised. ''Ah, hell,'' he muttered, reaching over to console the frightened kittens. They went willingly into his arms. ''Sorry about that.''

The kittens purred and rubbed their small bodies into him. They'd grown some, Cash noted, marking the time that he had been here.

He'd overstayed his welcome. Yet he couldn't leave the farm until Ben felt better. Cash knew Ben wouldn't be of much help building Antonio a small house, but understandably the man wanted to help his son. Cash's offer to help had been sincere. He'd been happy for Antonio and wanted to help the boy and Ben with the building.

Besides, the danger might still be present. If the Wendells were still in the area searching for him, he had no choice but to stay on at Twin Oaks. He'd weighed his options again, knowing full well it would be better for Jenna if he left. She might have a chance at that future she'd talked about, without him here, stirring up emotions, leaving them both frustrated and confused.

She might find someone to love.

Hell, Cash thought, one thing he knew for sure, he didn't want to be around to watch that happen. Seeing Jenna smitten with another man would tear his gut in two.

Cash set the kittens aside. He reached for his boots and threw his arms into his shirt. He wasn't going to get much sleep tonight. Climbing down the loft, he headed for Queen's stall. "Want to go for a fast ride?" he asked, grabbing for Queen's tack.

She hadn't been exercised today and Cash was too darn restless to sleep. The ride would do them both good. After saddling her up, he led her out of the barn.

He mounted quietly and lifted his head toward Jenna's bedroom. The lights were out. She'd never know he was gone. "We'll make it a short ride," he said to his mare. Although all indications were that Jenna was safe, he didn't like chancing leaving her alone at night.

He rode his horse hard, out the gates, past the fields, circling around Turner's Pond and back. Wind wiped at him, nearly blowing his hat from his head. He bent low, was one with the animal, gliding, racing, pushing Queen faster and faster. The excitement, the exhilaration helped clear his head.

He'd been right. It had been what both needed, a good hard ride.

Jenna had only been asleep a short time when noises from the yard had her snapping her eyes open. She listened carefully. Sounds of commotion, of animals shuffling and anguished cries, seemed to be coming from outside, somewhere.

Jenna rose quickly and dressed, shoving her boots on. She reached under her mattress, pulling out a gun. As she palmed it in her hand, the weapon felt strange. She hadn't given that gun much thought lately, since Cash had arrived. But for weeks after that awful man had come to claim ownership of Twin Oaks, Jenna had slept with it under her mattress each night.

She raced down the stairs, but was more wary

once she stepped out her front door. She listened
again and followed the sounds. They seemed to be
coming from the sheep pen. Her hands trembling
with fear, Jenna tightened her grip on the gun. She
moved with cautious deliberation, listening, winc-
ing at the terrible sounds she heard.

She rounded the corner of the barn and froze. A
pair of shocking eyes met her gaze. A wolf. Jenna
barely contained a scream upon witnessing the
wolf's heinous actions. One sheep was down already and before she'd caught the wolf's attention,
he'd been stalking another. The animals moaned in
their way, pressing their innocent bodies as far
from their predator as possible.

"Go! Get away!" Jenna pointed the gun, ready
to shoot.

The animal turned to face her, his eyes menac-
ing. Slowly, he came toward her, preying upon her
as he would any other animal. Everything inside
of her went black with fear. Her heart thumped
hard, her breathing sped up. She pulled her finger
back on the trigger and took her shot.

Nothing.

She tried again.

Nothing.

The wolf made ready to leap the fence, preparing to attack. Jenna cried out and pulled the trigger
a third time. Nothing.

The wolf jumped and Jenna stumbled back.

A shot rang out.

Jenna witnessed the animal's forward progression stop in midair. The wolf's piercing yelp of pain echoed in the night. Lifelessly, he fell to the ground.

All of the life went out of her as well. She fell onto the hard cold dirt, shaking.

"Jenna!" Cash's voice, filled with anger, boomed in her ears, causing her to nearly jump out of her skin. He lifted her up hurriedly and carried her into the house.

Chapter Sixteen

Cash placed Jenna, none too gently, on the sofa in the parlor. Noting her body trembling, he tossed her a quilt. "Cover up," he commanded, then began to pace in front of her.

"Of all the damn fool things to do, Jenna. Don't you know better than to argue with a wolf?"

The question required no answer. He didn't look at her, didn't want to see the stark fear on her face or admit to himself if he'd been one minute later, Jenna would have met with a horrendous death.

Cash paced some more, splaying his hands through his hair, his mind rushing with images of Jenna on the ground, the wolf ready to attack.

One minute later, and he would have lost her.

"You don't go running into the night with an unloaded gun."

He continued to pace, staring straight ahead, shaking his head, attempting without much success to tamp down his anger.

"Why didn't you check the gun, Jenna? Why? Tell me why?"

Her silence mystified him. Jenna usually spoke her mind. When he turned to her, the look of sheer, unbridled terror on her face did him in. Tears spilled down her cheeks, streaming fast and silently. Her whole body shook, shoulders, arms and legs.

Cash let out a quiet curse. "Wait here," he said, taking his leave. Moments later he entered the parlor, carrying a bottle of whiskey and a glass. He sat down next to her and poured the amber liquid and handed her the glass. "Drink this." She gulped it down then sputtered. "Whoa. Not so fast. Sip it slowly, sugar."

"I d-don't w-want to." She shoved it away, pushing at his hand.

He pressed it to her lips one more time. "Sip it slowly. You'll see. It will calm you."

Jenna stared into his eyes, hers swollen and reddened from tears.

"Trust me," he said, asking her to do something she'd never done before. After all this time on the farm, he hadn't gained Jenna's trust.

Her gaze on him unwavering, she took the offered glass and sipped slowly. He watched the delicate muscles on her throat work as the liquor flowed down smoothly. "Better?"

Jenna nodded, handing him back the glass.

He leaned back and nudged Jenna into his arms.

More than anything else, she needed his comfort. She needed to be held and reassured. But, Cash admitted, he, too, needed reassuring. Holding her in his arms meant she was alive and safe. Thinking of what might have happened, of how close she'd come to losing her life, had Cash covering them both with the quilt and tightening his hold. He held her that way for a long time.

Finally, she said, "I t-thought the gun was loaded."

"No matter. You shouldn't have faced down the wolf."

"I didn't know there was a wolf out there. I heard noises."

"It's not for you to go into the night, investigating."

"Yes," Jenna said with sadness, "it is my responsibility. This is my farm now. The animals—"

"Wouldn't survive with you dead. You shouldn't take such chances with your life."

"The gambler advising me not to take a chance?"

"That's different, Jenna. No one would expect you to confront a wolf. Your life is worth more than that."

"My life doesn't seem to be worth all that much," she said.

Cash had never heard her speak with such disillusionment before. Her admission rattled his bones. "Your life is worth *everything*."

Jenna snuggled deeper in, seeking his warmth and comfort, it seemed. "Thank you for saying that and for saving my life. You think we're even now?"

"I still owe you." He said this without explanation, but he meant it with his whole heart. Jenna had saved his life, but she'd also given him more in the short time he'd known her than she could ever imagine. Cash stroked her head, letting his fingers trail through the softness of her long blond hair. "I faced a wolf once," he confided.

Jenna lifted her head up slightly, to look into his eyes. He nodded. "I did. I was just a boy."

"Tell me."

Cash would offer up the story to Jenna, giving to her a part of himself, a part of his life that he'd never shared with another person. Not only did Cash find the experience cleansing but also he found it more intimate and heartwarming than any sexual favor Jenna might grant him. In Jenna, he'd found a woman he'd wanted in his bed, yes, but he'd also found a friend, someone in whom he could confide and trust with his most personal experiences.

And after he shared his wolf story, Jenna whispered in a voice filled with awe. "You've had the most amazing adventures."

He chuckled and the movement tossed her off his chest. He reclaimed her quickly, pressing her head back to where it had been. Where he wanted her. She snuggled in. "Adventures? Sugar, it's called survival."

"I know, but I mean, you have so many stories. Tell me more, Cash. Tell me all about your childhood."

Cash let out a breath. He had dead animals outside to tend as well as other chores to do, but nothing on heaven or earth could have torn him away from Jenna at the moment. He adjusted his hold on her and began sharing stories of his youth. And in the telling he found the only real healing of his childhood, Cash had ever known.

The next weeks flew by for Jenna as preparations were made for Antonio and Marcie's wedding. Elias Bender had finally come around, agreeing to have the marriage take place on his farm. It was to be the biggest shindig the town of Goodwill had ever seen.

Cash and Ben spent most of their free time with Antonio, helping him build a small cabin on a plot of land not too far from Ben's house. Jenna saw little of any of them. Her time was spent doing daily chores: milking Larabeth, mucking out the barn, collecting eggs from the henhouse and slopping the hogs.

On occasion, she'd make up a lunchtime meal and deliver her baskets to the men working on Antonio's house. They ate heartily, but their minds were on their work and Jenna didn't want to intrude. It warmed her heart to see Cash getting along so well with Ben. The two men seemed to have struck up a friendship and Antonio just plain thought the sun rose and set on Cash's shoulders.

Jenna understood her young friend's fascination with Cash. What she didn't fathom was her own. She'd convinced herself that Cash Callahan, gambler, wasn't worth the time of day. She'd thought him a callous, calculating man who had used her in a terrible way. He ruined her life. He took away her future. At one time, she'd hated him.

But no longer.

Her feelings for him ran deep, so much so that the stirrings in her heart frightened her. She'd tried to deny them, tried to will them away, yet feelings so strong weren't easy to ignore.

But Jenna had to try. So rather than think about all that Cash had been through in his life, all the heart-wrenching stories he'd confided in her in the name of survival, she'd set her concentration on the wedding. The excitement had become contagious. Jenna poured her efforts into helping Rosalinda with some surprises for Antonio and his new wife. Today after completing her chores, she'd spent time helping Rosalinda make a mattress for the newlyweds. Once the fabric was sewn, they took dried corn husks, cut them up into smaller pieces, then soaked them. When they had dried and were a bit softer she and Rosalinda stuffed the mattress. "A good strong bed and two loving souls is what makes a marriage," Rosalinda had said.

Alone in her house now, Jenna sat quietly on her sofa. Years ago, Rosalinda had taught her how to crochet, but Jenna had always been too busy to simply sit deep in thought and work the yarn. She hadn't known if she even remembered how, but as she hooked the yarn and made stitch after stitch, the patterns that she'd learned had come back to her.

"You think Antonio and Marcie will like my present?" she asked Button. Her lazy slumbering cat didn't budge on the sofa. "You think it will turn out pretty enough to put on their table?"

Jenna heard the back door open. Her heart sped up at the sound of Cash's boots hitting the floor. "Jenna?"

"I'm in the parlor."

He entered wearing a big smile. "It's all done. We've finished the house. Antonio is bringing Marcie out to see it tomorrow."

Jenna set down her crochet needle. "That's wonderful. She'll be surprised."

"Yeah, and we've finished up just in time. The wedding's day after tomorrow."

"I know," Jenna said, "I'm hoping to have this tablecloth finished. It's a gift for their wedding."

Cash looked it over. "It's pretty. Looks like it's almost done."

"Not really. I've got to work on it most of tomorrow, I'm afraid."

"You do that. Don't worry about the chores. I'll get to Larabeth in the morning and take care of everything."

Jenna tilted her head and cast him a smile. "You know, I think Larabeth prefers you over me now."

Cash chuckled. "I knew she'd come around. Most females do, once they get to know me." Cash winked, his charming grin entirely too disarming.

Jenna picked up her needle again and began working the yarn. "Female *cows,* you mean."

"Ah Jenna, that ain't nice," he replied with amusement.

Jenna stifled a chuckle of her own. "Just speaking the truth, Mr. Callahan, just speaking the truth."

"Well, tarnation woman, don't be so doggone honest."

Jenna put her head down, smiling. Heavens, if Cash only knew that she wasn't being honest at all. She had gotten to know him, and she'd certainly come around. Actually, she'd come full circle. Where at one point she couldn't abide having him live here on the farm, now Jenna couldn't imagine her life without him. She didn't want to think about the time he'd have to leave the farm. She couldn't envision saying goodbye to him. He'd become so much a part of Twin Oaks. He'd become so much a part of *her* as well.

Finally, yet with great reluctance, Jenna had come to the realization that she had fallen in love with Cash.

She had fallen in love with a gambler.

Chapter Seventeen

I want to see it on you. Just once.

Cash's sentiments were never far from her mind. Jenna sat on her bed, gazing up at the beautiful golden-yellow dress adorning her mirror. She had come to accept this gift from Cash slowly, day by day, in increments of which she had no real conscious recollection. She only knew that today, the day of Antonio's wedding, she would wear the dress proudly, without qualm or trepidation.

Jenna combed her hair to a luminous shine, leaving it down in waves, the ribbons Cash had given her on her birthday helping to keep the tresses in place. She put on her petticoats then stepped into the dress, taking time to do up each tiny pearl button. When she was completely dressed, Jenna approached the mirror.

"Oh, my," she whispered on a sigh. Surely, the reflection staring back at her wasn't Jenna Duncan, farm girl. Jenna continued to stare, her gaze roaming over each nuance of a dress that fit her to perfection. She lifted her arms and noted how the lace on the sleeves glided like a soft caress over her fingers. The bodice fit snugly, exposing a great deal of her skin, then flared out at the hips in a full skirt. Jenna perused her image in the mirror. She'd never owned a dress like this before. It was stunning, a work of art and being so made Jenna feel truly feminine.

"Stop your gawking, silly girl," Jenna said to her reflection. She grabbed the mantilla Rosalinda had given her. "Cash is waiting."

Jenna made her way to the top of the stairs when she heard Cash call out from below, "We're going to be late, Jen—"

Cash stood at the base of the stairs and when he gazed up, he took a step back, whipping the hat from his head. She saw him swallow and lock his gaze onto hers as she walked down the stairs. A flash of heat coursed through her body, causing commotion to her insides. Cash hadn't taken his eyes off of her, and the appreciation she witnessed in them turned up the heat considerably.

When she reached the last step, Cash was waiting there. He took her hands, his gaze flowing over her body like soft silk. "You look more than beautiful, sugar. The dress, well…I didn't forget anything about you."

The reminder of their time together as man and wife brought heat to her cheeks. Jenna drew in her bottom lip and took a deep breath. The movement brought Cash's attention to her chest and she became increasingly aware of the amount of skin the dress exposed. "Thank you," she said softly, nearly tongue-tied. "You look nice, too."

Nice? Cash looked positively handsome today, wearing the same suit he'd worn when he'd come back to the farm. A pressed white shirt contrasted sharply with the dark and dramatic cut of his suit and fancy vest. Even his boots were shined, almost as brightly as his eyes which gleamed deep blue and were constantly on her.

He came closer, his breath touching her throat and spoke quietly near her ear. "Thank you for wearing it," he said, his words spoken with sincerity.

Jenna took a swallow, but said nothing more.

"We'd better go," Cash announced and together, hand in hand, they headed for the wagon outside.

Cash was a dead man.

He held a losing hand. There was no way out. He couldn't fold yet he didn't hold the cards to win, he realized as he stood by Jenna's side as Antonio and Marcie spoke their vows. The wedding, held outside in a garden setting on Bender's farm, had more guests than the entire population of the town of Goodwill. Ranchers, farmers, shopkeepers, had all been invited. Bender was an influential man, having the biggest, most prosperous farm in the territory.

Painfully aware of the interest Jenna was attracting from the young males in attendance, Cash spent most of his time casting stern looks their way. He sidled up as close to Jenna as he could, yet he knew he was doing her a disservice. The honorable thing to do would be to leave Jenna's side. He'd taken away her future, perhaps now, he could give it back to her. With him out of the picture, Jenna could meet someone here, maybe even a farmer, who shared the same interests, had the same dreams as her.

But as his gaze flowed over the men eyeing her, Cash didn't know if he was that noble a man. To give Jenna up was a tremendous sacrifice to make, even though ultimately it was for her own good. He couldn't bear to let her go, yet he knew he couldn't have her. The day would come when he would leave.

And as her flowery scent rose up to tease his nostrils and stir his blood, Cash reminded himself once more that he held a losing hand.

Antonio stood facing Marcie, their hands entwined. Within minutes, the preacher concluded the ceremony by announcing that Antonio could kiss his bride. Jenna applauded as enthusiastically as the others then turned to him, her face glowing with joy. "Oh, it was such a lovely ceremony. I think they'll be very happy."

Peering down at her sweet expression, Cash could only nod in agreement. This was what Jenna wanted, a marriage, someone to love and a family one day. She deserved it, dammit. And if Cash were a different kind of man, he'd give it to her. Guilt assailed him, punching him hard in the gut. He had no right to Jenna. He had no right standing in the way of her happiness. "I'll be back later," he said, leaving her standing there alone.

Hell, she wouldn't be alone for long.

Cash wandered off, taking a look at Bender's enormous barn, his array of animals and his stables. He hiked quite a distance to where the fields began. The walk did him good, he mused. It helped to clear his head, which, oftentimes, got too dang dumbfounded when Jenna was around.

Less than an hour later, he returned to the gardens, watching the festivities as food and drink were offered up in abundance. He spotted Jenna amid some older ladies. Three young men hovered by her side, seeming to entertain them with their tales. Cash exhaled slowly, turning away. When he spotted Ben leaning on his cane by the food table, Cash headed over there. "Congratulations," he said, offering Ben his hand. "Antonio and Marcie make a real fine couple. I wish them well."

They shook hands, Ben's face beaming. "Thank you, thank you. It was quite a ceremony. And how about this feast? Old man Bender sure knows how to throw a party."

"Yeah, I suppose he does."

"Where's Jenna?" Ben asked. "Rosie said she's been asking for you. I thought by now you two would have found each other."

Cash shrugged and gestured toward the veranda. The other ladies had vanished, yet those three men still held Jenna's attention. "She's busy."

Ben peered over in that direction then slanted him a look. Cash knew that look. He'd come to know Ben quite well in the months since he'd been at Twin Oaks. "She's been asking for *you*."

"I'm not available."

"*Making* yourself not available is more like it."

Cash shrugged. "Maybe."

Ben shook his head. "Don't be a fool. How long do you think it'll take before one of those men over there is going to ask for Jenna? How long, Cash? Look at her. She's sweet and beautiful. That gal's got a heart of pure gold. They're just discovering something you've known all along."

"I'm hoping she likes one of them," Cash announced, his heart pounding against his chest. He was flat-out lying, to Ben and to himself.

Ben laughed. "You ain't fooling me. You want her for yourself."

Cash shook his head adamantly. "I'm not—"

"What? A farmer? If you're not a farmer, then I'll eat my boots, Cash Callahan. I ain't seen anybody work as hard, or take to the farm as quick or get on with the animals so well, as you. In your head you're not a farmer, but in your heart, maybe you are. Now, you gonna let them men take Jenna for a whirl around the dance floor? Go on," Ben urged with a hand to Cash's shoulder, "ask her to dance. The music's just starting."

"Don't expect much," Cash said, holding Jenna's hands as they waited for the music to begin. "I'm not such a good dancer, but I think I can manage not to crush your feet."

Jenna chuckled and with a tilt of her head, confessed, "I'm hoping not to crush yours, either, Cash. I haven't had much chance to go dancing."

He cast her a quick smile. "Well, then, we should do all right."

A small band of musicians began playing and Cash seemed to settle into a tempo that she could follow. They moved about the dance floor with surprising ease.

"I didn't see you after the ceremony. Where did you go?" Jenna asked, her gaze fixed on his. She'd been curious, dying to ask why he'd left her side as soon as he possibly could.

Cash pursed his lips and didn't reply right away. When he apparently made up his mind to answer, he asked, "You want the truth?"

Jenna blinked. Of course she wanted the truth, but suddenly she was fearful of his answer. "I believe I do."

"I left you alone so that you might meet up with someone new."

"Someone new?" Puzzled, Jenna slowed her steps.

"A man," Cash replied, his gaze fastened to hers. "I saw the joy on your face during the wedding ceremony. You want that for yourself and I don't blame you. You deserve it, Jenna. I figured—"

"You figured to abandon me." Hurt by his intentions, although she thought she understood why, but reason didn't weigh heavily when it came to matters of the heart. "Why'd you save me from the wolf the other night, Cash, if you intended to throw me to the wolves today anyway?"

"I'm not doing that!"

Jenna stopped dancing. "Aren't you? There's no one here for me, Cash. Not one man I'd like to spend time with, so you can stop your matchmaking."

Jenna turned to leave, but Cash grabbed her around the waist and spun her to face him. He searched her eyes steadily, but there was amusement in his tone. "Not one man?"

"Not a one," she confessed, folding her arms across her middle.

His lips twitched. "Not even me?"

"Especially you," she said matter-of-factly, her irritation slowly dissipating. Cash's gaze softened and he took her back into his arms. They moved around the dance floor again.

"Well, I can't let you go now. There're too many men ready to pounce. I've been staring each one of them down. It's tiresome." He sighed dramatically. "So long as there's no one here you'd like to spend time with, I suppose you're stuck with me today."

"Mmmm, stuck," she repeated. Jenna's heart clenched tight when Cash grinned and pulled her body up to his. He whirled her around the dance floor once again, their argument and his ridiculous notions forgotten.

Three hours later when the celebration was over, Jenna embraced Rosalinda in farewell. "Antonio made such a handsome groom. I know he's happy. Do you like Marcie?"

A winsome smile crossed Rosalinda's face. "*Sí.* She is good for my Antonio. She makes him happy. I only wish such happiness for you now, *querida.* Then, all will be well."

"All is well, Rosa. Don't worry over me."

Rosalinda, dressed in a lovely gown of blue satin, directed her gaze to Ben and Cash, who were hitching up their wagons. "You wear his dress, no? He has been very attentive today. I have eyes. I see the way he looks at you. He is a good man, Jenna."

This time, Jenna didn't deny it. "Yes."

Rosalinda's brows arched. "Ah, so now, you see it, too?"

"Yes, but he is happy to have me meet other men. He thinks I want to marry just anyone."

"Ah, but you have only one man in mind?"

"No, Rosa. I don't have anyone in mind. Cash isn't going to stay with me. I know that. He'll be gone soon, but I will never forget him."

Jenna understood that she and Cash had only a short time together. He seemed restless lately and was only staying on at Twin Oaks because he had no other choice.

Ben and Cash walked over to them, ending their conversation. "Ready?" Cash asked. "I've got the wagon hitched."

"Yes, I'm ready," Jenna said, placing a soft kiss on Rosalinda's cheek. "Goodbye and congratulations again," she offered to both the Markhams.

Cash embraced Rosalinda then turned to shake Ben's hand. "I'll be by tomorrow and we'll talk more about that idea I had."

Cash helped Jenna up onto the buckboard, then mounted the seat and took up the reins. Jenna waved until Ben and Rosalinda were out of sight. When she couldn't take Cash's silence another minute, she asked, "What idea are you going to talk to Ben about?"

Cash shrugged in that noncommittal way he had. "Just something I heard today, that's all."

By the finality in his voice, the conversation was

over, but Jenna's unyielding curiosity was sparked. Still, she didn't pry. She didn't have to know everything Cash did and said, did she?

He was pretty much a private man. Yet it warmed Jenna's heart that he'd opened up to her about his childhood. She'd never forget the stories he'd told and never again judge him so harshly for the life he had led.

Jenna wrapped the mantilla more snugly around her shoulders. The day had surrendered to night and there was a slight chill in the air.

"Cold?" Cash asked, giving her a sideways glance.

"A little bit."

"Come closer," he suggested and when she did, he wrapped an arm around her. His body gave off heat but Jenna experienced a different sort of heat, one that came from being near the man she wanted. One that came from longing, from hope and from desire.

"Better now?"

"Much better," she said, leaning her head against his chest. They rode home in silence, Jenna happy to have this time alone to share with Cash.

All too soon, they entered the gates of Twin Oaks. Cash reined in his horse, then jumped down from the wagon. He walked over to Jenna, his hands taking hold of her waist and lifting. Once he set her down, she gazed up into his eyes, his expression unreadable, yet his hold on her hips had tightened some. "You go in. I'll see to the wagon."

Jenna didn't want him to let go his hold. "Aren't you coming inside?"

Light from the half moon cast shadows on his face, but shadows of doubt entered his eyes as well. "No, better not."

"It's early. I'll make coffee."

Cash blew out a sharp breath, contemplating, as though there was a war going on inside his head. "Jenna, if I come inside—"

"We'll have coffee," Jenna finished for him.

He stared at her for a long moment. "Okay, I'll be in, in a few minutes."

Relieved, Jenna smiled then entered her house. She didn't know what she expected, or why it was so important to her, but she didn't want her evening with Cash to end.

Jenna set about brewing the real coffee Cash preferred. She stood by the cookstove, watching flames rise up, but her mind wasn't on Arbuckle's coffee. Tonight her mind was on Cash, the handsome stranger whose life she'd saved, the gambler, the man who had ridden back into her life, causing chaos and havoc to her heart.

She felt his presence from behind before she actually heard his footsteps. "Jenna, I can't do this," he whispered in her ear. His hands once again were on her hips, but she sensed he used them as a brace to anchor her, so that she wouldn't turn around.

Jenna put her head down, her whole body aching to lean back, against his strong chest. "What can't you do?"

"I can't sit in this kitchen tonight, talking about wheat and cows and farm tools. I can't pretend anymore that I don't want you."

"Oh," Jenna said lamely, her mind racing for answers, her heart pounding up inside her head.

"I'm going now," he said as he released his grip on her.

The loss was near to unbearable. Jenna turned around when she heard the door close softly. On impulse, she raced to open the door. She took a step outside and saw Cash walking toward the barn. "I can't pretend anymore, either," she said into the quiet night.

Chapter Eighteen

Midway into the yard, Cash stopped, but didn't turn around. He stood motionless and Jenna wondered if he'd heard her. "Guess I'll just *pretend* I didn't hear that," he said, his voice grim. He began walking again toward the barn.

"Pretend all you want, Cash Callahan, but you did hear me," Jenna said, taunting him. "I didn't take you for a coward."

Cash did turn then, slowly, eyeing her from just below the brim of his hat. "I'm no coward, sugar. It's killing me, not coming over there."

Jenna knew in her heart, this was the right thing to do. This was what she wanted. If only for one night, she wanted to know the joy of being in Cash's arms once again. She knew the consequences. She understood that when Cash left, her heart would shatter, but at least, she'd have this one memory to call upon, when life, with all its uncertainties, got too intolerable. "It's killing me, too, Cash." She put out her arms, beckoning him.

Cash was beside her instantly, picking her up, carrying her into the house, planting kisses on her mouth, her cheeks, stroking his hands through her hair. He didn't let up, didn't stop kissing her until he closed the door to her bedroom.

Cash held her close, nestling her in his arms. She heard him sigh, reining in his passion. With a hand, he stroked her back then rested it upon her waist. He spoke with quiet calm now, as if a settling balm had taken hold of him. "You know what I thought when I saw you wearing this dress?" he asked.

Jenna shook her head and pulled away enough to gaze up into his eyes.

"That maybe I could claim you as mine."

"I am yours," she said in a whisper, "tonight."

He smiled, a flash of teeth in the moonlit shadows of the room. "You look so beautiful in your dress, it's nearly a shame to take it off you."

He worked a button, then another, his soft touch causing her skin to prickle in anticipation. With the bodice open, cool air descended upon her.

"'Course, it would be more of a shame *not* to take it off you," he said, bending down to kiss her throat. His lips warmed her instantly and Jenna let out a little sound of pleasure. "I've missed you, Jenna. Missed being like this with you. I've wanted you for so long."

Jenna reached for him, her long slow kiss the only reply she had to offer him. She'd wanted him, too, daydreamed about his kiss and fantasized about his touch. Somewhere between hate and mistrust, between anger and disappointment, between hurt and betrayal, Cash had entered her heart. He'd managed to find a small opening, a tiny crevice that Jenna hadn't closed off and he'd inched his way in, day by day, deed by deed, until she no longer had the will nor the strength to battle her feelings for him.

Under Cash's expert ministrations, her dress fell gracefully to the floor and she stepped out of it. It wasn't long before Cash had removed the rest of her clothes. He carried her to the bed, setting her down with care, as if she was the most precious of gems.

Jenna swallowed hard when Cash began to undress. She watched him remove his jacket, undo the buckle on his gun belt and guide the holster to the ground. He removed the remaining clothes quickly. She marveled at his form, the perfection of his body, the solid strength he carried about him like a shield of armor. He came to her then, lowering himself down, taking her into his arms and murmuring soft exquisite words. His lips claimed hers, his hands sought her body, and as their limbs entwined, their hearts came together as one.

Sensation upon sensation stirred her blood as Cash found ways to pleasure her. She moaned and cried out and when they joined, his body finally claiming hers, Jenna knew great and unequaled satisfaction.

Cash turned to draw her close from behind, pressing his body to hers, his hand finding her breast and gently rubbing in a sensual caress between two lovers. Jenna sighed, blissfully happy. She didn't know what tomorrow would bring, so she didn't dwell, but rather relished the sweet surrender of her body to the man she loved.

A short time later, Cash made love to her again with such slow and precise deliberation that Jenna wanted to scream from the torturous delights he evoked from her. He claimed her heart, her body, her soul, and when they moved together as one, reaching the pinnacle of overwhelming pleasure, both of them screamed, calling out into the night each other's names with fury and passion and love.

They collapsed onto the bed, sated and happy. Cash took her into his arms and spoke with pained resolve. "I'm never going to leave you, Jenna. I promise."

Jenna kissed him, wanting so much to believe him. She tried with all of her might and she wondered about her cold, wretched heart when it wouldn't allow him her trust. What sort of woman was she? Why couldn't she believe him? But deep down she knew, Cash *would* leave her and take with him, everything she held inside. He'd leave her crushed and broken and she would never, ever recover.

Jenna tossed and turned in bed, her vivid dream so vile, so unsettling, that she had to clamp down on her mouth so she wouldn't call out to Cash. She didn't want to wake him, but instead, curled her body around his, seeking shelter and protection. Cash immediately wrapped his arms around her and Jenna closed her eyes, hoping to sleep.

But the violence she'd dreamed, the terrible noises that had upset her, didn't stop. She snapped her eyes open. Vulgar shouts and warnings, *threats* she only knew by tone, since she couldn't manage the words, made her skin crawl. They were real and coming from outside!

Jenna shook Cash awake. He snapped his eyes open to the shouts and immediately bounded from the bed.

He went to the window and swore violently. Jenna knew immediately, sensed by the rigid stance of his body, that they were in danger.

"Get dressed, Jenna. Quick. And get down onto the floor."

"What is it?"

"The men who nearly killed me. The Wendells. They're trampling the fields, setting fires. One of them just torched the barn."

Shocked, Jenna sat up, motionless.

He picked up his gun and checked it, then threw

on his clothes. "Get dressed, Jenna and lay on the floor. And no matter what, don't leave this room!"

"What are you doing?" she asked in a panic, jumping out of bed and putting on her clothes.

"I can't let them destroy the farm. All we've worked for. I'm going downstairs."

"No! Cash, please. You can't!"

"I can't let them destroy everything." He fastened his belt and holstered his gun.

"I don't care!" she pleaded, tears streaming down her face. "Let them! Let them do what they want."

"They're not going to stop there, Jenna. They won't be satisfied until we're both dead."

Jenna gasped, her hand flying to her mouth. She ran to the window and peered out, unmindful of the devastation before her, the wheat fields trampled and in flames, the barn starting to catch fire and penned animals panicking. She only thought of Cash. She couldn't lose him. "There're four of them!"

Cash grabbed her and pulled her away from the window. "Get down! I'm going to try to even up the odds a bit." He kissed her quickly. "Don't cry. Stay up here. I'm sorry, Jenna. I didn't want this for you."

Jenna clung to him. "Please, Cash. Be careful."

He nodded, then was out the door. Jenna couldn't let him face them alone. She couldn't live with herself if she didn't try to help. She raced to her wooden chest and opened it. After the wolf incident, Cash had made her lock her gun away. She lifted the gun out and loaded the chambers. Grabbing the box of ammunition with gun in hand, she ran down the stairs.

Cash cursed when he saw her. "Don't argue with me, Cash," she said in the most forceful tone she'd ever used in her life. "I'm staying."

Cash stared for one moment, then nodded. "The doors are locked up and—"

Shouts from outside interrupted him. He peered out the parlor window.

"Cash C-Callahan, you m-murdering son-of-a-bitch, come on out h-here."

"D-don't take a m-man to hide behind a w-woman's skirts."

Others shouted obscenities, all slurring their speech.

Cash turned to her. "Sounds like they've been drinking. That's a good thing."

"What are you going to do?"

"Got to get the animals out of the barn. I'll steal over there. It's dark enough and with the barn on fire, they aren't about to stick close by. I'll mount Queen and lead them away from here."

Jenna shook her head, pleading with him to change his mind. "Don't, Cash. Please don't go out there! It's safer in here. We can both fight them off. I can shoot, Cash. I'll—"

"Listen to me, Jenna. This is the only way. We

can't stay in here. How long before they figure to set the house on fire? If they do that, they'll get us both. You stay in here. Keep the gun ready. Protect yourself. If all goes well, I'll reach my horse and lead them off the property. When you think it's safe, head on over to Ben's place. You got that? I'll meet up with you there.''

Jenna nodded, holding back her tears. She had to be brave, for Cash. "I'll meet you at Ben's," she said.

"That's my girl." Cash crushed his lips to hers one last time, then headed for the back door.

Crouching down as low as he could, Cash waited until the horsemen were out of view, then dashed to the barn. He hoped it was dark enough, and that the movement wouldn't arouse attention. He needed just a short amount of time to get the animals out safely, before he led the Wendells on a not-so-merry chase.

He slipped into the barn unnoticed and immediately was struck by fierce smoke rising up in layers, choking his lungs. He coughed several times before catching his breath. After that, he moved efficiently, leading Mac, then Larabeth and the others out the back of the barn. Scrappy bounded at his heels, grateful to be let out of the smoky barn.

Shouts and taunts continued on, and as he peered out, Cash noticed one man heading to the house with a torch. With haste, Cash mounted

Queen and riding low without benefit of saddle, he charged out the front of the barn, making his way into the yard.

"There he is!"

"Let's get him!"

Immediately all four men became alert.

Cash had the benefit of surprise and managed to take a shot at one of the men as he raced by. He witnessed his target fall from his horse. The others began shooting, but Cash kept low and urged Queen on. Cash made it out the gates of Twin Oaks and rounded the bend in the road.

That's when he noticed two men on horseback, with guns ready, heading straight for him. Cash swore, a sense of impending dread assailing him. He was completely outnumbered. Trapped, with three men at his back and two in front.

Then Cash recognized one of the riders facing him. Ben. The other man he couldn't make out. They rode straight toward him, firing shots at his assailants. As they neared, there was no time to comprehend his surprise when he recognized the second rider. Jenna's brother, Bobby Joe Duncan, rode fast and hard beside Ben.

With help by his side, Cash reined his mount around, facing the Wendells. Shots rang out from both sides. One of the three men went down.

The others made a swift turn and headed back toward the farm.

"They're going after Jenna," Cash shouted. He

pushed Queen to her limit, riding as fast as he could. Both Ben and Bobby Joe were behind him, all three taking aim and shooting at the riders heading back to the farm. Another man went down, the bullet hitting his shoulder.

By the time the third man reached the farmhouse, Jenna had him in her sights, aiming her gun from the porch. With the three of them behind him and Jenna facing him, Rex Wendell had no choice but to drop from his mount and lift his arms in surrender.

Cash rushed over with gun trained and tied him up with a rope. When he stood to face her, Jenna dropped her gun and ran straight into his arms, tears cascading down her face. "Everything's all right," he said to reassure her.

She clung to him. "Oh, thank God. Thank God."

Cash brushed a kiss to her forehead. "Are you okay?"

She nodded, both arms wrapping snuggly around his neck. He held her tight for a moment then peered over at the barn.

"We've got to put out that fire," Cash said, hoping it wasn't a futile notion. Half the barn had already succumbed to the flames.

But a moan from the yard had them shifting attention. Bobby Joe had fallen from his horse, landing on the hard dirt. He gripped his bloody leg.

"He's been hit," Cash said. Both he and Jenna ran over to him.

Jenna bent down to meet his eyes. "Bobby Joe," she whispered, her surprise at seeing him here as great as Cash's had been. "It'll be okay. We'll get you fixed up."

Bobby Joe took hold of her hand. "I didn't lead them here, Jen. I didn't," he said, his voice barely audible.

"Shhhh. Don't worry about that. I've got to get you into the house."

"No, you have to listen first. I got wind that they found out about you and Callahan." He paused to take a breath. "I knew they'd head over here real quick. I left word with the sheriff in Goose Creek, then came here fast as I could to warn you. I found Ben along the road. He'd seen the flames and was coming to help."

"I'm glad you came home," Jenna said, caressing his face. She turned to Cash. "Can you get him into the house? I've got to stop the bleeding."

Ben helped with Bobby Joe, both of them lifting the injured man. Once Cash settled him onto the parlor sofa, he turned to Ben. "Jenna will tend him. Think you can help me put out that fire?"

"I'm fine, Cash. Let's get to it." Ben and Cash worked into the night. Others joined them, neighbors and farmhands alike. It took three hours to tamp down all the embers. Cash was grateful for one thing—the animals had survived. But as far as the farm went, they'd know by daylight the extent of the damage.

Yet there was no doubt in Cash's mind that the farm Jenna loved with her whole heart, was in ruins. And the blame rested entirely on his shoulders.

It was all his fault.

Chapter Nineteen

In the late hours of the night, before dawn showered the sky with light, Cash walked into the parlor, noting Jenna had fallen into an exhausted sleep on a chair. She'd been spending her time between tending Bobby Joe and helping put out the fire. But Cash saw beneath the smudges of soot and grime on her face to the pale ashen woman lying there, her spirit all but broken.

She didn't deserve this. She shouldn't have to pay for his crimes with such a high price, her beloved farm. Cash watched her wiggle uncomfortably in the chair, a weary sigh escaping her lips.

He went to her, lifted her and carried her up the stairs to her bed. Gently, he lowered her down and covered her. He turned to walk out, to leave her with whatever peace she might find in her sleep.

"Cash," she called out, her voice soft and sweet. "Don't leave."

"You need your sleep, sweetheart."

She sat up a little, her eyes hazy as she struggled to keep them open. "So do you. Stay with me. I need you to hold me."

Cash could deny her nothing. He returned to the bed. Lowering himself down, he took her into his arms. She fit snugly, tucking her chin under his and resting her hand on his chest.

"Bobby Joe is going to be all right. The bullet grazed his skin and there'll be a scar, but he'll be up and around soon," she said.

"I'm glad to hear it. If it wasn't for him and Ben, it wouldn't have been long before the Wendells hunted me down. They would have hurt you, too, Jenna. They came here for revenge, wanting to see me dead. Bobby Joe saved my life."

"I know. I thanked the Lord a thousand times," she said with deep heartfelt emotion Cash didn't deserve. She shouldn't be thanking anyone for his life. She should loathe him for bringing her nothing but destruction. "What happened to them?" she asked with a whisper.

"The sheriff showed up a few hours ago with his deputies. They hauled them all off. He said they were wanted in four states. Three were wounded, but they'll live, hopefully to hang for their crimes."

Jenna shivered and Cash brought her tighter into his embrace. He kissed her brow and reassured her, "It's over now. It's all over. Try to sleep."

Cash held her until she fell asleep and as the

dawn blinked upon the horizon, he left her to see to the farm and all the destruction.

Cash walked the fields, his gut tight with grief. Jenna's wheat, the tiny young stalks just making their way into the world, had been trampled. Those that weren't had caught fire, or were singed so badly, they'd never produce a healthy enough crop to bring to sale.

Cash stood gazing out, a solitary life on this blackened countryside that had been once been so full of hope and promise. Nearly three fourths of the fields were destroyed and along with it, Jenna's dream. The farm had been all she'd had left.

Now she had nothing.

Cash wouldn't allow it. He'd see to it that Jenna had her dream again. Her farm would prosper. He'd make sure she'd survive the winter with plenty of food and clothing and with all the supplies and equipment she'd need to rebuild the farm next season. They'd rebuild the barn and add even more livestock. Twin Oaks would be better than ever before.

Cash had to see to it. He couldn't abide living, knowing the devastation he'd caused her. And he knew of only one way to earn the money for Jenna. He'd always been a survivor. This time, his life and his heart depended solely on one thing.

His skills as a gambler.

Jenna came to him then, as quietly as a spirit,

her footsteps no longer careful as she treaded over the land. Tears filled her eyes. Cash could tell she tried not to cry, but he saw the moisture welling up. And as the morning sunshine shed light over the fields, Jenna gazed out to what was once her future.

Her expression faltered. On her face, Cash read bleakness and loss of all faith. He witnessed her anguish, the pain darkening her golden eyes, and it tore at him as nothing else ever had.

She took his hand. Cash wondered why she'd even want to touch him, why she'd need him now, when both knew he'd brought this upon her. Yet he held her, because to let go would truly destroy him.

They stood together in the fields, hands entwined, quiet and somber. Cash made a solemn vow then, to make this right.

Even if it meant losing Jenna in the end.

The next day, Jenna stood on the porch, saying goodbye to her brother. "Are you sure, Bobby Joe? You could stay on a while longer."

"I'm sure, Jenna. Thanks for fixing me up."

Jenna smiled with sadness in her heart. "I should thank you. We all might have died if you hadn't come to warn me."

Bobby Joe shook his head as he looked at the smoke still rising up from the barn. "I was too late for some things."

"But not for others," she said.

"No, not for others." Bobby Joe took a wobbly step, his leg still wrapped with bandages. He caught sight of Cash, out by the barn. "You love him, Jen?"

Jenna turned in the direction of the barn. Cash was shoveling dirt on the low-lying embers still smoldering. "I think I do."

"I only hope he doesn't break your heart."

"I don't believe he will, Bobby Joe," Jenna said in earnest. Through all the bleakness, the loss of her farm, Jenna had gained perhaps one good thing. Her hope. She believed in Cash Callahan. She loved him. She never thought she'd ever feel hope or love again, but he'd shown her how to live, not merely exist.

"Bobby Joe, I wish you'd stay on a while," she said, realizing how much she'd like to get to know her brother again.

"Jenna, I'm not a farmer. I'm a gambler. There's no changing that. We don't stay in one place long. Gambling's in our blood. It's all we know, all we want to know."

Jenna nodded, trying hard to understand.

"I'll try to send you money for the farm. Can't promise anything, though. All depends on how my luck's running. I'm sorry, Jen," he said, his eyes meeting hers. Jenna believed him. Perhaps her brother had learned a thing or two; perhaps he'd grown up a little bit as well. "I'm sorry for everything."

"I'll miss you."

"I'll write and I might even come back one day, but Jen, I hope you understand why I can't stay on."

"I'm trying to, Bobby Joe." Jenna curved her lips up, trying for a smile. "You take care of that leg now."

"I will." Bobby Joe kissed her on the cheek, then mounted his horse and rode off Twin Oaks property.

The following morning, Jenna set out a mug of coffee for Cash. He sat down at the kitchen table, taking a sip, but he didn't touch his food. He'd been quiet lately, spending his time with Ben, assessing the damages to the farm, hardly speaking to her, though at night, he'd hold her in his arms and try to reassure her with soft words. They'd been through a lot together, but Jenna had never seen him so deep in thought, so completely absorbed before.

"Cash? Aren't you hungry?"

He lifted his head up and sighed deeply. "I've got something to say, Jenna. And I'd like you to hear me out."

Jenna's heart nearly stopped from his tone. All she could do was to give him a slight nod of her head.

"I figure you can't make it through the winter without the crop."

"Maybe, if we—"

"No, Jenna. I've been talking to Ben. I know where you stand. You're not going to make it. Now, I figure I've got the means to make a lot of money. I'm the only one who can set this all to rights."

Dread crept in, an overwhelming sensation, attacking her insides, creating fear and doubt. "What do you plan to do?" she asked, her voice raspy.

"The only thing I know to do, Jenna. I'm going back to Texas. I'm going to make you enough money to get this farm going again."

Jenna bolted out of her chair. "No!"

Cash stood, too, bracing his hands on the table, leaning in. "My mind is made up. I'm leaving."

Jenna laughed, an eerie sound of wry amusement. "Just a few nights ago, you said you'd never leave me, Cash. Is that all your word's good for?"

Cash inhaled sharply, his body rigid. "Jenna, that was before your farm was destroyed. I can't live with that. I can't let you lose everything you worked for, because of me. I'm responsible and I'm going to make it right."

"You're going off to gamble, Cash. That's what got you in trouble first off. No good comes from gambling."

"It's all I know how to do, Jenna."

"That's not true. You know how to farm this

land, Cash. I've watched you. And you're good with the animals. Larabeth favors you over me now. You *do* know more than gambling.''

"You need money for the farm. None of those things are going to make a difference if you can't make it through the winter," he argued, his voice as determined as ever.

"What if I won't accept the money?"

Cash cursed. "Dammit, Jenna. You'd let your stubborn pride get in the way of rebuilding your farm? What about Rosalinda and Ben? It's their farm, too. I owe this to all of you. You won't change my mind.''

Cash was right. She couldn't allow her stubborn notions to ruin Ben and Rosalinda's life. Winter would be cold and hard if they didn't do something, but gambling still wasn't the answer. "There are other ways," she said.

"What other ways, Jenna? Tell me."

She couldn't think, her mind sifting through thoughts rushing in, but nothing came to her. "There *must* be other ways. I know there must be.''

"This is one time your faith fails you, Jenna. I have to be practical minded. I can make enough money to see you through the winter.''

Jenna swallowed, her arguments futile. Cash really would leave her. "How long will you be gone?''

He let out his breath slowly, perhaps as a sign that she'd conceded. "A month, maybe two."

Jenna turned away from him, her eyes misting up with tears. Bobby Joe's words came back to torment her, a haunting reminder of what Jenna had known all along.

We don't stay in one place long. Gambling's in our blood.

Bobby Joe had also claimed that once a gambler, always a gambler. "There's no changing that," he'd said.

Jenna knew that truth from the beginning. Foolishly, she'd thought Cash had changed and now she knew differently. Hope had come back into her life, for just a short time, but now Jenna felt empty inside.

Jenna knew Cash wouldn't come back. She had no doubt he'd send money. He'd do the responsible thing. But he thought of himself as a gambler, not a farmer, just like Bobby Joe. He'd return to the only way of life he'd known, the farm and the time they shared together being only a shallow memory in Cash's mind.

He came close to stand behind her. Gently, he grabbed her shoulders and whispered in her ear as though he could read her thoughts. "I'll be back, Jenna. I swear. And you'll have your farm."

Jenna closed her eyes. Cash had been right about one other thing. Her faith *had* failed her. She didn't know if she could trust his word. With Cash gone, she'd have nothing left, no hope and no dreams for the future. "When will you leave?"

"Later this morning. I've spoken to Ben. He knows. He's going to watch out for you, like always, sweetheart, but the danger has passed. You'll do fine."

Jenna turned to look him in the eyes, her stomach churning and her mind filled with grief. "You think you're doing the right thing, Cash. But I know there are other ways. You just won't see it. And yes, I'll do fine. I guess I'm a survivor, just like you, Cash Callahan."

Cash blinked hard, staring into her eyes. When he bent his head, Jenna knew she couldn't deny herself his kiss. His lips took hers, the familiar taste and feel of him a bleak reminder of all that she had lost. "I'll be back," he vowed, then took his leave.

Jenna slumped into the kitchen chair, her body limp, her heart aching. Losing the wheat crop she could deal with, but losing Cash was more painful than she could ever have imagined.

Cash reached the town of Blackwater in three days. Familiar surroundings and a friendly face, just the balm he needed now. He'd pushed Queen to her limit, each mile that took him off the farm harder and harder to handle. His thoughts were of Jenna and only Jenna. He'd never forget the look on her face when he'd ridden off. She wasn't one to hide her emotions, and what he read on her face spoke of doubt and fear. Jenna doubted him. She didn't trust him. She didn't believe he'd return. He'd seen all of that on her face, and so much more. He'd seen disappointment. He'd seen her hopes shattered. Cash had been so bent on getting her the money she needed to rebuild her farm, he'd ignored what Jenna truly wanted.

What she'd *always* wanted.

She hadn't asked for much, just someone to love, a partner to help raise a family, work the farm and share her dreams. That's what she really needed.

Cash's words to Jenna silently screamed inside his head, hitting him hard with the truth.

All of life is a gamble with the choices we make.

Cash reined in his mount with those thoughts close at hand. He tied Queen to the post and entered The Palace saloon, taking off his hat.

Louella greeted him with her usual coy smile. "Hello, handsome. Glad to see you back again. There's a game just starting. You're in as soon as you take everything off."

Cash stood there, his mind reeling as notions entered his head. Ideas that stuck with him and wouldn't let go. He realized then that Jenna had been right. There *were* other ways. Grinning at Louella, he unfastened his gun belt and handed it to her. As he sat down at the table, dawning knowledge gripped him tight, a clear vivid picture of what he was going to do. He lifted his gaze to meet hers. "Just a meal, Louella. That's all I came for."

With eyebrows raised, Louella nodded. "Guess that tells all, Cash."

"Yep, it sure does," he said, unable to keep a big smile from his face.

And right then, Cash Callahan knew he'd made the right choice.

Jenna sat in the kitchen, staring at the bowl of stew before her. She wasn't a bit hungry, but lifted the spoon to her mouth because she knew she had to eat. In the week that Cash had been gone, mealtime had become real lonely. She missed Cash, plain and simple. There was no use denying it.

Ben and Rosalinda had been so sweet, worrying over her, asking her to supper. Jenna had to get used to being alone again, so she didn't accept their offers. Still, Ben paid her a visit every day, frowning at her when she refused his help.

Jenna had always made do. Just like Cash, she'd always found a way to survive. Only, this time, pure loneliness ate at her, sapping her will. She had only Cash's word to bank on that he'd return. Did she have enough faith in him? The man she loved was a gambler. He hadn't changed and she could never hope to have him love farming the way she did.

When trouble settled on the farm, he'd turned to gambling, as he always had in the past. He

wouldn't even consider another option. Cash knew
only one way of dealing with life and that was by
gambling.

She had no doubt Cash would bring the money
they needed to the farm. He was a man of talent
and determination. But what then? Dare she hope
he would stay on? When would he tire of the farm
and of her?

"Stop driving yourself crazy, Jenna," she said,
taking her plate to the washbasin. She glanced out
the window, watching Scrappy bark and jump at
Button. Her confident feline just stared at the dog,
before lifting her head in regal fashion, then saun-
tering away. Scrappy flopped onto the ground, his
black face in a pout, resting on his paws. But instantly, he lifted his head, tail wagging, bounding
up and raced down the path.

Jenna spotted a man, making his way under the
twin oaks, heading toward the house. "Cash!"

She untied her apron, flinging it and racing out
the door. He was on foot, and Jenna's mind mud-
dled with worrisome thoughts. Had something happened to him? Was he injured? Where was Queen?

Scrappy reached him first. He bent to scratch his
dog's head, then lifted up when she approached.

"Cash," she said breathlessly.

"Damn, Jenna. You get more beautiful every
time I see you." He walked over to her and took
her hands in his. "Come here and kiss me. It's all
I've been thinking about for the last five miles."

Jenna flowed into his arms. Warm lips, gentle, yet rooted in passion, took hers in a thorough kiss that nearly buckled her knees. She pulled away a bit, gazing up at him. "Cash, why are you on foot? Are you hurt?" She searched him for signs of injury. "Where's Queen?"

Cash laughed, taking her hand and tugging her toward the house. "Come on. Let's get home. I'll tell you everything."

Once inside the house, Cash emptied his pockets. Bills and silver coins hit the kitchen table. Jenna stared at the money.

"I made it to Blackwater, Jenna. I stood there, looking at my life at those gaming tables and knew that what I had here with you was worth so much more than that. I didn't sit down at those tables, Jenna. I couldn't. I wanted more for you. I wanted your respect…and trust."

Jenna's heart filled with joy, hearing Cash's admission that he hadn't gambled. He'd come back to her and hadn't gambled, but she remained puzzled. "Where did the money come from?"

Cash rubbed his chin. "Bender. I sold him my horse and saddle."

"You sold Queen?" Jenna couldn't believe he'd done it, but Cash's firm nod and gleaming eyes told her he'd spoken the truth.

"Got nearly three hundred dollars and the old guy made me promise I wouldn't bet him for anything ever again."

Jenna chuckled. "Oh, Cash."

"This is enough to see us through the bad times, Jenna. But listen, I have an idea. When we were at Antonio's wedding, I heard talk. There's a new seed coming from the other side of the world. Winter wheat seed, Jenna, called Turkey Red. Bender's going to give it a try and I figure we will, too. We'll plant seeds this fall and harvest in the winter. Bender's going to let us know how to get our hands on it."

Jenna's heart overflowed with love. Cash had found a way. He'd turned his back on gambling, for her, for them both. He'd come back to her with a plan for the farm. She dared to ask, "Does that mean you're staying on?"

Cash took her hand and the look in his dark indigo eyes stole her heart. "Jenna, I've never had a real home until I met you. You…you're my home. I'm asking you to do something for me, sweetheart. I'm asking you to gamble one time only."

"You want me to gamble?" she asked, her mind filled so crazily with love that she couldn't comprehend, didn't know what he was saying.

"Yep. I want you to gamble that I'll stay on here at Twin Oaks. I want you to gamble that I'll be a good husband, for real this time, and a good father for our children. I love you, Jenna, with everything inside, everything I've got to give. I'm asking you to take the biggest gamble of your life. I'm asking you to bet on *me*."

Jenna thought of the boy, orphaned at a young age, having to invent ways to survive. She'd thought of the man whose life she'd saved. The man who'd never left a plate empty, but garnished it with a flower, a show of gratitude for a meal. She thought of the man, who had worked so diligently in the fields, claiming not to be a farmer, yet displaying those traits each and every day. She thought that she'd known love from words across a page with a man she hadn't met. But now she knew love differently; by working alongside of a man, toiling until the day becomes night and learning his heart and soul, knowing all his faults and still wanting him desperately. That was the true and full measure of love.

Jenna smiled, thinking of the bright future ahead. The future she'd always wanted. She had only one word, one reply for the man who held her heart. "Yes."

And she knew, it wasn't a gamble at all.

But a dream come true.

Epilogue

The setting sun cast one last glow across the fields, a beam of light falling onto golden grain, rising up waist-high, as bountiful as it was beautiful. Three children played silly games of hide-and-seek within its boundaries, giggling joyously as a gentle southerly breeze bent the tall stalks ever so slightly. A man and woman stood upon the land, their hands entwined, a mangy dog and regal feline at their feet. Their gazes flowed over the fields then focused together on two oaks, steady and sure, with branches bending, connecting so fiercely that no force of nature would ever part them. And their resilient leaves kissed one another, tenderly, heartily in a caress that would go unequaled.

Always.

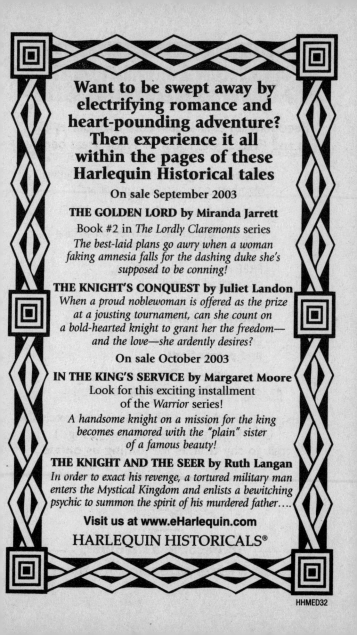

**Want to be swept away by
electrifying romance and
heart-pounding adventure?
Then experience it all
within the pages of these
Harlequin Historical tales**

On sale September 2003

THE GOLDEN LORD by Miranda Jarrett

Book #2 in *The Lordly Claremonts* series

*The best-laid plans go awry when a woman
faking amnesia falls for the dashing duke she's
supposed to be conning!*

THE KNIGHT'S CONQUEST by Juliet Landon

*When a proud noblewoman is offered as the prize
at a jousting tournament, can she count on
a bold-hearted knight to grant her the freedom—
and the love—she ardently desires?*

On sale October 2003

IN THE KING'S SERVICE by Margaret Moore

Look for this exciting installment
of the *Warrior* series!

*A handsome knight on a mission for the king
becomes enamored with the "plain" sister
of a famous beauty!*

THE KNIGHT AND THE SEER by Ruth Langan

*In order to exact his revenge, a tortured military man
enters the Mystical Kingdom and enlists a bewitching
psychic to summon the spirit of his murdered father....*

Visit us at www.eHarlequin.com

HARLEQUIN HISTORICALS®

ITCHIN' FOR SOME ROLLICKING ROMANCES SET ON THE AMERICAN FRONTIER? THEN TAKE A GANDER AT THESE TANTALIZING TALES FROM HARLEQUIN HISTORICALS

On sale September 2003

WINTER WOMAN by Jenna Kernan
(Colorado, 1835)

After braving the winter alone in the Rockies, a defiant woman is entrusted to the care of a gruff trapper!

THE MATCHMAKER by Lisa Plumley
(Arizona territory, 1882)

Will a confirmed bachelor be bitten by the love bug when he woos a young woman in order to flush out the mysterious Morrow Creek matchmaker?

On sale October 2003

WYOMING WILDCAT by Elizabeth Lane
(Wyoming, 1866)

A blizzard ignites hot-blooded passions between a white medicine woman and an amnesiac man, but an ominous secret looms on the horizon....

THE OTHER GROOM by Lisa Bingham
(Boston and New York, 1870)

When a penniless woman masquerades as the daughter of a powerful marquis, her intended groom risks it all to protect her from harm!

Visit us at www.eHarlequin.com

HARLEQUIN HISTORICALS®

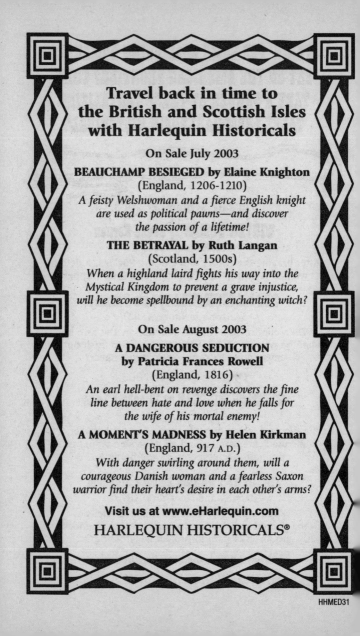